PACO
Night Rebels Motorcycle Club

CHIAH WILDER

Copyright © 2018 by Chiah Wilder
Print Edition

Editing by Hot Tree Editing and Lisa Cullian
Cover design by Cheeky Covers
Proofreading by Rose Holub

All rights reserved. This book or any portion thereof may not be reproduced or used in any manner whatsoever without the express written permission of the author except for the use of brief quotations in a book review. Please purchase only authorized additions, and do not participate in or encourage piracy of copyrighted materials.

Your support of the author's rights is appreciated.

Disclaimer: This is a work of fiction. Names, characters, businesses, places, events and incidents are either the products of the author's imagination or used in a fictitious manner. Any resemblance to actual persons, living or dead, or actual events is purely coincidental.

I love hearing from my readers. You can email me at chiahwilder@gmail.com.

Make sure you sign up for my newsletter so you can keep up with my new releases, special sales, free short stories, and other treats only available to newsletter readers. When you sign up, you will receive a FREE hot and steamy novella. Sign up at: http://eepurl.com/bACCL1.

Visit me on facebook at facebook.com/AuthorChiahWilder.

Insurgent MC Series:

Hawk's Property
Jax's Dilemma
Chas's Fervor
Axe's Fall
Banger's Ride
Jerry's Passion
Throttle's Seduction
Rock's Redemption
An Insurgent's Wedding
Outlaw Xmas
Insurgents MC Romance Series: Insurgents Motorcycle Club Box Set (Books 1 – 4)
Insurgents MC Romance Series: Insurgents Motorcycle Club Box Set (Books 5 – 8)

Night Rebels MC Series:

STEEL
MUERTO
DIABLO
GOLDIE

Steamy Contemporary Romance:

My Sexy Boss

Chapter One

STREAKS OF WHITE-HOT lightning broke the blackness, ripping the night sky like paper. Seconds later the rumbling thunder came. Another few miles down the highway, the lightning forked close to Paco's Harley. More booms reverberated overhead, and then the rain fell, slow and spattering at first and then lashing down, torrential, relentless.

Paco slowed down, cursing the semitrucks as they barreled past him, burying him in a blinding wave of water as their tires hit the puddles. He squeezed the water out of his foam grips and debated about pulling over and taking out his rain gear.

A second series of jagged lightning bolts zigzagged across the sky. *I gotta get out of this fucking storm.* Riding wet on a bike with lightning too close for comfort was just asking for trouble. The rain came down in sheets, obstructing his vision, pelleting his skin like bullets. The brake lights on several of the large trucks in front of him glowed eerily in the mist, and he decided to follow them, hoping they were headed to the nearest truck stop.

Sure enough, the semis took the next exit and turned right with Paco following behind them. Bright lights filtered through the thin mist and a yellow neon sign read "Eagle Truck Stop," the word "Diner" flashing in blue lettering underneath it. Three of the large trucks turned in and drove to the fuel pumps. After following them in, he veered to the right and parked in front of the eatery. The rain had soaked him, so he opened his saddlebag, took out a change of clothes, and rushed into the diner. Drops of water rolled down his face and neck, his feet squishing with every step he took.

"It sure is coming down," a woman behind the lunch counter said as her eyes traveled up and down his muscled body. "You need somewhere to dry off?"

"Yeah. Do you have showers here?" he replied.

She pointed to the right. "You gotta go next door for that. They got showers, plus a trucker lounge with TV and video games. No laundry though. The shower will cost you twelve bucks but that includes a towel, washcloth, soap, and a floor mat. Where're you coming from?" The redhead gave him a smile that said she was available. He'd seen that smile more times than he could count.

"Thanks for the info." A gust of wind blew past him when he opened the door, and, with head bent, he walked next door.

Thirty minutes later, Paco was back at the diner in a booth by the window, watching the trucks as they moved from the pumps to parking spaces that lined the large lot. The rain was steady now, and he saw several women move between the lanes of parked semis.

"My name's Holly," the redhead said as she handed him a menu. "I see you got yourself all dried off. Nice pair of jeans, by the way. When you came back in, I noticed you wear them real good." She licked her pink-stained lips.

"Get me a cup of black coffee," he said, looking at the menu.

"You got a name?"

"Yeah. Get me that coffee."

Holly snorted, then walked away. Several men came in yelling out greetings to her. Paco watched as she laughed and flirted with them, bending over the counter and playfully smacking a couple of them on their arms when they commented on her tits. Shaking his head, he pulled out his phone and shifted his focus to the parking lot. The door to a truck opened and an arm reached out to help hoist a woman with long dark hair inside.

"Hey, dude," he said to Steel.

"Where the hell are you?" the president answered.

"I got caught in a fucking storm so I pulled into a truck stop. I'm gonna wait it out. If it doesn't get better, I'll have to spend the night drinking coffee in the diner. How's the weather in Alina?"

"Clear. Are you still in Utah?"

"Yeah. I'm close to the Colorado border though."

"How's your sister?"

"Great. She had another boy."

"Here's your coffee," Holly said as she put the cup in front of him.

"I gotta go. I may not be back until tomorrow. Later."

"There's a motel behind the truck stop in case you stay the night. The beds are real comfy too." She undid the top two buttons on her uniform.

"Thanks. I may need a room."

"Holly, bring your sweet ass over here. My buddy Rich wants to ask you a question."

The waitress turned sideways and laughed. "You just hang on. I got a customer here." She looked at Paco and winked. "I'm popular with the men around here."

"I'll have a burger—medium—fries, and a cup of green chili."

Her brows knitted. "You're not very friendly, are you?"

"No, I'm not." He picked up his cup and took a sip. The coffee tasted stale and harsh, like it'd been sitting out all day. "Give me a fresh cup of coffee and bring me some cream."

"Don't you ever say 'please' when you want something?"

"No."

He scrolled through his texts as she walked away. The majority of them were from women he'd hooked up with in the past six months, asking when they could get together.

Shaking his head, he put his phone down on the table. The truth was he didn't want to see any of them again. He'd had fun for a while, but no one had interested him enough to pursue anything for more than a few weeks. It wasn't that he was against relationships; it was just that the one woman who'd captured his heart had also shattered it, and he wasn't looking to have that happen again.

"Here you go," Holly said, placing a steaming cup of coffee in front of him. "And I opened a new carton of creamer just for you."

"Thanks." He stirred a splash of cream in the coffee. The earthy scent filled his nostrils as he brought the cup to his lips and took a sip. Bitter sweetness snapped at the back of his throat as the hot liquid warmed him.

Glancing outside, he saw three women in short shorts huddled under the eaves of the diner as the rain poured down. A cold rush of wind swirled around him as the front door opened and a woman with too much makeup and too little clothing entered. Head down, she walked over to the booth next to his and slid in. Drops of water trickled down her face and neck, and she grabbed a napkin and wiped them away before running it through her long dark hair.

Then she looked up and locked gazes with him. Her eyes were like an endless stretch of midnight sky. A bundle of sorrow, pain, and loneliness swam in their inky depths along with threads of fierceness and pride. They drew him in. Something down deep, very deep inside him stirred faintly. He sucked in a breath. *Damn.*

"Here you go, handsome." Holly put a plate in front of him. "I'll be right back with your green chili. Can I freshen up your coffee?"

Dragging his eyes away from the woman, he nodded slightly as he pushed his cup toward her. "I need ketchup."

"You got it," Holly said, walking away.

He glanced at the woman again. She stared down at her phone while she blew her nose. Bringing the phone to her ear, she looked over her shoulder at a group of men at the lunch counter who were talking with Holly.

"I'm real sick tonight," she said in a voice loud enough for Paco to hear. "I made about a hundred bucks, but I'm burning up."

Paco picked up a fry and put it in his mouth. The woman looked like she was about twenty-three or so, and from the way she was dressed and the amount of makeup she had on, he guessed her to be a working woman. The other women still huddled under the eaves were older and looked worn out. Two of them had the signs of meth on their faces: sores, scarring, gaunt.

"Please, Bobby. I promise to work extra hard tomorrow. I just need to sleep. I'm really sick." Tears trickled down her face, and she grabbed a napkin and wiped her nose.

"Here's your chili and some fresh coffee." Instead of putting the bowl of chili down next to his plate, Holly leaned way over and set it on the other side. Her chest brushed against him and she giggled. "Sorry. My boobs are so big that they always get in the way. I noticed your jacket when you walked out earlier to go next door for your shower. Is the Night Rebels a motorcycle club?"

Paco nodded while he squirted ketchup over his burger.

"Is your club one of them one-percenters?"

One of the truckers had swiveled around on his stool and stared at her. "I think one of your customers wants you," Paco said.

She looked over her shoulder. "Oh. Him. He can wait. It's not every day that a biker comes in here, especially one as good-looking as you. I love seeing a guy on a big Harley. I mean, you guys must be pretty strong to handle such a powerful motorcycle."

"Okay. Don't freak out. I was just asking if I could take tonight off. Forget about it." The young woman set her phone down, then blew her nose again.

Paco glanced back at Holly. "I've got everything I need."

The waitress narrowed her eyes. "You trying to tell me you wanna be left alone?"

"Yeah." He picked up his burger and took a big bite. The woman in the booth watched him.

"Whatever." Holly walked away.

"Can I have a cup of chicken noodle soup?" the woman asked the waitress.

Holly stopped at her table. "You got any money?"

She shook her head. "Put it on my tab."

"Carl told me not to serve you anything until your tab's paid up."

"Didn't Bobby pay it?" she asked in a small voice.

"Nope. And since you don't have any money and can't order anything, you gotta get outta here. You're taking a booth away from paying customers."

The woman glanced around. "There's hardly anyone here. I don't feel so good right now. Can I have a glass of water?"

Holly shook her head. "Carl doesn't want your kind taking up space unless you're gonna pay. You need to move on."

Paco watched as the woman's chin trembled, her lashes blinked, and her hand clutched at her throat. "Put whatever she wants on my tab," he said.

Holly spun around, her mouth gaping, her brown eyes flashing. "What?"

The woman cleared her throat. "I don't want any charity," she said as pride shone in her eyes.

A smile twitched on his lips. "I'm not giving any."

Holly came over to him. "Are you sure about this? She's a lot lizard."

Anger burned inside him as the waitress smiled smugly. "I don't like repeating myself. Put her order on my tab." He turned away and pulled the bowl of chili closer to him.

Mumbling something incomprehensible under her breath, she stormed away. "Remember the bowl of chicken soup, and bring me a cup of tea, please," the woman said as Holly passed her table.

"Unbelievable," Holly said, looking behind her shoulder at Paco.

When she'd gone to the kitchen, the woman stared at him. He kept eating, acting like he didn't know she was watching him, but he was acutely aware of her. A woman had never had such an effect on him after only a few minutes. Even when he'd met Cassie, he hadn't been immediately drawn to her.

What the hell's going on? I must be tired or something.

Holly slammed the soup and tea down and rushed away. The woman grabbed several crackers, and the crinkling sound as she opened them made him smile. He looked at her.

"Thanks for this," she said. "I'll pay you back tomorrow. I promise."

"You don't have to. You sound like you're sick."

"I am. I feel like shit. I'm sure once I finish the soup and tea, I'll feel a lot better." Steam rose from the bowl. She looked up. "I've never seen you around here before. You new to the road?" With the spoon near her mouth, she blew.

"I'm not sure I know what you're asking."

"I mean are you new to long-haul driving?"

"I'm not a trucker. I'm just passing through. I got caught up in the storm."

Holly came back over. She darted her eyes from him to the woman, then back to him. "I thought you weren't the friendly type," she said as she picked up his empty bowl.

Ignoring her, he said, "Give me a piece of apple pie and warm it up."

"Fucking unbelievable," she muttered as she walked away.

The woman's phone rang and she grimaced. Slowly she picked it up. "I'm having some hot tea before I go back out there." A long pause. "I know. I understand. I'll have the money." She placed the phone on the table, then wrapped her hands around her cup.

From where he sat, Paco saw tracks of fear streak her face. Something about the way she sat, her eyes watering and her hands clinging around the mug, hit a chord inside him. *She's scared to death. I bet this Bobby fuck is her pimp.* Sensing she was in trouble, he wanted to help her. *I should just pay my bill and forget about her.* But he couldn't. There was something about her that grounded him. He didn't know what it was, but he wanted to make sure she was okay.

"Here's your piece of pie. Did you decide to stay at the motel? The rain's still coming down pretty good." Holly leaned in closer.

He glanced out the window. "Yeah, it's still raining. You can bring the bill." He jerked his head toward the small woman in the booth. "Make sure she doesn't want anything more."

When Holly went up to her table, he saw the woman shake her head and then take out a mirror from her purse. She wiped her face and took out what looked like lipstick and a pencil.

The waitress walked over to his table. "Here you go. You pay up front. I wrote my number on the back, just in case you want some company tonight." Holly smiled widely.

"Don't want any." He stood up and shrugged his jacket on. Picking up the bill, he glanced at her taut face. "The pie was good." She glared at him, and he gestured her to walk in front of him.

When he went by the woman's table, he jerked his head at her.

"Thanks for the soup and tea," she said, her mesmerizing eyes stopping him.

"You're welcome. You got somewhere to stay?"

Nodding slowly, she chewed on her lower lip.

"I overheard your conversation on the phone. You really gonna haul your ass outside in this freezing rain?"

Sinking down in the faux-leather seat, she broke eye contact. "I don't have a choice," she whispered.

"Are you gonna pay your bill?" Irritation laced Holly's voice.

Ignoring her, he stood silent by the woman's table. She looked up at him. "What? We all gotta do junk we don't want to sometimes." She resumed chewing the corner of her bottom lip.

"I'm getting a room at the motel for the night. Come stay with me."

Her eyes widened. "I need to bring in some money tonight, but thanks."

"I'll take care of that. You're all stuffed up, and you look like you're miserable." He shoved his hands into his pockets. "It's your call."

She watched him for a few seconds, suspicion shining in her eyes. And then she ran her gaze over him, slow and unabashedly. The ringing phone broke in on her assessment of him, and she groaned when she looked down at the screen.

"What do you want now?" She brought her slender fingers to the base of her throat. "Who told you I was still in the diner? You got people spying on me? Really, Bobby? Anyway, I'm just getting ready to go back out."

Paco saw her face tighten and her fist clench. *I should take off. Why the fuck am I getting in the middle of this shit she has going on?* The truth was he wanted to help her. She seemed as if she'd stumbled into a world in which she didn't belong. It was like she lost her way, and for reasons he couldn't articulate or even understand, there was something about her that touched him.

She placed the phone inside her skimpy short jacket. "You're not a serial killer, are you?"

He chuckled. "No. Are you?"

Shaking her head, she laughed, and it was sweet and soft and sparkling like dew on green grass in the spring. Scooting toward him, she grabbed her purse and stood up.

Without saying anything, he walked over to the cashier and paid the bill. Holly reclined against the wall, watching him intently. Several men at the counter stared at the young woman who stayed close to him. He told the cashier to give Holly her tip, and then he walked outside into the freezing rain, the woman following.

He opened one of the saddlebags and took out his waterproof motorcycle jacket. "Here," he said, handing it to her. "Put it on. It'll keep you dry." She slipped it on and jumped on behind him. The roar of his Harley competed with the howling wind, and as he rode away, he caught a glimpse of Holly standing by the window, her face pinched.

Roady's Motel looked like hundreds of others off interstate highways strewn across the country. It had two sets of external metal stairs leading to the second floor. It wasn't a total dump from the outside, but it looked like the type of place that travel-weary people stayed alongside drug dealers, pimps, and prostitutes.

Fitting the key into the doorknob, Paco turned it, opened the door, and switched on the overhead light. The room had one large bed, two chairs, and a small table. A TV sat on top of a scratched-up long dresser. He closed the door behind him and looked sideways at the woman, who stood quietly by the bed.

"What's your name?" he asked as he dropped a small satchel on the table.

She jumped. "Misty. What's yours?"

"Paco. You need to use the bathroom?" She shook her head. "I'm gonna get out of these wet clothes." Before he closed the bathroom door, he looked behind him. "And don't think of stealing any of my shit. I'm not gonna be happy if I have to track you down in the rain." Without waiting for her to answer, he closed the door.

Twenty minutes later, he came out with a towel wrapped around his waist, his wet clothes in hand. Going over to the closet, he saw that Misty hadn't moved an inch since he'd gone into the bathroom. "Have a seat. You want something hot to drink?"

"I'm good," she said, going over to the bed and sitting on the edge of it. "I'm not feeling so good."

"Don't mind me. Go to sleep if you want."

From the corner of his eye, he saw her watching him, her gaze focused on his bare chest as he hung up his clothes. He turned toward her. "Like what you see?"

Quickly, she averted her gaze and stood up. "I'm going to take a warm shower. I'll be done soon." She scurried out of the room.

Grabbing the remote control, he went over to the satchel on the table and took out a bottle of whiskey. Spotting four glasses next to the television set, he nabbed one and poured a generous amount of booze into it. He propped a pillow behind his back and leaned against it, switched on the TV, and then took a deep drink. The whiskey tasted smoky and sharp, and it burned its way down his throat into his belly. *Fuck that's good.* He poured a bit more into the glass.

Misty came out of the bathroom, a towel wrapped around her small frame. Her hair was damp and smelled like almond and cherries, and he was glad he'd left the complimentary bottle of shampoo for her. Her hair looked darker than it had in the diner. It was long, shiny, and almost black. Her skin was smooth, and he figured she wasn't a meth user like a lot of the women he'd seen sniffing around the trucks earlier when at the diner. Her complexion was clear, her lips heart-shaped, her brows perfectly formed, and her dark lashes framed the most amazing eyes he'd ever seen. The tattoo of a crown with the initials "EZR" underneath was interesting, and he wanted to see what other tats she had on her body, underneath the towel.

"Do you like what you see?" she asked, a smile tugging at the corners of her mouth as she walked over to the bed.

Fuck yeah, sweetheart. "You feel better?"

"Yes." She began to take off her towel.

He stood up, went over to his case, and took out a T-shirt. "Put this on," he said, handing it to her.

Confusion crossed her face. "Why? Don't you want me naked when you fuck me?"

"I'm not gonna fuck you. Why don't you try and get some rest?"

"Wait. I thought you wanted me to stay with you so I could earn my quota. I'm not in the habit of giving freebies. If you're not going to pay me, then I need to get back to the truck stop." Her voice quivered slightly.

"Don't get so fucking bent out of shape. I said I'd pay you. I just don't wanna fuck you. You're sick and you need to sleep. I'm just helping you out."

Placing her hands on her hips, she thumped her foot on the carpet. "You pity me?"

"I didn't say that." He sat back on the edge of the bed and took another long drink.

"You don't find me attractive? I'll have you know I have no problem getting plenty of men who want sex."

Quirking his lips, he eased his eyes up and down her body. "I don't doubt that. And I think you're damn attractive, but I don't pay to fuck, sweetheart. I'm offering you a warm room, a good night's sleep, and no worries about hustling your ass with a lot of old men with beer guts who probably haven't showered in a while." He switched the channel on the TV.

She stood there for several minutes, holding the T-shirt, staring at him. He kept watching the screen, keenly aware of her presence, the scent of cherry blossom roping around him. *Fuck, she smells good.* He adjusted his boxers, trying to ease some of the ache in his groin. *I could bang her and relieve some stress.*

For the past three weeks, he'd been at his sister's in Richfield, Utah, helping her out while she gave birth to a third boy. His brother-in-law was in Afghanistan, and when Kendra called and asked him to be with her when her baby was born, he didn't hesitate; he jumped on his Harley and made a beeline for Richfield. Kendra was the only family he had. He'd always looked after her, especially after their father murdered their mother.

Images of blood-smeared walls pushed through his mind, and he closed his eyes tightly as if to squeeze the memory out of his brain.

The bed moving brought him out of the past, and he looked sideways and saw Misty slip between the covers. A low chuckle escaped from her lips. "I've never been in bed with a guy without fucking him."

It wasn't that he didn't want her, it was just that he didn't want it like *that*.

What the hell's up with me?

"Get some sleep. You'll feel better."

The guys at the club would never believe that he was next to a pretty woman who was naked under his T-shirt, willing to fuck, and he didn't go for it. *Hell, I don't believe I'm just sitting here, drinking whiskey and staring at the TV instead of fucking her good.*

Turning toward her, he saw her body move up and down with each breath she took, and he could feel the warmth radiating from her. *Shit.*

Her breathing became deeper, and he knew she'd fallen asleep. He watched her for a long while, finished the whiskey, and then switched off the lights.

SUNLIGHT FILTERED THROUGH the tears in the worn curtains, illuminating the shadowy corners of the room. Paco glanced over at Misty, watching the way the rays danced over her body before finally resting softly on her skin. In the morning light, her hair was as black and glossy as a puddle of spilled ink, her slightly parted lips pink like strawberry ice cream. Without thinking, he reached out and stroked her cheek, and her eyes flew open as she jerked backward.

"I didn't mean to wake you," he said, getting up from the bed. His head felt like it weighed a thousand pounds as he went into the bathroom and splashed cold water on his face. When he came back into the room, her back was against the headboard, her knees drawn up close to her chest. "It stopped raining." He looked out at the parking lot and saw several large trucks heading to the highway.

"Where do you live?" she asked.

"By the four corners in Colorado. Have you ever been there?" He kept his back to her, watching the convoy of semis leaving the truck stop across the street.

"Yeah, but I didn't see much."

"Where're you from?" There was no answer. He turned around and looked at her. She smiled weakly, pulled at the sheet, and shrugged. "You don't know where you're from?"

"I gotta get going. I didn't mean to spend the night." She threw off the sheet and, as if on cue, her phone rang. Fear etched her face as she stared at her phone on the nightstand. "I better answer this," she mumbled as she grabbed the phone and headed to the bathroom.

Paco stuffed his dry clothes into his satchel, then slipped his boots on. Glancing at his watch, he figured he'd make it back to Alina in a little over two hours.

"You going?" Misty asked.

He whirled around and saw her propped against the wall, arms hugging her small frame. "Yeah. I paid for the room, so you got a few more hours until checkout. How're you feeling?"

"Better. Thanks." She fidgeted in placed. "Uh... didn't you say you were gonna pay me?" He opened his wallet and counted out five hundred dollars, then tossed the money on the bed. With wide eyes, she shook her head. "That's too much. He's gonna know something's up."

"How much is normal for you?"

"A really good night, I can bring in five hundred bucks, but last night was raining, so about two hundred fifty. I already have a hundred, so one fifty's good."

Surprised at her honesty, he held her gaze. "Take the rest for tonight. You can spend another night here. You still sound sick."

"I don't want you feeling sorry for me. I can take care of myself." She picked up the money, took what she needed, and threw the rest back on the blanket along with his T-shirt.

"Go ahead and keep the shirt."

"I can't."

He shrugged and picked up the T-shirt and money except for two fifties. "You can pay your tab and have something just in case you don't feel good tonight."

Slowly she stretched out her arm and snatched the two bills. "You must be rich. What do you do?"

"I own a surplus store." He picked up his leather jacket.

"What's that?"

"I sell military surplus clothing and gear. I also have a large biker section for leather cuts, jackets, boots, and other things."

"I never heard of a surplus store. Do you sell camouflage shorts and T-shirts for women?"

"No shorts, some tees."

"Where's your store at?"

"Alina. I gotta get going." He bent over and picked up his satchel. A soft hand touched the top of his; he looked down and then at her.

"Thanks for everything. I mean it. I don't meet people who don't want something from me." She leaned over and brushed her lips across his cheek.

Straightening up, he ran his fingers through her soft hair. "Take care." He opened the door and left the room. As he walked to his Harley, he felt her eyes on him, but he didn't look back. He had no reason to take one last look at her before he left. She wasn't anything to him, just a girl who'd felt like shit and needed the night off. When he was hitchhiking around the country—after his return from Afghanistan—he'd depended on the kindness of strangers when he was broke. He'd now paid it forward by helping a stranger in need.

Swinging his leg over the seat, he switched on the engine and drove away, fighting the urge to see her one last time. Blending into traffic, he welcomed the rush of the cool air as he soared down the highway. As far as Paco was concerned, he couldn't get back to the clubhouse fast enough.

Chapter Two

MISTY STOOD IN front of the Walmart bulletin board, scanning the flyers of missing persons. A picture of a smiling teenage girl with long dark hair and eyes stared at her. It was an achingly ordinary school portrait with the branches of green leaves background. The girl's smile was self-conscious, her hair too perfect. Above the picture, the word "Missing" was in bold, red lettering. The flyer listed the girl's age to be fifteen at the time she went missing and indicated that she had pierced ears.

Bile burned its way up her throat, and it felt like she was in a box where the walls kept closing in on her. Black spots floated before her eyes and she looked over her shoulder. *I know Bobby's found parking by now. I can't let him see this.* Grabbing the flyer from the board, she ripped it in half and then again. Dashing over to a trash can, she saw him coming into the store. She threw away the pieces of paper and took several deep breaths.

"Whatcha doin'?" he asked, a look of suspicion in his eyes.

"Just throwing away a tissue. Did you have to park far?"

He looked down into the trash can, then back at her. "Not too far. Let's go check out the lingerie." Bobby gripped her hand and they went into the store.

Ever since she'd turned over the money Paco had given her, Bobby had been in a good mood. He'd even let her stay in and sleep the night before, making Crystal and Amber Jade hustle even harder. The two women hated her anyway, and she was sure they were going to plan something to get back at her. They blamed her for Bobby making her his special woman. She was allowed to stay with him in the RV while the other two women had to share a small camper. He never spent the night with them, though he occasionally had sex with them to spite her when she made him mad.

"You like this?" He picked up a purple lace mesh top with a G-string.

"It's pretty," she said, but her mind was on the picture of the girl on the bulletin board.

Chelsea Sullivan. I was her a lifetime ago.

"You seem distracted. What's going on?" Bobby stared at her intently.

Her stomach twisted in several knots. Under no circumstances did she want to break the good mood he'd been in. When he was in a foul mood, he could be very cruel. Forcing a smile she didn't feel, she stroked his cheek. "I'm just happy you're buying me something so pretty, that's all."

A tense pause filled the space between them, and then he tugged her to him and hugged her. "You're my good girl. You want some cold medicine?"

"That'd be great. I know if I had some, I'd feel so much better faster."

"Yeah. Tonight I need you out there. I can't keep giving you time off." Her heart sank but she kept her smile and nodded. "You can wear this under your coat. No way any of those whores can compete with you." He dropped the lingerie set into the cart and steered it toward the pharmacy.

As they maneuvered the aisles, she saw a man ahead of them wearing a leather jacket with writing on the back. The bottom read "Colorado." *Is Paco back in town?* Butterflies erupted inside her as they passed the tall man. She looked quickly at him and her heart felt like it was shrinking. It wasn't him.

Since he'd left the day before, all she could think about was him. He was different from any man she'd ever met. When she'd entered the diner that stormy night, she noticed him immediately. How could she not? With his dark brown hair, chocolate-brown eyes, and square jaw covered in just the right amount of scruff, at first she thought he was a figment of her fevered state. But then he looked at her, and the way Holly—that bitch—kept flirting with him told her that he looked as she saw him: rugged and gorgeous.

"You want cough drops too?" Bobby asked.

"Uh… yeah. Yeah. That's good." She turned away, pretending to be looking at the bottles on the shelf. The fact that Paco ignored Holly's advances told Misty he was different from any of the guys who pulled into the truck stop. And when she saw him with a towel around his waist, his chest perfectly sculpted and sprinkled with wicked tats, and the trail of dark hair suggesting something wonderful, she *wanted* to fuck him. But he said no. She couldn't fathom it. He'd paid her to sleep and feel better. It'd blown her mind, and she still couldn't believe it.

"I think this one will do. What the fuck's up with you?" Irritation laced Bobby's question.

Focus. Don't make him mad. "I guess I just need the medicine. I'm feeling a little out of it."

His face softened. "We'll go back and you can take it and sleep before you get out there tonight." He steered the cart toward the checkout counters and she followed. *Maybe Paco will be in the diner tonight.* She knew it was a long shot; he'd told her he lived near the four corners in Colorado, and that was over a hundred miles away. She wondered if she'd ever see him again.

Just stop it. Even if you saw him again, so what? It's not like you can go away with him. It's not like you're free.

Images of her jumping up in the air shaking her pom-poms during a game at Roosevelt High flitted through her mind. Back then she'd been free. She shook her head in a vain attempt to scramble the memory. Allowing herself to remember wasn't good; it made her sad and resigned. She'd done a good job of erasing her past, but sometimes it shoved its way front and center. Meeting Paco had stirred the walk down memory lane, and seeing herself at fifteen on the flyer had opened the floodgates.

But remembering was dangerous, and as shitty as her life was, she still wanted to keep living.

Bobby's lips on her skin were cool and soothing. The past scurried away to the shadowy corners of her mind.

"You're burning up." He took out the cold medicine and opened it as they walked to his car. Stopping in the middle of the parking lot, he poured out a thick red liquid into the plastic cup. "Here, drink up."

She threw it back and crinkled her nose as the sweet medicinal liquid coated the back of her mouth. "Thanks."

"I always look out for my special girl. You know that." He leaned in and kissed her cheek again.

On the drive back to the RV park, she watched the wind blow the sand and tumbleweeds across the desolate landscape. It was so different from the fertile rolling plains of Ohio.

Stop remembering! I wonder what Paco's doing right now. He said he owned a store. What did he call it?

"You're pretty quiet. Is the medicine doing its thing?"

She nodded.

He said he sold biker stuff and military things. I'll have to google it tonight. I'm just curious. It's nothing more than that. Gives me something different to think about.

"Here we are." Bobby turned into the RV park, about twenty RVs scattered around the dirt lot. All of them were there to work the truck stop for a while before moving on to another one. Misty had been there for the past three months, and she knew Bobby would be pulling up stakes soon. Working the truck stop route was a very transitory life.

She went into their quarters and walked directly to the bedroom. Stripping down to her underwear, she slid under the covers and pulled them over her head. The medicine had begun to take effect, and her heavy eyelids drooped until she succumbed to sleep.

Chapter Three

THE ENCROACHING DARKNESS brought the cold air swirling around Paco, pushing away every lick of warmth it could. Tucking his chin downward, he tugged his jacket tighter around him as he walked toward the clubhouse. Beneath his boots, the ground was slick with ice, and the wind whipped his loose hair about his face, bringing soft pellets of water. He quickened his pace, reaching the front door before the storm hit. A clap of thunder echoed above as he entered the toasty main room.

Glancing at the bar, he saw Steel and Roughneck talking, a bottle of beer in each of their hands. If the president of the Fallen Slayers was there, then something was wrong in Silverado.

"Hey, dude. You're back. How's Kendra?" Goldie asked.

"Good. She had another boy. What's Roughneck doing here?" Paco replied.

"He and Brick came by this morning. Seems like they're having trouble with the little shits in Silverado. These punk gangs are nothing but a pain in the ass. I heard you got caught in the storm a few days ago."

"Yeah. It was fucking brutal. I've been back a couple of days. You been keeping busy with the tattoo shop and Hailey?" Paco motioned to the prospect for a double shot of whiskey.

Goldie laughed. "Yeah. Having an old lady keeps you busier than hell."

Another clash of thunder and then the sound of rain hammering the roof, beating at the windows, and bouncing off every hard surface.

Steel turned around and jerked his head at Paco. "You got back from the store just in time."

"I must be a fucking magnet for the rain." He took the whiskey Patches handed him and took a long drink. "How're things in your neck of the woods?" he asked Roughneck.

Brick came over and leaned against the bar next to Roughneck. The president shook his head. "Not so good. I was just telling Steel about the trouble we're having with that punk gang, the West Avenue Bandits."

"You got your arsenal stocked, didn't you? I remember we put you in touch with Liam." Paco took another gulp.

"We got the guns, but the problem is they're building up their fuckin' gun stock. They're getting their shit from the Los Malos Gang out of Pueblo. We heard they're working with the Satan's Pistons." Roughneck popped a few spicy peanuts in his mouth.

"How in the fuck do the Pistons have any clout right now? We took them out pretty damn good." Paco motioned for another round of drinks.

"They're buying the guns after the idiots give them the money. The punks are so stupid they don't even know the Pistons are ripping them off," Steel said.

"How're they getting their money?" Diablo asked as he came up to the bar.

"They've set up shop and are dealing in drugs and women. They just opened a new strip bar. We've heard rumblings about them wanting to expand their territory and dip into Alina and the rest of the county."

"No way that shit's gonna happen," Paco said, slamming his fist on the counter.

"That's for fucking sure," Steel added.

"We'll chase their asses outta here like we did the Skull Crushers and Satan's Pistons." Diablo crossed his arms.

"That's the way we feel too, but we don't have the numbers to fight them the way we'd like," Brick said.

"These sonsofbitches are actively recruiting from around the county. We've got the experience, but these wannabes are increasing in numbers. They just react without thinking or strategizing. We may need your help, but for now we'll see what they're going to do." Roughneck picked up his beer.

"We wanna see if they're full of shit or are a real threat," Brick added.

Steel shook his head. "They're going to take over Silverado if you don't do something. You need to show them you're not putting up with their bullshit. If you wait around, they'll think they can do what the fuck they want."

"I'm with Steel," Paco said. "You need to come up with a plan, and then either take them out or run them out of the county." Diablo nodded in agreement.

Roughneck ran his hand over his face. "We don't have enough brothers to go head-to-head with them."

"We'll jump in," Steel said.

"Okay. Why don't you guys come to Silverado next weekend and check it out? We can update you then," Roughneck said.

"They gotta be stopped. If they get a stronghold in Silverado, then we'll have a damn mess on our hands. And the West Avenue Bandits need to stick to stealing and shit. We need to show them we don't want them involved in our county, or yours, even if it's only indirectly." Paco gritted his teeth. If he had it his way, he'd get a group of them together, ride to Silverado, and blow the assholes straight to Hell.

"If you need us sooner, let me know," Steel said, clasping Roughneck's shoulder.

"You're fuckin' cheating." Goldie's voice bounced off the walls. The men at the bar turned toward the pool tables.

"I told you Raven's been teaching me some moves. I warned you." Muerto laughed.

"So now you're a pool hustler like your old lady?" Goldie leaned over and took a shot.

Steel, Diablo, and Paco sniggered. Roughneck turned away, his brows knitted. Paco figured he was remembering when Raven hustled in Max's bar. It still seemed to piss him off. "You got some chow around here?" Roughneck asked.

"Lena and the girls are getting ready to bring it out," Steel replied.

"Ruby doesn't look like she's gonna help," Diablo said, pointing to the club girl sitting in Army's lap.

"She's a looker. I may want to get cozy with her after I eat. You got any hang-arounds coming tonight?" Roughneck asked.

"I'm pretty sure Army, Eagle, and Brutus got the word out that we have the president of the Fallen Slayers spending the night. The chicks will be coming in soon," Paco answered.

The Night Rebels waited until Steel and Roughneck filled their plates before they went over to the table. Fried chicken, mashed potatoes, corn, coleslaw, and biscuits enticed them. Paco filled his plate and sat down next to Army, Jigger, Goldie, and Muerto.

"You wanna go to the bike rally this weekend?' Army asked as he buttered his biscuit.

Paco picked up a chicken leg. "Where's it at?"

"Utah. Not too far from where your sister lives," Army replied.

"It's not going to be a big one, but some of the smaller ones have some badass bikes," Goldie said.

Misty's dark eyes flashed through his mind. *I can stop off and see her again to make sure she's doing okay.* "Count me in." He took a swig of beer.

"Cool. We can ride together. I think there're about six of us who are going." Army shoved in a forkful of mashed potatoes.

"Are you going?" Paco asked Jigger.

"I want to but I can't. I'm going to Durango to see my kid for the weekend."

"How's that going with your ex? Did the judge increase her alimony?" Goldie said.

Shaking his head, Jigger coated his potatoes in black pepper. "Nah. He set it to expire at the end of the year. She about shit a brick. Serves her right. She wanted to get more money outta me so she could sit home and watch TV. Fuck that. I'm glad the judge saw through it. I wish I had Abe full time."

"Does she treat him all right?" Paco asked.

"Morgan's a royal bitch, but she's a good mom. I just wish I saw him more, that's all." Jigger pushed his plate away. "Some of the chicks are coming in. Man, the blonde in the short leopard skirt is fuckin' hot."

Paco craned his neck and saw a stacked woman in her thirties wearing a tight skirt and a clingy top walk toward the bar. He smiled. "She's just your type, dude. Built and older." Jigger was twenty-six years old, and Paco noticed he shied away from women his own age and went for those who were in their mid-thirties and older.

"Older women are more grounded than the ones around my age, and they have more experience, which makes it real fun." He chuckled.

"I love older women," Army said as he ran his eyes over the blonde's curves.

"Age doesn't mean shit if you hit it off," Paco said as he rose to his feet. "You want any more drinks? I'll have Rusty bring you another round."

Goldie held up his hands. "None for me. I'm taking off."

"I want to get to know the blonde hottie," Jigger said, standing up.

"I'll go over to the bar with you," Army said.

With his back against the bar, Paco scanned the crowd. In a short time, the room had become packed with hang-arounds, all looking to have a good time with a brother. Some of them were there for the excitement of being with a rough biker, some loved having sex with a lot of men, and some came for the drugs and the intimacy, even if it was just for a short time. He saw Roughneck and Alma, one of the club girls, kissing up a storm before Roughneck stood up, grabbed her hand, and walk out of the room.

"Hey, bro, how's it going?" Sangre asked as he approached Paco.

"Good. The store's been busy, which is good."

"I heard you got caught in that crazy storm that blew into Utah over the weekend. It fuckin' sucks to be on a bike in a downpour."

"Yeah, but I was able to pull off pretty soon after it started." He picked up his beer and brought it to his lips. *If it wasn't for the rain, I wouldn't have met Misty. Shit, I've got to stop thinking about her.* But he couldn't help it. She'd been on his mind since the morning he'd left. There was such sadness in her eyes, but also a solid determination; he couldn't help but want to know her backstory. *How the hell did she get mixed up with a pimp?* That question had been on his mind for the last few days. *How did she end up in a truck stop selling her body?*

"You listening, man?" Sangre's loud voice in his ear made Misty's face fade away.

"What did you say?"

"I asked if you're going to the rally in Utah this weekend."

"Army just told me about it. I'm in. You?"

"I got too much shit to do at the grow store."

"Hey, baby. You want some company?" Lucy ran her nails up and down his forearm. He shook his head and the club girl's face fell. "What's wrong?"

"I have some things on my mind, that's all."

Leaning in close, she wrapped her arms around his neck. "I can make sure you forget, even if it's just for a little bit." She licked his earlobe.

His dick twitched, but he pulled away. "Just not feeling it tonight, Lucy. Another time."

"I'll hold you to that." She kissed his cheek and walked over to Eagle, who was chatting with Brick and Diablo.

"Why the hell didn't you go for Lucy? She's been wanting to jump you since you got back. You know you're her favorite." Sangre turned around and gestured to Rusty. "Two more here."

Paco rested his elbows on top of the bar. "Lucy will be available whenever I want." He picked up the whiskey the prospect put in front of him. "Two new guys want to prospect for the club."

"Are they the ones who've been hanging around for the last six months?"

Paco nodded. "Tattoo Mike and Rooster recommended them. They said they've known the guys for years and they're solid. Chains did backgrounds on them and they look good."

"Cool. We need a few more members, especially with all the shit these punk gangs are trying to pull. Do you know if Steel is letting Patches and Rusty patch in?"

"We've talked about it. It'll probably happen at the summer rally."

"So you gonna party tonight or just drink and check out the women?" Sangre turned around and leaned against the bar.

Following suit, Paco's gaze landed on a small woman with long black hair. Sucking in his breath, excitement rushed through his veins. *It's Misty. What the fuck is she doing here?* Staring fixedly at her, he picked up his drink and took a big gulp. *Think, man. There's no way it's her. She lives over a hundred miles away.*

Even though he knew it wasn't her, adrenaline shot through him in anticipation of seeing her amazing eyes again. Then, as if sensing she was being watched, she slowly turned around, and the adrenaline drained out of him. *It's not her.* The woman walked toward him, and he clasped Sangre's shoulder.

"Later, bro." He pushed away from the bar.

"Hey," a throaty voice said behind him.

He turned around and saw the woman he'd thought was Misty. "Not interested," he said, taking a few steps away from her.

Her lips turned downward. "You don't remember me, do you?"

Slowly shaking his head, he searched her face. "No. I don't."

"It was a few months ago. My hair was lighter. Remember… Charlotte?"

He racked his brain but nothing came up. "Maybe you're mistaking me for one of the other brothers."

"Oh, honey, there's no way I'd mistake you. You kept licking shooters off my tits. Does that jog your memory?"

Scrubbing his face, he jerked his head back. "Oh, yeah. Fuck, I'm sorry. You look different. When we hooked up, your hair wasn't as long as it is now."

She leaned in close, the scent of nutmeg swirling around him. The softness of her tits pressed against him made his dick jerk. Placing her index finger on her lips, she said, "Shh… don't tell anyone, but I'm wearing a wig."

"I'll be damned."

"You game for some shooters?" She ran her hand over his.

"Not tonight. I have some stuff to do. Maybe another time."

"Really? I was hoping we could hook up again. I should be mad at you for never calling me."

He chuckled. "I don't usually call chicks. As I recall, you gave me your number and told me to call you. That never works for me. If I wanna call a chick, I ask for her number."

"I just thought we had something, you know?"

"It was fun."

"You sure you don't want this?" She ran her hands over her curves and squeezed her breasts.

"My brother Sangre would love what you're giving away." With his elbow, he nudged Sangre.

"Yo. What's up?" Sangre said, swiveling around.

"Charlotte's feeling real frisky and wants some fun," Paco replied.

Sangre ran his eyes over her body and Paco sniggered. "Is that so, baby?"

"Well, I really wanted to have some fun with Paco, but he doesn't want to." Her gaze went to Sangre's tight muscular arms. "You look like you wouldn't pass up some fun with me."

"My brother here is a fuckin' idiot. I'd love to party with you, baby." Sangre wrapped his arm around her and winked at Paco. "Thanks, dude. I owe you." He led Charlotte away and they disappeared into the crowd.

After putting the empty glass on the bar, Paco headed up to his room, kicked off his boots, and went over to a chest of drawers. Opening the first drawer, he took out two Jack shooters and several joints. He went over to the CD player and switched it on, turning the volume down. Sinking down in the recliner by the picture window, he looked out. In the distance, headlights from random vehicles glowed eerily through the thin mist. Specks of light filled the inky sky, but in the darkened haze, the San Juan Mountains weren't visible. It was like a pitch-black curtain had been draped over them.

He put the joint between his lips and lit it, enjoying the first long drag. The lyrics from Twisted Sister's "We're Not Gonna Take It" sang out and he picked up his phone.

"What's wrong?" he asked Kendra, dread weaving through him.

"Nothing. I've been meaning to call you since you left a few days ago. I just wanted to make sure you made it back okay."

"I'm good. How's the baby?"

"Great. Matt and Diego are loving their new brother. It's so adorable. Vicky said she can stay a couple more weeks. I'm happy. I can use the help."

"I told you I'd give you the money to hire someone to help you out."

"I know. I appreciate the offer, and I may take you up on it after Vicky leaves. You do so much for us as it is. I hate to take anything more from you."

"I offered, so it's no problem. Anyway, I remember how the pay sucked when I was in the Army. Jesse's not sending enough home for you and the boys."

A small pause. "Thank you. You're a wonderful brother. I don't know what I'd do without you. You've been there for me ever since Mom died," she said softly.

He didn't want to think about their mother, about the red-smeared walls and furniture, about finding her sprawled on the floor swimming in her own blood. He didn't want to revisit the scene he conjured up most days and nights.

It'd been sixteen years since he came home from school and walked into a nightmare, his mother's body bruised and stabbed on the dining room floor. He'd been fourteen and had come home early because of an injury he'd sustained when he and some of his buddies were roughhousing during lunch. When he'd first seen his mother, the reality of what had happened hadn't sunk in. He'd called his father right away and then the police. His father had made it to their house before the police, and when he came in and saw his slain wife, he'd fallen to his knees and wept uncontrollably. Paco's father's cries still echoed through his brain all these years later. He'd never be able to expunge them.

"Hello? Are you still with me?"

"Yeah. Sorry."

"You were thinking about Mom and the horrible thing Dad did to her, weren't you?" she whispered.

Taking a deep breath, he blew it out slowly. "No point in recalling all that shit. I'll be near Richfield this weekend. I'm going to a biker rally. I'll stop in and see how you and the kids are doing."

"Another visit from you so soon. I love it! I know the boys will be ecstatic about seeing you again."

"I'll call you toward the end of the week and let you know when I'm coming. Take care of yourself, and call me if you need anything."

"I will. I love you," she said.

"Yeah. See you."

He put the phone on the end table and twisted off the cap on the whiskey shooter, downing it in one long drink before lighting another joint, stretching his legs out in front of him. He wasn't going back to Utah for the rally or to see his sister; he was going because a dark-haired woman had captured his imagination. With one glance, her soulful eyes pulled him in, and he wanted to see her again.

A billow of smoke ribboned around him as he blew out. Paco had no idea what it was about this particular woman that intrigued him so much, didn't know why he couldn't get her out of his head. A part of him feared the deep stirrings inside him, but he ignored the unease.

Maybe when I see her again, I won't feel anything. I bet I was just tired from the long ride and the storm. I'll see her, make sure she's okay, and then move on. When I get back, I'll party with Lucy. I may even ask her to spend the night with me. I'll be back on track. I just need to see Misty one last time, and then all will be good.

Watching the mist thicken outside, he rested his head back against the cushion and closed his eyes.

Chapter Four

THE CHILLY WIND'S harsh bite whipped around Misty, making its way through her leggings, and she pressed her knees close to ward off the cold. Her hair fell loose around her face and shoulders, tousled, tangled. She bowed her head, wrapped her arms tighter around herself, and headed to the diner.

The heat calmed her chattering teeth as she stepped into the restaurant, walked quickly to the first booth, and slid inside. She glanced out the window and saw Crystal and Amber Jade moving between the lanes of trucks. She knew she should be out there hustling, but it was so cold, and she was so tired.

Earlier, several men had taken the bait when Bobby had her get on the CB to see who was interested in what she was offering. She had some men lined up, but she didn't feel like being with any of them. She was sick of what her life had become. When she'd been back home, she'd never dreamed her life would turn out like this. She'd wanted to go to college and study theater. One of the things she'd loved best was acting in the school plays at Roosevelt High.

Misty supposed she was getting plenty of acting experience every time she pretended to like what she was doing, and most of her interactions with Bobby were lies. The truth was she couldn't stand the bastard, and it repulsed her whenever he touched her.

In the beginning, she'd fought hard, but after a long time, he'd broken her. She'd been resigned to the fact that her life would always be this way until she'd met Paco. For that brief slice of time she'd spent with him, he'd made her want to get away from the shame and filth her life had become. But she knew she really couldn't escape without harm coming to her family.

Sighing, she rubbed her hands together to warm them up. *You have no idea what an impact you had on me, Paco.* She hadn't been to the diner since the night she'd met him, and she was half hoping he'd be there, drinking a cup of coffee.

"Unless you got money, your skank ass is outta here," Holly said.

The nasty woman's voice shattered her thoughts. "Bobby paid the tab," she replied.

"No, he didn't. He probably spent the money you fuck for on a woman who isn't a whore. Do you got money?"

Misty's insides tightened as she opened her coin purse.

"And the biker isn't here to feel sorry for you, so either show me the money or get the hell outta here."

Taking out three dollars in quarters, she threw the coins on the table. "A cup of hot tea. Bring me some honey and a glass of water with lemon."

"I oughta throw your ass out, you filthy lot lizard." She whirled around and walked toward the kitchen.

Her words stung as hard as if she'd slapped Misty across the face. *She's right. I'm nothing but scum. The bottom of the barrel, even for sex workers.* She wiped her eyes and pretended to be looking for something in her purse when Holly came back and slammed down the cup of tea. The brown liquid sloshed over the rim and spilled on the table. Without looking at her, Misty pulled out a few napkins from the dispenser and wiped up the mess before ripping open a packet of honey.

As she drank her tea, she looked down at her phone. She'd googled the keywords "surplus store" and "Alina," and two stores had popped up in the town. She'd been toying with the idea of calling him for the past couple of days, but each time she tapped in the number, she'd chickened out.

What would I say to him, and where would it get me? I can't escape. She stirred her tea. *It's better to forget all about him and give up on the crazy notion that I'll be freed. If I want to avoid a beating from Bobby, I have to focus on earning enough money tonight. I know Crystal and Amber Jade will tell Bobby they saw me in the diner. Those bitches.*

The fantasy of Paco rescuing her from her shitty life didn't get her anywhere. *That shit only happens in fairy tales, the ones Mom used to read to me. Fuck... that was such a long time ago.*

"Can I sit with you?" an older woman asked as she slid in the seat across from Misty. "I gotta get off my feet for a while."

Her thoughts splintered and she looked at the woman. Misty had seen her hauling her ass in and out of cabs since she'd arrived at the truck stop with Bobby, Crystal, and Amber Jade three months before. The woman looked to be in her early fifties, her face lined and weathered from too much sun, her teeth rotted. Misty was pretty sure she was a meth user like most of the women on the lot. She felt sorry for her because she had to compete with the younger flesh flocking to the lot night after night. Misty often saw the woman hustling during the day. She probably knew the younger women preferred the nights when they could do shameful things under the cover of darkness.

"Are you having a good night?" Misty asked as she stirred another packet of honey into her tea.

"Not so good. My feet are killing me. What about you?"

Misty shrugged. "Okay, I guess."

"You doing this 'cause it pays better than some crappy-ass minimum-wage job, or are you forced to do it?" She stared fixedly at her.

Misty cleared her throat and sat up straighter. "It pays the bills. What about you?"

"I've been flying solo for almost thirty years. I was about your age when I started. I've quit so many times, but I always come back. The pay is good, and I don't have to declare shit to the government." She guffawed, then leaned back. "I'm Shirley."

"Misty."

"Hey, Shirley. What can I get you?" Holly asked.

"I'll have the BLT with extra mayo. Bring me some coffee."

"Black, right?" Holly smiled, and Shirley nodded.

"Can I have some more hot water?" Misty asked.

Holly rolled her eyes. "Aren't you the big spender? I can't have you taking up space drinking hot water."

"Just bring me the water. I fuckin' paid for it." Holly glared at her, then marched away. "She's such a fuckin' bitch."

Shirley chuckled. "She thinks she's better than us because she doesn't get paid to fuck. Actually, she's pretty stupid. She's been giving it out for free to all the long-haul drivers for the past three years, and she's still stuck in this shithole."

"She doesn't seem to have a problem with you. I hate the bitch."

"Look at me, sweetie. Would you be jealous of me? She hates you because you're pretty and clean. I can tell you don't use. And the way that biker stood up for you made her madder than hell. She wanted to fuck him so bad." Shirley laughed.

"How'd you know about Paco?"

"She told me and anyone who would listen. She couldn't believe that he picked you over her. I just wished I was here to see it."

"He was just helping me out. Nothing happened. I was so sick that night, I just fell asleep, and he was a real gentleman."

"That's a first. I used to party hard with bikers when I was younger. I worked in some of their strip clubs, and 'gentlemen' isn't a word I'd use in describing them. But they sure know how to party and give a gal a good time. I had some great times when I was younger."

Holly put the BLT in front of Shirley. "Can I get you anything else?"

The woman glanced at Misty. "You want something to eat?"

Holly scowled.

A low growl rumbled from Misty's stomach, and she squirmed in her seat trying to quiet it. "I'm good."

Shirley shook her head. "No you ain't. Do you like BLTs?"

With eyes cast downward, Misty nodded. Holly huffed out an exaggerated breath and stomped away.

"Thanks," Misty said softly. "I'll pay you back."

"I know you will. No rush. Where you from?"

She raised her eyes and met Shirley's pale blue ones. "Why?"

The woman took a big bite of her sandwich and chewed for a few seconds. "I was just wondering. I'm from Arizona, but I've been traveling all around the country. I've been here for about three years. It's the longest I've ever stayed in one place in a real long time." She popped a potato chip in her mouth and crunched down on it.

"We do a lot of traveling too. Especially in Texas, Louisiana, and Mississippi. It's not so humid here, so I like that."

Holly slammed the plate down in front of Misty and stalked away.

"So you're not gonna tell me where you come from. Are you sure you're here 'cause you wanna be?" Shirley looked at her pointedly.

"Yeah." She bit into the BLT. "This is really good. I can't remember the last time I had a BLT." In a couple of minutes, she'd finished her sandwich and chips. "I guess I was hungry." She laughed dryly.

"You gotta eat."

"Thanks, Shirley." Misty glanced at the flashing screen on her phone.

Bobby: *Y the fuck r u in the diner?*

"Those bitches," she muttered under her breath.

Misty: *Just stopped in 4 hot tea. Still sick. Leaving now.*

Bobby: *U better bring home 500 bucks or I'll be pissed.*

A shiver of fear wrapped around her spine.

Misty: *I will. No worries.*

Bobby: *Move ur fuckin' ass. NOW.*

Sliding her phone in her jacket pocket, she scooted to the edge of the booth. "I have to get back out there. Thanks again, Shirley. I'll pay you back. Promise." She pushed the coins over to her. "That's for my tea."

"Take care of yourself. Be careful whose cab you go into."

Misty smiled. It'd been a long time since someone cared about her well-being. For a split second, Shirley reminded her of her mom. "I will. See you around."

The wind slashed through her as she rushed over to the middle row of trucks. Several of the drivers honked, and a couple flashed their lights. She waved at them, holding up her hand indicating that she was going to visit them all. *Someone's on my side tonight. I'll definitely make more than what Bobby's expecting.*

Happy that she'd avoided a beating, she opened the door of a semi and pulled herself in.

AT FOUR IN the morning, she quietly turned the doorknob and went inside the RV. Bobby's snores greeted her, and she hoped he'd stay sleeping when she was ready to slip between the sheets. The last thing she wanted was to have him paw her.

Turning on a small lamp on the counter, she saw numerous beer cans strewn across the counter and the small table. Elation coursed through her—he'd passed out and would be out cold for the next several hours.

After drinking a bottle of water, she went into the bathroom and jumped into the shower. The warm water made her relax for the first time in the past several hours, and she rubbed her skin over and over, trying to wash off the memories of that night. Taking a shower after her shift had become a ritual she looked forward to every night. It gave her order in a life filled with chaos.

She padded to the bed and gingerly slid between the sheets. Bobby kept snoring. She closed her eyes, waiting for the refuge of sleep to take her away for a few hours.

RAYS OF SUNLIGHT pierced her eyes as she slowly opened them. The scent of coffee permeated the room, and she heard the clang of pans and the low sizzle of something frying in a pan. *Breakfast links.* How she hated them. The smell alone made her want to puke. She pulled the covers over her head to block out the sun and the smells.

"Get up, lazy bones." The bed dipped, Bobby's hand running over her hip and leg. "You did real good, baby. Seven hundred and fifty bucks. Fuck, you must've been on fire last night. Crystal and Amber Jade didn't bring that much in for the two of them. You hungry?"

"Not really. I'd rather sleep for a few more hours. I got in late last night."

"You can sleep while I drive."

A knot formed in the pit of her stomach. "Why're you driving?"

"We're pulling outta here."

It was as if he'd thrown a bucket of ice water at her. Her heart beat in overtime, hitting against her chest so hard she feared her ribs would break and her skin would rip apart.

I can't leave. How will Paco know where I am?

"Although, I'm tempted to stay after the money you brought in last night. If I hadn't made the arrangement, we'd stay a bit longer." He pulled down the covers and stroked her hair.

Don't touch me, you disgusting asshole. I can't go. Then his thin, cold lips kissed her. It was a sloppy kiss, and it turned her stomach. *You're being ridiculous. You've moved so many times. Why is this any different? And don't you dare think about Paco. You're being ridiculous. Like he'd ever come back here looking for you.*

"What's the matter? Did you give it all away last night?" He laughed and roughly squeezed her breast under her thin nightshirt.

"Do we have to go? I don't want to."

Suddenly he wrapped his fist around her hair and yanked it hard. Her eyes watered and she cried out before he brought his face inches away from hers. "I'm not asking you what the fuck you want. You don't have an opinion. You don't think. All you do is fuck. I own you, and I tell you what the fuck to do, when to do it, and where to do it." Spit from his mouth wet her face. For good measure, he pulled her hair so hard she feared it'd rip out of her scalp.

"Okay. I'm sorry."

"Don't ever question me again, slut," he growled as he smacked her hard across the face then walked out of the room.

She rubbed her tingling scalp, then buried her face in the pillow, suppressing her sobs.

Thirty minutes later, Misty sat in the front passenger seat as Bobby pulled away from the gas pump. Hitting the highway, she glanced in the rearview mirror and stared at the truck stop as it became smaller and smaller, then eventually disappeared. She put on her sunglasses and focused on the mountains in the distance as the sand and sagebrush blew across the highway.

Chapter Five

WITH TWO BLACK saddlebags in hand, Paco zipped them on the yoke and tightened the belt to make sure there was enough clearance from the bottom of the packs to the top of the rear tire. He glanced over at Shotgun, who had just finished installing his bags. Normally, Paco and the other bikers would dismount the satchels when they returned from a longer trip. Paco pulled on the packs to make sure they were secure, then slid his leather gloves on while he waited for Goldie, Army, Chains, and Cueball to come out.

"No rain in the forecast," Shotgun said as he tightened the screws on his bags.

"Glad of that." Paco leaned against his bike and lit a joint. Winters in Alina were a combination of bitter winds, rain, and sometimes snow. The San Juan Mountains could be treacherous in the winter with all the snow and ice that covered them, and it would be a pain in the ass to ride if it started raining.

"Are you finished, Shotgun?" Army asked, walking over to a shiny amber Harley.

"Just about," Shotgun replied.

"I'm gonna ride with you guys until we get to Moab, and then I'll join you at the rally." Paco opened one of the bags and took out his sunglasses.

"Whatcha got going in Moab?" Army asked.

"Just something personal." He put on his sunglasses and swung his leg over his Harley.

"Doesn't your sister live in Richfield?" Chains asked as he pushed up his bike's kickstand with his boot.

"Yeah. I'll see her on the way back. You wanna come with me?"

Chains nodded. "Yep. You staying the night?"

"Planning on it."

"Doesn't that chick you used to bang all the time live in Richfield?" Army asked.

"That's right, she does. That fuckin' works out for me." Chains switched on the engine and the low rumble of his Harley filled the space between them.

Shotgun straddled his bike and turned on the engine. Soon a loud rumble from all the idling bikes made some of the club girls come outside to see what was going on. Paco was glad the conversation had been cut off. He wasn't in the mood for twenty questions, and some of the brothers were nosy as hell, especially Army. He was way worse than any of the club girls.

The six bikers left the club's grounds and headed to the highway. They rode in formation, two by two, and drivers slowed down when their powerful iron machines roared past them. As the traffic thinned out, Paco relaxed a bit, enjoying the coyote-meets-road-runner desertscape of southern Utah. Red rocky cliffs and buttes abounded, and high above, pale against the blue sky, king birds rode the thermals in a graceful dance. Gnarled branches of ironwood trees had dropped their leaves, making them look almost dead among the green cacti and agave plants that rose from the coarse ground. As they passed through Monticello, sagebrush-covered cattle ranches dotted the landscape.

Up ahead, amazing red rock formations signaled that Moab was coming up. Paco raised his arm and pointed to an exit, indicating that he was going to turn off. The truck stop was there, and anticipation crawled up his spine. Goldie nodded and pointed toward his bike's gas tank as if to say he needed to refuel. Soon Paco's brothers followed him into the truck stop, pulling up to the gas pumps.

"It's been a while since I rode this route. I forgot how fuckin' beautiful it is," Goldie said as he walked inside the convenience store with Paco.

"Even though I come through here quite a bit, it always blows me away. You getting something to drink?" Paco picked up an energy drink and went over to the counter.

"Hailey and I were out late last night, so an energy drink is just what I need."

Paco took out his money clip. "Twenty on four," he said to the pasty-faced man behind the counter. "And this." He slid the can toward him.

After paying up, he stood by the gas pump, filling his tank while he scanned the area where the semis parked. Several women walked in front and between the trucks, but there was no sign of Misty.

"Awesome ride," Shotgun said as he grabbed the nozzle and fit it into his gas tank.

"So what do you have going on in Moab? I never heard you mention it before." Army took a bite out of a Snickers bar.

Paco clenched his jaw. "Like I said, it's personal."

"Did you get some first-class pussy when you came by this way last week? You coming back for more? Does she have a friend?"

"Fuck off." Paco put the nozzle back in its cradle.

"I was just screwin' with you, but I think I hit a nerve. Who is she?"

"I told you to fuck off." Paco crushed the energy drink can and tossed it in the trash bin. "I'll meet up with you guys later," he said to Chains and Cueball. They nodded.

He watched them turn onto the highway, and then he rode over to the diner. So far he hadn't seen Misty. *Maybe she just comes out at night.* He'd find out where she was staying and go talk to her.

The diner had more people in it than when he'd been there the previous week, but it was earlier in the day and the weather was good. A few people looked like tourists who'd stopped for a bite to eat, and the rest of the customers were truckers. He scanned the room, hoping to see a woman with long hair and soulful eyes.

Misty's not here. Fuck.

"Just one?" an older woman asked, a menu in her hand.

He jerked his head and followed her to a booth by the window. She gave him the menu. "Someone will be with you in a moment."

A young woman of about twenty started coming over to him. She held a small notepad and had a pen tucked behind her ear. Behind her, he saw Holly wearing a large smile. Practically knocking down the young waitress, she rushed over to his table.

"I've got this one, Annie."

"But it's my table," Paco heard her say in a low voice.

"I know him. I'll give you one of my tables. That guy with the big gut. He's a great tipper. Just unbutton your top a little and bend down real low." She turned to Paco. "Hi, stranger. How've you been?"

"Fine."

"I didn't think I'd ever see you again."

From the way she looked at him, he knew she thought he'd come back to see her. "Just passing through."

"You a salesman or something? Do you sell shoes or vacuums?"

"On a Harley?" *What a dumbass.*

She giggled and placed her hands behind her back, pushing out her chest. "What can I get you to eat?"

"Where can I find Misty?"

The smile vanished, her shoulders drooped, and her eyes narrowed. "What?"

"Where can I find Misty?"

"Are you fuckin' serious? You came back here for someone like *that*?"

"I didn't ask for your damn opinion. Where is she?"

"How do I know? I don't keep track of *them*. What's your deal? Are you one of them guys who has a thing for dirty women?"

"Bring me a cup of coffee and some cream." He turned away and looked out the window. Beyond the truck stop, he saw an RV park and wondered if that's where she lived.

Holly slammed the coffee down and it spilled. He grabbed her wrist and squeezed it.

"What the hell? You're hurting me."

"You show me respect. We can do this the easy way or the hard way, but believe me, the hard way isn't gonna be the way you wanna go with me."

"I just can't believe you're interested in a girl like that. Besides, she's gone."

A sudden coldness hit at his core. *Gone?* "What the fuck does that mean?" He gripped her wrist tighter.

"I haven't seen her in a couple of nights. I heard that she and two other skanks left with her boyfriend, Bobby. I have no idea where they went. People come and go from here all the time." She blinked quickly. "You're really hurting me."

He slowly relaxed his fingers and she pulled away from him. Rubbing her wrist, she offered him a small smile. "I get off in an hour if you want somewhere to crash."

He looked out the window. "I'm leaving. Bring the bill." Sitting on a rusted chair in front of the diner was an older woman. She had her leg crossed over her thigh, and her hand kneaded her bare foot.

So Misty's gone. Why the hell do I feel so shitty about it? I should've asked for her number. This is lame as hell. I should be riding with my brothers instead of drinking shitty coffee and hoping the bitch waitress lied to me. Fucking pitiful. I'm outta here.

With force, he pushed the coffee away from him, the dark liquid spilling onto the table. He grabbed the bill and went to the cashier. Without a glance at Holly, who'd positioned herself right next to the cash register, he paid and went outside.

He looked at all the trucks, and at the women who walked back and forth around them.

"You're good-looking. Where did you come from? I've never seen you before."

He looked over his shoulder at the woman in the rusty chair. "Just passing through."

"You a long-haul driver?"

"Nope."

"I could tell you weren't. I bet that gorgeous dark green Harley's yours."

"It is. Do you know Misty?"

Holding her hand up to block the sun, she nodded. "You looking for her?"

"Yeah."

Shaking her head, she clucked her tongue. "The young ones have the tight asses and perky tits, but I've got the experience. I can give you a better time than she ever could."

"I'm not looking for that. I just need to talk to her."

She scrunched her face. "You her brother or something?"

"Do you know where she is or not?"

"You don't go in for small talk, do you?" She chuckled and resumed rubbing her feet. "She took off with that no-good pimp Bobby. They left a couple of days ago in the early hours."

Fuck. The bitch told me the truth. "Where were they going?"

"I dunno. I just saw him and the three women take off. A lot of them people just stay around for a few months and then move on to another lot. I've been here for a long time, seen all sorts of people come and go. It's the nature of the business."

That's it, then. "Thanks." He went over to his Harley.

"Hey. My name's Shirley."

Without looking at her, he adjusted his rearview mirror.

"You got a name?"

"Yeah." He switched on the engine.

She walked over to him. "If you were around when I was younger, you'd be all up my ass." She smiled, her stained and rotted teeth peeking out from behind her lips.

He jerked his head at her, backed up, and rode away.

Three hours later, he pulled into a large grassy area where booths, a couple of stages, and a lot of cool bikes filled the space. Spotting Cueball's silver Harley, he made his way over.

"Dude," Cueball said as he bumped fists with him. "We thought you'd be a lot longer. Army said you were getting some pussy."

"Army's a fucking asshole. Do you see the tents?" Cueball nodded.

A lot of the bike rallies rented out tents, especially the smaller ones, and Goldie had reserved a few of them a couple of weeks before. They'd spend the weekend at the rally, and then he and Chains would stop by and spend a night or two with Kendra.

Paco hated that he gave a shit about Misty leaving so much so that he wasn't really into the rally. The way he was reacting to never seeing her again surprised him. He barely knew her, and he'd placed his heart in a rock-solid steel case ever since he and Cassie had broken up. *Now why the fuck am I thinking about* her? *Ever since Misty and I crossed paths, all sorts of shit's been brewing inside me.*

"I found some chicks we can party with tonight," Army said, handing him a beer. "They've been into us since we first got here. And when they find out you're the VP of the club, they'll be willing to do anything."

"Are they the ones in Daisy Dukes and almost see-through T-shirts?" Shotgun asked as he opened a bottle of Jack.

"Those are the ones. And when the sun goes down, it'll get fuckin' cold, and we'll have to keep them real warm," Cueball added as he flipped the cap off his beer bottle.

Paco looked over to a group of women who matched Shotgun's description and smiled. *Fucking a bunch of biker groupies hard is just what I need. That'll knock some sense into me and get me out of this funk I've been in.*

"You in, bro?" Army asked.

"Yeah, sure," Paco answered, but the truth was he wasn't really feeling it. He was talking himself into it, but he had no interest in the group of giggling women who kept pointing at him. All they really wanted was a mind-blowing experience they could tell their friends about when they got back home. Every biker chick wanted to screw a vice president. Lately, all of it had become so mundane and predictable.

When he'd first become a Night Rebel, he couldn't believe how the women flocked to the club, wanting to experience the wild side even if it was only for a night. And he loved it. He could have sex whenever and as many times as he wanted. It had been what he needed to rid Cassie from his mind, his body, and his heart. He'd thought he'd never tire of the life, but he had. Suddenly having any chick he wanted didn't mean that much to him, especially since most of them just wanted to fuck a biker. Something was missing, but he wasn't sure what it was until he'd helped out Misty. Their interaction wasn't sexual. She needed help. He gave it. And in that solitary moment when she let him help her without any strings attached, he knew he needed something more than banging a different woman every night.

He looked around at his fellow club members and knew they wouldn't understand. *Maybe Goldie would since he has Hailey now, but Army and Shotgun would have a field day with this one.* Truth be told, he didn't even understand it, but something had clicked deep inside him that night he'd met Misty. Something he'd gone out of his way to keep buried and apart from the rest of him had started to crack, and he wasn't sure if he was ready to deal with it. Part of him wanted to keep his familiar lifestyle, but another part craved more. So much more.

As they checked out the bikes and chatted up old friends they hadn't seen for a while, Paco ignored the women who kept staring and pointing at him.

"You're not into the chicks, are you?" Goldie asked as he handed him a joint.

"Not really." He inhaled deeply.

"Wanna tell me what's going on with you?" Goldie lit another one and put it between his lips.

Paco shook his head. "I don't know. It's just some shit came up that's got me thinking too much. Scorpio called me a few nights ago."

Scorpio was doing a six-year stint in state prison for selling stolen bike parts to an undercover cop when he'd been in Denver helping out with his sick dad. It was bad luck, and Paco had told him that he should've called him or Steel if he needed the extra money to pay his dad's medical bills.

"How's he doing?"

"Good. He's counting the days until he's outta there. It'll be good to have him back at the club. He and I prospected together."

"I know you guys are real tight." Goldie went over and bought two more beers from a booth, handing one to Paco. "Life can really suck, but then kickass shit happens that blows your mind. Like Hailey for me."

"Yeah. You got a good woman. We gotta make sure the West Avenue Bandits don't start shit in our county. I can't believe Roughneck wants to wait around and see what these punk gangs are gonna do. He's gotten soft."

Goldie laughed. "Don't let him hear you say that, but I agree. The whole club's acting like pussies. We gotta set them straight. Are you going to Silverado next weekend?"

"Yeah. We can't let shit start. Steel's one hundred percent on board with this. If Roughneck and his brothers won't do anything, we will."

At the end of the evening, Goldie and Paco sat inside their tent and talked about motorcycles—their favorite subject—while the rest of the brothers partied hard with the giggling groupies.

A SMALL YELLOW sign emblazoned with "Army Surplus" in black lettering hung from the corrugated metal roof. The only other surplus store in town was near the outskirts, and it was half the size of Paco's store in downtown Alina.

The store had the perpetual scent of musty canvas mixed with metal, rubber, and leather. Not only did he carry a large assortment of military-issued clothing and gear, but there was a large section devoted to riding on the road. Leather jackets for men and women, riding boots, motorcycle gear, and funky accessories for the woman who had a rebel streak in her lined the walls and shelves in the back section of the store.

Glancing down at his phone, he opened the text and smiled when he saw the picture of Tommy that his sister had just texted him. He'd only been back a day and Kendra was already asking when he was going to come for another visit. He wished she and the boys would move to Alina. Jesse had another five years on his contract which meant Kendra and the kids would be alone a lot.

The door chimed as Army, Eagle, and Chains walked in, Army making a beeline for the cute clerk Paco had just hired.

"What brings you guys in? Just bored?" Paco stood up from the stool behind the counter.

"We were in the neighborhood, and Army's looking for a flag," Eagle said.

"Hey, honey. Do you have a 'Don't Tread on Me' flag?" Army asked the girl as she blushed ten shades of red.

"There's one hanging from the ceiling right in front of your face. Leave Jillian alone. She's got real work to do." Paco pointed behind him. "Can you open the boxes that came in this morning and sort them out?"

With a look of relief, Jillian nodded and dashed away.

"What the fuck?" Army asked, reaching up to touch the flag.

"Don't mess with my employees. I've told you that before. Besides, she's too damn young for you. You wanna hang the flag up in your room?"

"Yeah. I'd love to mount it on my bike so the fuckin' badges could see it and know not to mess with my civil liberties." The brothers laughed.

"That'd be cool. Take it to Skid Marks. Maybe Shotgun or Diablo can get it mounted for you. Let me get you one." He bent down and pulled a crisply folded flag from a plastic bin.

"Do you have any Corozal Drystar gloves left?" Eagle asked.

"I just got another shipment in. They're in the back of the store."

At that moment, a trio of women came in and eyed the men. One of them smiled at Paco. "Hi."

"Hey. How's it going?"

"Okay. Well actually, I've been pretty bored lately." She ran the tip of her tongue over her top lip. "How've you been?"

"Good."

The woman's two friends laughed and went over to a rack of camouflage clothing. She winked at Paco and joined them.

"Who the hell is she?" Army asked, his eyes on her ass.

"A customer. She comes into the store a lot."

"From the signals she's giving out, she wants more than camouflage T-shirts and cut-offs."

Paco laughed. "Yeah, I've suspected that for a while."

"Then why the fuck haven't you ridden her?"

"I don't mix business with pleasure."

"Well since this isn't my business, I'm gonna check her out." Army started to walk away.

"Hold on. I'll go with you," Eagle said.

"Do you still want the gloves?" Paco asked.

"Yeah. Size large." He followed Army.

"Aren't you going to join them?" Paco asked Chains.

"Nah. I'm not into women outside of the club. You know how it is. With the club women they know the score. Citizens are a pain in the ass."

"You've got a point there." Paco knew Chains was still bitter about his wife leaving him for Cross Bones. Chains's old lady started having an affair with Cross Bones, whose old lady was Lena, the cook for the club. At first Chains hadn't believed it when brothers started telling him that Cross Bones and Brandy were cozying up, and Paco hadn't blamed him. Chains had thought he and Brandy were solid—Paco could relate to that. But then one night, Chains, Paco, Eagle, Army, and Sangre had come back early from a charity poker run and he'd found Brandy on all fours, her ass high in the air and Cross Bones's cock buried deep inside her. The brothers had let him beat the hell out of Cross Bones, only interfering when the fucking betrayer took out his gun.

Lena had been devastated. She'd loved Cross Bones since she was seventeen years old. Steel threw his ass out of the club, and Chains promptly filed divorce papers, but Paco knew it'd left a real bitter taste in his mouth and a huge crack in his heart. Even though it'd been four years, he still refused to fuck anyone but a club girl.

"I could use some of the Drystar gloves too. Where're they at?"

"At the back of the store with all the biker stuff. Jillian and I moved things around a couple of weeks ago. Grab a large pair for Eagle."

Army came up to the counter. "Put the flag on my tab. Can you bring it to the club tonight? Eagle and I are gonna be busy for a while."

Paco glanced over to Eagle, who had his arm around one of the women. "I'll put the gloves on his tab and bring them to the club. You gonna party at their house?"

"Nah. The blonde who has the hots for you is married, and her cute brunette friends have boyfriends. I think we'll get a room at the Starlight Motel. You sure you don't want to join us?"

"I've got work to do."

"Your loss. I'll let you know how it goes." Army went over to the women, and with his arms around the blonde and her friend, they walked out.

"He's gonna be worse than the club girls when they tell us their stories," Chains said as he put two sets of gloves on the counter.

Paco laughed. "You good with holding down the store this weekend? Jillian will be here, and Felix said he'd close up on Friday and Saturday. We should be back from Silverado by Sunday night."

"I'm good, though I may have to figure out where everything is since you changed it all around."

"Jillian will help you with that. She's the one who organized the store. I have to admit it looks better and makes more sense the way she did it."

"Okay, that should work. I'll see you at the clubhouse later." Chains walked out as Paco picked up a large box and began opening it.

A few hours later, Jillian came up to him. "Should I lock the front doors? It's past six."

Paco glanced at the wall clock: 6:20 p.m. "I didn't realize it was so late. I've been going through inventory and the time escaped me. You should've come over sooner."

"I'm good. I got caught up stocking the shelves. I'm almost done with all the new stuff. I can finish the last three boxes tomorrow."

"Yeah, sure. Go on, I'll see you in the morning."

"Are you doing anything fun tonight?" She slipped her arms through her down jacket.

"Nah, just the usual. What about you?"

Her cheeks colored red. "I'm going out with Carson Stuart. Do you know him?"

He whistled softly. "His dad owns Stuart Construction, right?" She nodded as she put on her gloves. "You're running around with the big bucks."

"Are you making fun of me?" She smiled.

"No, I think it's great. Just watch yourself. I heard his old man is a dick, and sometimes the apple doesn't fall far from the tree. If he messes with you, let me know. I'll straighten him out."

Now her entire face was bright red. "I'll keep that in mind. See you tomorrow," she said as she walked out of the store.

He watched her as she went to her car parked in front, making sure she took off okay. Ever since she'd told him she'd lost her dad when she was in high school, he'd felt protective of her. Jillian didn't have a brother, and from what she'd shared with him, it seemed like her mother had fallen apart after Jillian's father died. Being young and on your own was something he could relate to.

Straightening up, he rubbed the back of his neck and decided to call it quits. He grabbed his jacket, locked up the store, and went out back. Soon he was riding through town on his way to the clubhouse. Most of the stores closed at six o'clock; the only businesses that stayed open were the bars, restaurants, and tattoo parlors.

He stopped by Get Inked and bumped fists with Skull. "How's business tonight?"

"Slow. Goldie and Tattoo Mike took off, so it's just me and Jimmy."

"Where's Liberty?"

"She's taking her break. What're you up to?"

"I wanted to know if you or Goldie wanted to grab a beer at Cuervos before I headed to the club."

"I'd go, but we like one of the brothers being here at all times. Another time."

"That's cool."

"Why don't you go over to Lust? Brutus is working tonight, and he told me they got a new dancer that'll make you hard for a week." He laughed.

"Maybe I'll check it out sometime. See you." He walked out as Liberty came in.

"Hey, how've you been?" she said, stopping in the doorway.

"Good. Skull said the shop's slow."

"It is, but it can get busy at midnight when drunk people want to do something crazy." She laughed.

"The business can always count on that. See ya." He went over to his Harley, made a U-turn, and rode toward the club.

The aroma of green chili, slow-cooked pork, and cilantro wafted around him when he came into the main room. A growling stomach reminded him that he hadn't eaten since that morning, and he walked into the kitchen. Lena stood over a large pot, stirring as steam rose above it.

"Smells good in here."

She looked over her shoulder and smiled. "With the cold weather, I thought a big pot of pork green chili would hit the spot. That's what my mother always made in the winter or whenever one of us needed cheering up. It's my comfort food."

"Do you need cheering up?" Paco went over and looked down into the pot.

"No, but I'm freezing my ass off." She picked up a bowl and ladled some chili into it. "Here. Get a couple of tortillas in the warmer. I also made chile rellenos. I know you like them."

"My mom made them every Sunday when I was growing up. Yours

rival hers." Paco went over to the cupboard, took down a plate, and piled three crispy rellenos, a spoonful of rice, and two flour tortillas on it. Taking two beers from the fridge, he shoved them in the pockets of his leather jacket.

"I can help you bring something out," Lena said as she watched him.

"I'm going to my room. Thanks for the chow." He walked out of the kitchen and went upstairs.

As he ate, thoughts of Misty popped into his head. He still felt shitty that he'd missed her, and he wondered if her fucking pimp had moved her to another truck stop.

The phone ringing broke in on his musings and he picked it up. "Unknown" flashed on the screen before he brought it to his ear.

"This is a call from Canon City. The caller is Jason. Push seven to block this call or push five to accept."

Paco pressed five, and a second later a deep voice came over the phone. "How the hell are you?"

"Doing good, Scorpio. Eating a plate of Lena's chile rellenos. They're fucking awesome."

"When I get outta this shithole, I'm gonna eat Mexican every day. How're the brothers?"

"Good." Paco and Scorpio knew the score when speaking on the phone. They never revealed anything incriminating. Their conversations were general, bordering on insipid, but Paco knew that just connecting with a brother on the outside made the time inside more bearable.

"You getting some good pussy? Fuck, I miss that." Scorpio chuckled deeply.

Paco laughed. "You know it. Your cock still doing okay? I thought it would've shriveled up without any pussy."

Another chuckle. "You asshole." A brief pause. "Some dude transferred here from La Vista prison."

Paco's insides tightened. "Yeah. So."

"Says he's your dad. He latched on to me when he found out I was a Night Rebel. His name's Frank Rollins."

Bile rose in Paco's throat. "The sonofabitch is my dad. He's a lifer. I don't know how he found out I was a patch-holder."

"Said somethin' 'bout seeing your picture in the paper a while back."

That's right. The fucking reporters put my picture in the Durango Daily. It had been about the shootout the Night Rebels and the Insurgents had with the Deadly Demons in Durango at a bike rally seven years before. A damn reporter had taken some picture of him and other members, and it landed on the front page of the paper. Since no one had talked, and no witnesses had the courage to tell the damn badges what had happened, there weren't any arrests.

Paco cleared his throat. "I don't wanna hear about my old man again. As far as I'm concerned, he's dead. Do you ever see Diesel?" Diesel was a member of the Insurgents MC doing a stint in state prison.

"Yeah, we're in the same cell block. We should be getting outta this fuckin' place around the same time. I gotta go. I wanted to make sure the old man wasn't BSing me about being your dad because if he was, I'd have to kick his ass."

Paco clenched his jaw. "Kick his ass anyway. For me. Later, dude."

He put his phone down and finished his beer, then gathered the plates and put them out in the hallway, texting the prospects to come pick them up.

He turned off the lights, and a sliver of moonlight spilled into the room. Going over to the window, he leaned against the sill and stared out. In the distance, the mountains were silhouetted against the deep velvety sky. His mother's corpse jumped front and center in his mind. At first, he'd believed that the police were too lazy to find his mother's real killer and settled on an easy target—his father. Kendra hadn't been so quick to rule him out, but she hadn't been as close to their dad as he had. And that was the reason the betrayal had pained him more than it had her.

As time had passed, the evidence against his dad had mounted: an addiction to strip bars, affairs with women he'd met online, taking out a million-dollar life insurance policy on his mother two months before she'd died.

How the fuck could you have done that to Mom? To us? You were married for eighteen fucking years. She trusted and loved you. We all did.

Anger burned in his veins as he picked up the desk chair and hurled it against the wall. The wood splintered and the broken chair hit the floor with a thud.

"Fuck!" He ran his hand through his hair, stiffening when he heard a knock on his door. "What?" he gritted out.

"Everything okay?" Sangre asked.

"Yeah. Just fucking pissed."

"I hear you, bro."

Listening to Sangre's retreating footsteps, Paco went over and picked up the pieces of the chair. All of a sudden, the room seemed suffocating. He had to get the hell out of there. Grabbing his jacket, he scooped up his keys and dashed down the stairs.

The TV blasted as the brothers watched the boxing match televised from Mexico. He went over to Patches. "My desk chair broke. Make sure there's a new one in my room when I get back." Patches nodded.

"How'd your chair break?" Cueball asked as he stared at the television screen.

"I threw it against the wall."

"That'll do it."

"I'm outta here. Later."

Paco went outside. The sweet scent of the creosote bush, the eerie sounds of the screech owl blending with the yelps of the coyote, and the feel of the cool desert air beckoned him. Straddling his Harley, he sped out of the lot, steering his bike onto the back roads. He rode hard and fast until he reached that moment when everything came together. It was like his bike and he became one, a Zen-like state taking hold of him so he and the world were in total harmony. There was nothing like it. It was his addiction and his love.

And it was the only thing that kept the demons away for a while.

Chapter Six

THE SILVER SPUR Motel was one of those seedy places where men with beer guts went to bang other men's wives, promising them the world and giving them nothing but an hour or less of sweaty sex. A fight was going on in the room next door, and a couple more screaming matches came from the rooms down the hall.

Sitting in a straight-backed chair, Misty looked down at the parking lot where weeds grew through the cracks on the asphalt. Bobby stood there, arms crossed, talking to a guy with a moustache and huge biceps. From the look of his body, she figured the dude must be on steroids.

She was nervous. Bobby was up to something. Since they'd arrived in Colorado, he'd been stepping outside the motel room to take his calls, not wanting her to hear his conversations. The sourness in her stomach had been on overdrive, and she'd been living on antacids for the past week.

She'd googled the distance between where she was and where Paco lived—it was about seventy miles. Only seventy miles separated her from seeing him again. *I should call him. Maybe he'll come see me.* Bobby's loud voice made her heart skip a beat. She stared at him as he uncrossed his arms and waved them around while the big guy glared at him. *Paco probably doesn't even think about me. Why would he?* Bobby whirled around and ran up the metal stairs. *Please don't let him take out his anger on me.* She folded her legs underneath her butt and wrapped her arms around her as if trying to make herself smaller.

The door burst open. Bobby's face was mottled in anger as he paced back and forth, his eyes darting everywhere but on her. She knew better than to speak to him when he was like that, so she sat still, wishing she could disappear.

Abruptly he stopped. "We gotta get going. You've got a private party tonight. The guy giving the party wants you to be especially good to his friends."

Fear twisted her insides. "What does that mean?"

Glaring at her, he said, "It means you do what the fuck they want and act like you enjoy it. Anything goes tonight."

"Are Crystal and Amber Jade gonna be there too?" Placing her fingers against her lips, she tried to stop them from trembling.

"You're flying solo tonight. That's the way he wants it, and the customer always gets what he wants."

"Where's the party?"

"His house. From the way I heard it, he lives in a mansion. You're moving up, slut." He laughed as he went over to the dresser and opened the top drawer, taking out a baggie filled with white powder. As he set up his snorting station, she looked back at the parking lot. *What does he mean 'anything goes'?* Images of handcuffs and whips swirled in her head, and she gripped the windowsill to steady herself.

"You better go in the shower and get ready. I gotta drop you off in a couple of hours. You'll want to look your prettiest." He bent his head down and snorted the white powder with a rolled-up dollar bill.

Numb, she walked to the bathroom. For the past eight years she'd been someone's property. Bobby was her second owner. Her body belonged to him, not to her. He rented her out so men could do anything they wanted to her. For the allotted time, they took temporary custody of her body.

After turning on the water, she stepped into the tub and unpeeled the bar soap, wishing Bobby had bought her some shower gel when they'd gone to the store the other day. He told her it was too expensive, but she knew he was just being mean. Sometimes he acted like he was her boyfriend and he loved her, but other times he was cruel and demeaning and made her feel insecure.

She let the hot water roll off her back, pretending she was getting ready for a date like a normal woman. Sometimes, if she concentrated real hard on what she wished her life was, she could forget what she was doing with different men, and then it wasn't so bad.

Squeezing out some shampoo, she closed her eyes as she brought her hands to her hair.

LYING ON THE cold floor, bruised, naked, and bound, Misty tried to moisten her cracked lips but her mouth was dry. The ball gag she'd had on for what seemed like hours had split the sides of her mouth, leaving them sore. Her arms burned and throbbed from being suspended by a rope from the ceiling. She stiffened when she heard hinges creak, a metal door click shut, and then heavy footfalls on the stairs leading to the dungeon. The footsteps stopped, and the scent of mahogany, lavender, and musk wafted in the room, and she knew *he* was there, watching her.

She'd learned the owner of the house was the mustached and muscular man Bobby had been talking with in the parking lot earlier that day. She'd heard a few of the men call him Victor, but he'd told her to call him Sir. He'd been brutal, and she hoped he wasn't coming in for another round. It seemed like the rest of the men had all left; it'd just been him and her for the past two hours.

"You did good, fucktoy." His words felt like slime on her skin. She lay there silently, knowing better than to answer without permission to speak. Heels clacking on the concrete floor, the odor of his cologne grew stronger as he came closer. The sensitive skin on her lower back itched when his wool pants rubbed against it. Leaning over, he trapped her nipples between his fingers and rolled them back and forth then pinched and pulled them roughly. Her body tried to resist the flurry of pain, and she twisted and squirmed in her bondage, trying to keep from crying out. Muffled squeaks erupted from her clenched teeth, and he laughed while he palmed her breasts with his smooth hands. Feeling his weight as he pressed against her, she scooted away but his arm yanked her back. "I didn't give you permission to move, slut," he snarled, freezing her in place. Silence weighed down on her and her nerve endings snapped in feared anticipation of what he was going to do. Bending down, he licked her behind her ear. "Now that's a good fucktoy," he whispered. Then he ran his fingers up her arms, her skin pebbling from his touch. "You like that? You may answer, slut."

"Yes, Sir." The truth was she hated him touching her, but sometimes her body would react even when she didn't want it to.

He untied her and turned her so she was on her back. The chilling coldness in his eyes made her shiver. "Get dressed and get out of here, slut." He stood up and walked away.

She slowly got up and went over to a metal cabinet to get her clothes. Wincing when her bra straps touched the cuts on her shoulders, she flung off her bra and slipped her dress on. Deciding to forgo the stiletto heels, she walked barefoot up the stairs. The house was quiet, and Victor was nowhere around.

She opened the large wooden front door and stepped out into the cold air, seeing the RV parked on the street. The tip of Bobby's cigarette glowed in the dark. Misty made her way down the long driveway, feeling someone staring at her. Pausing, she looked over her shoulder and saw a pretty woman in her thirties watching her from a window on the second floor. For a single moment, their eyes locked, and then Victor came into view. He tugged the woman to him, and she broke eye contact with Misty and hooked her arms around his neck. The couple kissed deeply as Misty turned away and hurried down the walkway.

She slid into the passenger seat and stared ahead. From the corner of her eye, she saw Bobby looking at her, but she didn't move a muscle or say a word. The RV started up and they rode in silence back to the motel. She scrambled up the stairs, anxious to get inside and forget about the evening.

"What's your hurry?" Bobby asked, ambling toward the door.

"I have to go to the bathroom," she lied. He smirked and let her in.

She rushed inside and locked the door behind her. For a while, the room would be her refuge. Taking off her clothes she stared at the reflection of her body in the mirror: bruises, welts from the cane, thin lines from the flogger, and red marks from the paddle covered her skin. Biting her lower lip, she turned away and went to the shower, turning the water on. The hot spray stung and made her eyes water, but she didn't flinch. She took it like a good girl.

After soaping up the washcloth, she scrubbed her skin over and over, trying to rid herself of his scent.

Chapter Seven

"Yo," Knuckles said as Paco and Sangre came into the Fallen Slayers' clubhouse.

Paco tipped his head at the sergeant-at-arms. "You made the room bigger."

"We knocked down some walls. We need more space for all the bitches who come to the parties."

"Hot ones, right?" Army said as he walked over to the bar.

"Of course. How was the ride?"

"Good," Paco replied. He watched as Steel, Diablo, Chains, Eagle, and Brutus placed their saddlebags down on two tables before joining him and Sangre at the bar.

"So when does the partying begin?" Eagle asked.

"Tonight we're going to Satin Dolls Gentlemen's Club. It's the strip bar I was telling you all about when Brick and me were in Alina," Roughneck said. "Knuckles just found out that it's owned by a guy named Victor Bustos. He's head honcho of the Los Malos Gang. Satan's Pistons are in thick with the 39th Street Gang, who hate Los Malos and the West Avenue Bandits."

"So the fuckin' Pistons are dealing in arms with the 39th Street fucks, Los assholes, and West Avenue dumb shits?" Paco said.

"You got it," Roughneck replied.

"How's business at the strip bar?" Steel asked.

Patriot, the Fallen Slayer's vice president, shook his head. "Real good. It's taking away business from our bar, Lusty Lady. They paid someone off to get the permits in record time."

"What time are we planning to head out?" Eagle said.

"Around nine. We'll leave our jackets and cuts at the clubhouse. I don't want them to know we're from biker clubs." Roughneck picked up his drink.

"It's gonna be hard for them not to know, dude. We look like bikers," Paco said.

"Or rockers," Patriot added.

"If anyone asks, we can say we're in rock bands on tour. I always wanted to be a fuckin' rock star," Army said. The brothers burst out laughing.

"We gotta come up with names for our bands," Chains said.

"The first thing we gotta do is not take our Harleys. We'll split in three SUVs." Knuckles picked up the beer bottle the prospect put on the bar.

"That's fuckin' obvious, dude," Sangre said as Knuckles bristled.

Paco chuckled. Knuckles wasn't the brightest one in the group. Too many fights and blows to the head probably contributed to that. Diablo was always complaining about how thick he was, preferring to work with Brick and Patriot when it came to security and maneuvers.

"You got any chicks around here? I could go for some relaxing before we head out." Brutus raised his eyebrows as he scanned the room.

"The club girls will show you where you can put your bags and crash. I'm sure they're up for some fun with some new brothers." Roughneck whistled and four women came out.

"Now that's what I'm talking about." Brutus elbowed Paco.

"I'll drop off my shit first. Who's up for a pool game against Diablo and me?" Paco asked the Fallen Slayers members.

"I'm in," Patriot said.

"Me too." Brick walked toward the pool table.

"Sounds good." Paco followed one of the club girls downstairs. She stopped in front of a closed door.

"This is where you'll be staying." She ran her blue eyes over him, checking him out. "You're the VP, right?"

"Yeah. What's your name?" Paco turned the doorknob.

"Lila. How many club girls you guys got?" She stood in the doorway watching him.

Throwing his bag on the double bed, he glanced over at her. "Six. Why? Aren't the brothers treating you right around here?"

"They're okay, but I've always found your club members to be more respectful to the women." Lila stepped inside the room. "Please don't tell anyone I said that."

"No worries 'bout that."

"I was thinking about moving to Alina. It's bigger than here, and I have some cousins who live in Tula, which is way closer to Alina than it is to Silverado. I like being a club girl. Would you have room for me?"

He ran his gaze over her quickly—she had nice tits, curves, and long golden hair. "Maybe. If you're serious, come see me sometime when you're in Alina. I can see what we can work out."

A wide smile broke over her face. "Excellent. While you're here, maybe you'd like a sneak peek of what I can do."

"Maybe. I'll let you know. Right now I'm aiming to win some bucks on a pool game." He took out a comb and ran it through his dark hair. "Thanks for showing me my room."

He pushed the lock and went back upstairs, joining Diablo, Patriot, and Brick at the pool table. Glancing at the clock, he figured he had three hours to make some money off Patriot and Brick. The two of them were cocky as hell and thought they were the best pool players in the two counties. Paco chuckled inwardly as he remembered how Raven had hustled Brick a couple of years before when they were all at Trick Shots. Brick had been so livid that a woman had outsmarted him.

"You ready to lose some money?" Brick asked as he set up the balls in the rack.

Paco smirked, then wrapped his fingers around a cue stick and glanced at Diablo who gave him a knowing look. The game was on.

IN THE MAIN room, the chairs were in ruby-red plush velvet, and warm vanilla scents from flickering candles in private nooks and alcoves wafted around the establishment. A tall skinny woman with perfect breasts walked across the neon-lit room inside Satin Dolls Gentlemen's Club dressed in see-through black lingerie. Another woman wearing pink panties and a short cutoff shirt exposing the bottom half of her breasts mingled with customers as two women twirled, ground, and spread their legs on the smoky stage.

"This is classy," Sangre said as he sat at a table near the stage.

"And packed. These assholes are killing our business," Roughneck replied.

A scantily clad woman came over and asked for their drink order. Army jabbed Paco with his elbow. "The Fallen Slayers have some serious competition. I can see why this place is crowded. The dancers are fuckin' hot."

"Yeah, but letting these assholes get away with this is opening the gate for all kinds of shit to go down. Besides, some of the women look too young." He jerked his head toward a girl who stood by the stage in a barely there school uniform. "I'd bet all the money I won at pool tonight that she's not even sixteen."

Army looked at the girl and red blotches appeared on his taut face. "You're fuckin' right. Underage girls usually means they don't wanna be here." Looking around, he bobbed his head. "Yeah… we gotta help the Slayers close this damn place."

Anger licked at Paco as well. Dancing because a woman wanted to was one thing, but doing it because she had no choice pissed him and his brothers off real bad. Chains had done some digging into Los Malos and the West Avenue Bandits, and it seemed that Los Malos was into buying and selling women. The West Avenue Bandits were more into selling drugs, stolen bike and car parts, and petty thefts, but Los Malos's biggest revenue came from the flesh trade. If Paco had to guess, he'd bet that a third of the women in the club weren't there by choice. The thought disgusted and angered him. *The fuckin' badges are probably in on this too.*

"Here you go." The waitress put the drinks down on the table. "You want to start a tab?"

"We'll pay as we drink," Steel said, opening his wallet.

"I'm gonna walk around," Paco said to Army and Steel. He stood up, and Diablo and Brick followed suit. They walked around the club, noticing the long hallway with numerous closed doors. Paco figured that was where the private lap dances happened.

The trio went over to the bar and ordered beers. "They've got underage girls working the place," Paco said to Brick.

"I noticed that. Shit. I have a sister about the age of some of these girls." Brick wrapped his fingers tightly around the beer bottle.

"They don't look like they're having fun. Not like the older one on stage. I'd say they don't want to be here." A frown creased Diablo's forehead.

The crowd erupted in applause and another hard-hitting song came over the speakers. Paco leaned on the bar, his back to the stage. Seeing the underage girls and knowing they were probably being forced to take off their clothes gave him a real bad taste.

Loud whistles and hoots pulled his attention back. He spun around and saw the back of a woman in a G-string and stiletto heels swaying her hips. The cool beer slid down his throat. The woman bent backward and the tips of her long hair brushed the stage. Then she straightened up and spun around, her breasts jiggling with her movements.

Paco looked at her, then did a double take. *Misty. What the* fuck? A flush of adrenaline tingled through his body. Men cheered. Men ogled. Men whistled. And fire rushed in his veins as he glared at the crowd. Part of him was pissed as hell that the men watched her intently. He ground his teeth. *This is stupid, man. She's not your woman.* But for reasons he couldn't understand, he felt protective of her.

Standing next to the bar, a muscled man with a mustache stared fixedly at Misty, lust clouding his eyes. Paco got a bad vibe from him. The way he watched Misty looked like he wanted to possess every inch of her, even her soul.

"What's up, dude?" Diablo asked.

Tearing his gaze from the jerk, he looked at Diablo. "Whaddaya mean?"

"You look like you're ready to beat the shit outta that guy." Diablo jerked his head to the mustached muscle man. "Did he disrespect you?"

"I just don't like the fucker's looks."

"We gotta play it cool. Unless he disrespected you, we don't wanna start shit right now. We don't want these assholes to know that we're checking them out."

"I'm not gonna start anything."

Army came over with an arm around one of the women. "And we're headed to Pueblo to do a concert. This here is the bass player." He pointed to Paco.

"I love bass players," she said.

Paco rolled his eyes and focused back on the stage. "I'm going out for a smoke," he said to Diablo.

The cold air blew away the shock of seeing Misty on stage. How the hell she ended up on a stripper stage in Silverado was a mystery to him. *At least she's not hauling her ass in a truck stop.*

He walked around the back of the building and saw a slatted fence surrounding most of the backside that looked to be a little over five feet. He grabbed the top of it and hoisted himself up, then dropped down on the pavement. The back door to the club was propped open. Pushing it wide with the toe of his boot, he went inside. Several women rushed around, stuffing their tits in tight bras and putting on stilettos. A few of them winked at him, and he lifted his chin in their direction.

A well-endowed brunette in a skimpy purple metallic top and sheer G-string smiled at him, then turned to a redhead. "You're on next, Reds."

The redhead adjusted her bra and threw on a long cape. "Hope they're tipping good tonight," she said as she waited to go on.

The lights dimmed and he saw Misty coming down the stage steps. She grabbed a robe hanging near the curtain and shrugged it on.

"Here," one of the women said to her. "You look like you need one."

Paco saw her hand Misty a joint.

"Thanks." She took it and, with her head bent down, walked right past him and out the back door. Following her out, he watched her light up and take a deep drag.

"I never thought I'd see you in this place," he said, walking toward her.

She whirled around, suspicion etching her face until recognition danced across it. "Paco!" Her lips turned upward into a wide smile.

"What the fuck are you doing here?"

"I work here. Do you live in Silverado now?"

"No… I'm just visiting some friends. I stopped by Moab last week when I was riding through. Some older woman told me you'd left. You hadn't mentioned you were moving on when we met."

"Well, things change fast. I live a very transient life." She pulled her gaze away from him.

He stared at her intently. "You okay?"

"Of course."

He heard her words, but her eyes, her posture, and her movements told him she was lying. "You being forced to do this shit?"

"Misty! What the fuck are you doing out here?" A tall man came onto the back patio. Under the glow of the glittering white string lights, the man's face was pockmarked, and Paco saw scratch marks on his bared arms.

"I was just smoking a joint." She moved closer to the man.

"Who the fuck are you?" he grumbled to Paco.

Paco's gaze darted to her, and he saw sweat trickling down her face, her body stiffening, and her fingers curling into a fist. He decided not to slam his fist into the asshole's face, but only because he'd promised his brothers.

"None of your fucking business." Paco took a step closer to him.

The man glanced at him, then turned to Misty. "Do you know him?" Paco was sure that the yellow-bellied fucker decided he was no match for him.

Misty shook her head. "No, Bobby. He was out here smoking a joint when I came outside."

So that's her fucking pimp. I want to pulverize him.

"You work here?" Bobby asked him.

"You ask me one more question and I'm gonna make sure it'll be your last." He took another step toward him. Twitching legs and erratic breathing told Paco the pussy was scared.

Turning to Misty, Bobby said, "Get your ass back inside."

Without a glance, she went back into the club. Before Bobby could follow her, Paco stepped in front of him, blocking his way.

"I don't want any trouble," he said, trying to walk around Paco.

"That's too fucking bad, 'cause you're gonna get it." With one swift movement, he buried his fist in Bobby's stomach. The man bent over, gulping for air. "Don't ever question me again." His knee made contact with the wheezing man's face, and the crunch of bones was music to Paco's ears.

"Fuck! I think my nose is broken." He looked up, blood streaming over his lips and dripping down his chin.

"You're fucking lucky that's the only thing I broke. Asshole." He went inside, hoping to see Misty again, but she was nowhere around.

"Where's Misty?" he asked one of the women.

"Who? Look, honey, I'm about ready to go on. After I get finished, I'll show you a better time than this Misty chick. I'll give you a lap dance you'll never forget." She winked, then brushed past him as she headed for the stage.

He ran his fingers through his hair while scanning the room. His gaze landed on Diablo's. "What the fuck are you doing back here?" Diablo asked.

"I'm looking for someone."

"There're plenty of women out there. Roughneck doesn't want any unnecessary attention, dude."

A door slammed behind him and he whirled around. Bobby leaned against it, his eyes flashing, a wad of red-stained tissues in his hand. Not wanting to jeopardize anything, Paco followed Diablo back into the main room and ordered a double Jack at the bar. As he drank, he kept his gaze glued to the curtain, but Misty never came out; she never even peeked from behind the black drapes.

What the fuck's wrong with me? I don't even know her.

By the time last call rolled around, Paco was ready to jump on his Harley, haul ass back to Alina, and forget all about strippers, lot lizards, and Misty. He was done thinking about her. He'd helped her out when she'd been sick and down. End of story.

Finished.

Done.

Chapter Eight

FROM THE SECOND floor, in an empty room with dirty windows, Misty watched Paco walk out of the club. She wanted to call out to him but she didn't dare. Bobby was furious. When he'd come back inside, he'd stumbled into the dressing room she shared with Crystal and Amber Jade, hopping mad. For almost an hour, he grilled her on who the "asshole" was who'd broken his nose, and she kept repeating over and over like a mantra, "I don't know. I've never seen him. He was out there smoking a joint just like I was." She hadn't changed her story once, hadn't flinched when Bobby raised his hand and struck her, and hadn't acted like her insides were a melting mess of anxiety and excitement. As Bobby ranted, she'd thought of the handsome biker, unable to believe he was at the club. She never thought she'd see him again.

Then Bobby had stopped, and silence pressed down on her. She'd looked up into his glowering face. "What the fuck are you thinking about? That fuckin' asshole who broke my nose?"

"No. I was thinking how awful it is that you're in a lot of pain." Even to her, she'd sounded insincere.

Bobby had held her gaze as tension crackled around them. Not moving a muscle, she'd willed herself not to show any weakness. *Bobby can't read my mind.* Then the door flew open and she jumped as her hands flew to her throat. The pig from the night before came into the room.

He'd smiled widely, his straight white teeth gleaming. "You looked good out there." His eyes ran up and down her body, and she felt like scrubbing her skin off. He'd turned to Bobby. "What the hell happened to you?"

"Nothing. I didn't see a door, that's all. So you like my women?"

Victor had taken a few steps closer to her. "I like this one."

"Get out. Victor and I need to talk."

She'd walked away, cringing when Victor squeezed her butt as she passed him. And now, watching Paco leave, a heaviness settled in her limbs. "Don't go," she whispered. Her shoulders curled forward and she swallowed several times, trying to get rid of the lump in her throat.

He was so close. It felt like she could reach out and touch him. *I could open the window and yell out to him, but Bobby would hear... and Victor.* She didn't want him to get hurt, although he'd held his own with Bobby. When she'd seen blood on his face, her insides had a party, and she liked Paco even more for doing what she'd wanted to do for a very long time. *And he asked me if I was being forced to be here. I almost told him.* And she may have if Bobby hadn't come out. There was something about Paco that made her believe that maybe she could trust him. Since her kidnapping, trust in people, especially men, had eroded until it no longer existed.

A car door slamming brought her out of her thoughts and she saw him in the front seat, staring straight ahead. That was the way she'd remember him. She pressed her fingers to her throat, trying to stop the lump from getting bigger. The SUV drove away, and she stood watching long after it'd disappeared from her sight.

"What're you doing up here?" Pixie, one of the dancers, asked her. "You don't want one of the guys to come up here and find you. A cute, new girl like you would have a bad time. Come on back to the club."

Misty nodded and followed her downstairs. Bobby was still talking to Victor, and when she passed by, Victor reached out for her, but Bobby stepped over and yanked her to him. "She's not available for tonight."

Nodding, he laughed. "You gave me a taste of her last night and teased me tonight when she danced. I can see why. She's prime real estate."

You fuckin' pig. I'm a person. I'm me. "Chelsea Sullivan," she said under her breath. A soft cry escaped through her lips. *Oh shit. I haven't said my name in years.* She dug her fingernails into her palms. *Focus. You need to know what the hell's going down. Something doesn't feel right.*

Victor came over and stroked her cheek; she cringed under his touch. "That's okay. I can wait. You know, waiting can be a powerful aphrodisiac. It makes me imagine all sorts of things I want to do to a fucktoy."

She stepped away from him, and his thin smile turned into a sneer.

"Be a good girl and wait in the bar. Victor and me are finishing up some business." Bobby pushed her in the direction of the bar. Darting her eyes between them, her shoulders tightened and she twisted a strand of hair around her finger. "Go on now." Harshness seeped into his voice, and she walked away.

Inside the club area, she saw Crystal, Amber Jade, and a few other women laughing and drinking with a group of guys wearing green bandanas. The letters "WAB" were tattooed on their arms. She'd learned earlier that evening that the place was run by a gang called the West Avenue Bandits, and Victor owned it. The night before, she'd seen the roman numeral "XXV" tattooed on his upper arm and back. When she'd asked Bobby about it, he'd told her it referenced the letters in the alphabet, so "L" and "M" added up to twenty-five. She'd learned that one question was about all she could ask without Bobby flipping out on her, so she didn't ask what the "L" and "M" stood for.

"Chica, you want a drink?" one of the men asked her. She shook her head. "I loved the way you danced. Next time we have to make sure the lights are brighter so we can see more."

You have your fuckin' boss to thank for giving me all the marks. Concealer and makeup could only hide so much, so she'd asked the sound and light man to crank up the smoke and turn down the lights.

"Let's party, chica." He hung his arm around her.

In one fluid move, she slid from under it. "Thanks for asking, but I can't party with anyone."

Two other men came over with their arms snaked around girls who looked to be fifteen. Emptiness reflected from their eyes. Misty saw the same thing in hers when she looked in the mirror—it was the look of resignation, enslavement, and despair.

"Let's go back to the clubhouse," one of the men said to the guy who kept bugging her.

Gripping her arm tightly, he jerked her to him. "I'm ready."

Misty tried to push away, but his hold was like iron. "No. I can't. Let go of me."

"Shut the fuck up, *puta*. You do what I tell you to do."

"Leave her alone, *cabrón*," Victor said.

The man instantly let go of her. "I didn't mean any disrespect. I didn't know she was yours." He stalked back to the bar.

"I always take care of what's mine." The way Victor looked at her set off a thousand five-alarm bells inside her.

"Crystal, Amber Jade, get your asses over here. We're heading out," Bobby said, walking into the room.

"They want to party with us," Amber Jade pouted.

"Not without paying." Bobby motioned for Misty to come over.

"How much you want for the three girls to party with us?" a short burly man asked.

Bobby hooked his arm around Misty. "This one's not available. For the other two, give me two grand."

"That's too much," the man said.

"That's the price." Bending down, he whispered in her ear, "You want a drink?"

A single shiver ran up her spine. *Why's he being nice to me?* "Sure." She really didn't want anything but to get out of the club. Some strange tension and energy was going around, making her nerves snap.

"Give my favorite girl a rum and Coke." Guiding her to the bar, she trembled as her smooth skin prickled to goose bumps. "You cold? Lemme give you my jacket." He draped it around her, then helped her onto the bar stool.

Her stomach churned. *He's up to something.* Light-headedness overcame her and she clutched the side of the bar, fearful she would topple over or faint.

"Here you go," Bobby said, handing her a tall glass.

She curled her fingers around it and brought it to her forehead, the coolness of the glass soothing her. Across the bar, Victor sat at a table, his dark eyes boring into her. The neon lights picked up glints of cruelty in that cold gaze.

She took a sip and thought she'd upchuck right there. "Bobby, I'm so tired. Can we just go back to the motel?" Holding her breath, she braced herself for his reaction.

"No problem." He threw a ten-dollar bill on the counter. "Keep the change." He helped her down and snapped his fingers. Crystal and Amber Jade rushed over.

"What about a thousand?" the short man asked.

"Two grand is the amount. Take it or leave it."

The man grumbled something inaudible under his breath, and a few other gang members threw dirty looks at Bobby.

"Come on, girls. We're outta here." With his arm curled around Misty, they walked out, the other two women shuffling behind them.

When they arrived at the motel room, Bobby took out a bottle of scotch and several bottles of prescription pain pills. "Why don't you take a warm shower before you go to bed? I know you like your showers."

What are you hiding from me, Bobby? "Okay." Sitting on the edge of the bed, she kicked off her stilettos and rubbed her feet. "Is your nose feeling better?"

"It will after I take a few of these." He poured out several white pills in the palm of his hand. "You want some?" She shook her head. "It'll make you sleep real good." Another shake of her head. Lifting his shoulders up and down, he poured scotch into a plastic cup. "Suit yourself." He popped the pills in his mouth and washed them down, then went over to the bed, turned on the television, and settled back on the pillows.

After her long shower, she came back into the room and saw Bobby conked out on the bed, the TV still on and the plastic cup on the floor. She padded over to the window and looked out. There weren't any lights on, and the parking lot was quiet. A dull ache pulled at her, and she wondered if Paco was still in Silverado.

Pressing her forehead against the cool windowpane, she closed her eyes. It'd been a long time since she'd felt the pull toward a man—eight years, to be exact. She'd been fifteen years old when she'd had a massive crush on Tyler Tarleton. He'd been the quarterback for the Roosevelt Raiders, and all the girls wanted to get his attention. Priscilla Mitchum had been head cheerleader and the most popular girl in the sophomore class. It hadn't been a secret that she had her sights on Tyler. According to her, since she was head cheerleader, popular, pretty, and rich, it made sense that she and Tyler should be a couple. Whenever she'd laugh and flirt with Tyler, Misty—*no, Chelsea. I was Chelsea back then, and I never thought I stood a chance with Tyler, not with Priscilla in the picture.*

But Tyler had started coming over to her during lunch and between classes, and when she'd bumped into him at a party and he'd asked her to dance, she'd been over the moon. He'd made her feel special and pretty.

How fucking naïve I was.

A loud grunt yanked her back from memory lane to the present. She looked over her shoulder and saw Bobby sleeping on his back, his mouth open; he looked like a fish gasping for air. *I wonder if he'd wake up if I put a pillow over his face.* Another loud grunt and then he turned on his side. For several minutes, she watched him sleep, and when she was convinced that he wasn't waking up, she tiptoed over to his jacket and slipped her hand inside the inner pocket. Her fingers curled around a fat envelope and she pulled it out, going into the bathroom and locking the door behind her. As she sat on the toilet, she opened the manila envelope to find stacks of bills. Ice ran through her veins, her ears pounded, and she couldn't move. Sitting there, just staring at the money, sourness filled her mouth and she thought she was going to lose it. Then, with shaky fingers, she pulled out the bundles of money and counted. When she reached $65,000, she knew.

There was no doubt.

Bobby had sold her to Victor.

Chapter Nine

PACO WATCHED LILA swaying her hips as she sauntered toward him. She was a pretty woman and he should be all over her, but the only woman he had on his mind was Misty. When he'd seen her at Satin Dolls, he'd been shocked but inexplicably excited at the same time. When she ignored him after they'd spoken briefly on the back patio, he'd been pissed and decided he was done with whatever was going on between him and her. But sitting at the bar, her sad eyes burning a hole in his mind, he knew he couldn't forget her that easily.

I gotta get the fuck outta here. Paco couldn't stand to pass the night in Silverado knowing Misty was so close. He didn't want to keep thinking about her and why the hell he cared. He needed the cold air whipping around him to numb his thoughts, needed to put distance between her and him.

Before Lila reached him, he slid off the stool and went over to Steel, who was leaning against the wall with a beer in his hand.

"Hey," Steel said.

"Hey. I'm gonna head back to Alina unless you need me here."

His eyes widened. "Really? Is everything okay?"

Paco drew in a long breath and exhaled. "I just got some shit going on in my head that I need to clear away. A good ride always does the trick."

"I hear you. Roughneck's calling church tomorrow morning. I'll fill you in on what goes on. From what I saw at the club, Los Malos Gang is all over the strip bar, even though they're based in Pueblo and Colorado Springs. The fucking punks in West Avenue Bandits are just their front. The dumb shits don't even know they're being used. Los Malos' handprints are all over the drug trade that's starting here. And they're trafficking women. Too many underage ones at the club tonight that didn't seem like they wanted to be there."

"I agree. West Avenue Bandits are just a bunch of punks who want pussy, drugs, and booze. Los Malos is calling the shots. I saw a lot of assholes with the number twenty-five tatted on them. They need to be shut down."

Steel's face grew taut. "I don't think Roughneck gets how serious this is. He and his brothers think this is about a strip joint and some drug buys, but we know it's just a matter of time before they start moving into Alina and the surrounding area. We gotta stop it."

"Yeah, I don't think Roughneck gets how important it is to act fast."

"That's what I'll discuss tomorrow with the Fallen Slayers. If they don't step up to the plate, we're gonna have to go in without them."

"Chains said they've got a lot of members between the two cities. We're gonna need some help from the Insurgents if the Fallen Slayers don't agree with us. I know Banger and his brothers aren't gonna want these assholes claiming biker territory." Paco took out a couple of joints and handed one to Steel.

Steel lifted his chin. "I'll give you the heads-up when we come back. I want an emergency church called."

Paco nodded and reclined against the wall as he watched men and women dance, drink, and screw. He stubbed out his joint, clasped Steel's shoulder, and made his way downstairs to pack up his stuff.

Darkness surrounded him. On that moonless night, the stars were somewhere behind the haze of black clouds stretching thinly above. Paco zipped the saddlebag onto the mount and started his bike. After wrapping his scarf around his neck, he pulled away from the clubhouse.

About fifteen minutes into the ride, when he was leaving the edge of town, he saw a figure walking on the side of the road. Immediately he stiffened. It wasn't common to see someone on the road at three thirty in the morning in a small town on a cold night. Adrenaline rushed through him as his senses heightened. Slowing down, he eased his foot off the accelerator. The person scurried away into the brush.

Paco stopped, opened his jacket, and slipped his hand inside his cut, taking out a 9mm. Nothing. The only sounds were the occasional hoot from an owl and the wind rustling through the trees. There was no sign of the person, but he sensed someone was watching him. More rustling, but it didn't sound like the wind. *Lizards? Jackrabbits? I doubt it.*

For many minutes he sat on his humming bike, gun in hand, scanning the area. Nothing. No one. Deciding it could've been a drifter, he pulled in the clutch and released the throttle.

As he rode away, the figure darted out from behind a large piñon pine tree, screaming, "Stop!"

Stopping short, he raised his gun at the approaching figure that had a blanket draped around it. From the size and shape, he was pretty sure it was a woman. When she came closer, her haunting eyes captured his and he lowered his gun. Without any questions, he got off his bike, took the plastic sack in her hand, stuffed it into one of the saddlebags, and then got back on his Harley.

He jerked his head back. "Get on." Misty scrambled onto the seat behind him. "Wrap and tuck the blanket under your legs." She complied then hooked her arms around him. He throttled the engine and pressed down on the gear shift as they rode toward the highway.

The cold air stung his eyes as they sped toward Alina. He was acutely aware of Misty's head resting on his shoulder, her tits pressed against his back, and her arms snug around him. He tried to focus on the road, but having her so warm and close to him was doing things to his dick that he didn't like. Finding her walking in the dark with a blanket wrapped around her shaking body was something he'd never figured would happen. It seemed like a force kept pushing her into his life. He wasn't sure he believed in fate, but it struck him as more than a coincidence that he'd bumped into her in the most random places.

Paco leaned into the curve and she held him tighter. He liked the way she felt behind him. He'd taken plenty of women on rides on his Harley over the years. When he'd first got interested in motorcycles, he'd been in high school, but he couldn't afford to get one. He and Kendra had been living with his mom's sister after their dad was arrested for hacking up their mom, and his aunt and uncle weren't too pleased to have two more mouths to feed on an already tight budget.

When he hit eighteen, he and a couple of his buddies got a place to live in town, and he found a better job at the local bowling alley. That's where he and Cassie had met. She worked concessions and he worked on the machines. They'd fallen hard for each other very fast, and they'd been inseparable. When he'd bought his first Harley, it was used, but he'd taken it out every chance he got, Cassie pressed next to him most of the time. Those had been good times, and her love for him had helped ease the pain of losing his mother.

A bump in the road made Misty's hand land on his dick. Instead of moving away, she kept it there. *Shit.* When he'd take Lucy or Ruby for bike rides, they'd tease his cock while he rode until he'd have to pull over and have them satisfy him. It was all in good fun; it didn't mean anything. He never once feared losing himself to any of the women, but Misty's hand on his dick was different. She made things he kept buried deep inside him stir, and he didn't like or want that. He reached down and slid her hand up. *I'm not going there with this one.*

In the distance, the lights of Alina glittered like a swarm of fireflies. Instead of going through the town, he opted to take the back road to the clubhouse. Soon he pulled in front and cut the engine.

"We're here," he said, and Misty's arms left him. He waited for her to get off before he did. Unzipping both saddlebags, he held them in his hands and went around back. He heard her footsteps crunching on the gravel behind him as he took out his keys and unlocked the back door. It was dark and quiet inside the club.

"I can't see too well," she whispered.

He handed her one of the satchels and then opened his lighter. Darkness turned into grayness, and he went upstairs with her close behind him. After opening the door to his room, he motioned for her to go inside. With her head down, she brushed past him and stood in the middle of the room, shifting from foot to foot.

With his boot, he closed the door and crossed the room to switch on a lamp on the nightstand. When he threw the keys down on the dresser, she jumped and glanced up at him. "Have a seat." He pointed to the chair by the window. She went over to the desk and pulled out the wooden chair.

Sitting down, she twisted her hair around her hands over and over. With eyes cast down, she licked her lips, then cleared her throat.

"You want something to drink?" he asked, walking over to the mini fridge across the room. He pulled out a can of Coke and handed it to her.

She popped open the top and took a sip. "Thanks," she said softly.

"You gonna tell me why the fuck you were walking around with a blanket wrapped around you in the middle of the night?"

For a few seconds the room was quiet, but then she sighed loudly. "Not much to tell. I had enough. I had to get away from Bobby." She took another sip.

Paco watched her as she sat hunched over in the chair, the blanket practically swallowing her. As if sensing his scrutiny, she fidgeted in her seat. The soft light from the lamp bathed her hair in a golden glow, making it shine like melting dark chocolate.

Silence stretched between them, and then, very slowly, she raised her eyes to his, and he sucked in his breath. Those smoky black eyes rimmed with long dark lashes seemed to draw more of him in every time he looked into them, captivating him. Dangerous. Intriguing. Beautiful. Unspoken emotions passed between them, and without thinking, he walked over and caressed her cheek, touching the corner of her eye. A hint of desire danced across her face as she closed her lids, her lashes sending sparks across his fingers. He jerked his hand back and moved away.

"You can crash here."

"Do you live here?" she asked softly.

"Yeah. I'll sleep in the recliner. We can talk about shit in the morning. It's late and I'm beat." He opened the top drawer of his dresser and took out a T-shirt. Holding it out to her, he said, "You can sleep in this. Did you bring any of your stuff?"

"Not really. Just my toothbrush, comb, makeup, and some clothes. Whatever I could put in the plastic bag."

"We can deal with that later. The bathroom's over here." He opened the door next to him, then went over to the recliner and kicked off his boots.

Clutching the T-shirt, she went toward the bathroom, then stopped and looked over her shoulder. "Thanks for helping me out, Paco."

"Sure. Now get changed so I can turn the damn lights off." He pulled his shirt over his head and unbuttoned his jeans. When she closed the bathroom door, he slipped on a pair of sweats and plopped down on the recliner. He didn't believe her story for one second. Something had happened that triggered her to run away in the middle of the night.

The bathroom door opened and she walked over to the bed. The way his T-shirt fell over her curves sucked him in immediately, making his cock thicken. *Fuck.* He was pretty sure that if he joined her in bed she wouldn't complain, but he didn't want her to fuck him because she felt obligated. He didn't want to get involved with her anyway. She wasn't a club girl, and the way she looked at him ensnared him and made his mind fall down into emotions he'd long buried, swearing he'd never resurrect them. *I'll give her some money and then send her packing tomorrow.*

"Did you want me to switch off the light?" she asked, pulling the covers down.

"Yeah."

The only light filtering in through the blinds was from the outside security lights that a raccoon or coyote had triggered.

"Good night, Paco."

He grunted, feigning drowsiness, but his body was as awake as if he'd drunk a gallon of coffee. For a long while he stared at her outline, listening to her breathing as it became deeper.

What the hell did I get myself into?

For reasons he couldn't articulate, it felt right having her in his room.

Don't go there. You gotta send her away.

With that thought on his mind, he closed his eyes.

THE METALLIC CLATTER of pots and pans and the aroma of bacon and pancakes wafting up the stairs woke Paco up. Weak threads of sunlight seeped in through the blinds, and he rubbed the sleep out of his eyes, trying to bring things into focus. Glancing at the bed, he saw Misty burrowed under the covers, her torso rising and falling systematically.

Standing up, he stretched as he tried to loosen the kinks in his muscles. He went over to the bathroom and closed the door. When he came out, a green towel around his waist and water trickling down his shoulders from his damp hair, he saw Misty standing by the opened window. A fresh breeze softly blew in.

"Did you sleep good?"

She turned to him, her cheeks rosy, eyes sparkling, and a wide smile on her face. "I haven't slept so well in years. It's amazing how wonderful it feels."

He laughed. She seemed so innocent on one hand, but on the other, she seemed so worldly. He suspected she'd lived and seen more of the seedier part of life than most of the women he knew. "So what're your plans?"

All at once, her face blanched, and he was sorry he'd asked the question. Raising her shoulder up and down, she shook her head. "I don't know. I didn't really think anything through."

"You got any money?"

She shifted her gaze from him to the corner of the room, then shook her head.

His gut told him she was lying, but he figured she couldn't have too much money since she had a pimp and they weren't known for being generous. "You can stay here for a few days until you figure it out."

She moved her gaze back to him. "Are you sure? I mean, aren't there other people living here, like your roommates?"

He chuckled. "The other guys will be cool with it. They aren't exactly my roommates, but for citizens it may seem like that."

"I'm not sure what you're talking about. Who are citizens?"

"You and anyone else who isn't a biker. Anyway, don't worry about the guys. Get ready and come down when you're done. I'm gonna talk to some of my brothers and get something to eat. Smells like Lena's making bacon and pancakes. She always makes breakfast burritos too, so you'll have a choice."

"Who's Lena?"

"Our kickass cook. She makes the best food."

"You have a cook? Wow."

"It's not what you're thinking. Come down when you're ready to have some chow." He dropped his towel and slipped on a pair of jeans over his boxers. Taking out a clean T-shirt, he tugged it over his head. He felt her eyes on him as he dressed, and it turned him on. Pulling his boots on, he glanced up at her. And just as he thought, she was looking at him; she met his gaze. A flirty smile danced on her lips. He winked at her and walked out. His dick was pissed as hell at him, but he'd told himself he wouldn't get involved with her. He couldn't afford to.

As he walked down the hall, he remembered his wallet. He had a wad of cash in it, and even though he didn't want to think he couldn't trust her, he wasn't stupid. She was broke, and her job was hustling guys. Turning back, he went to his room and opened it. Misty stood by the bed, naked. Her back was facing him, and the angry red streaks marking her body took him aback. *Fuck. Her pimp did a number on her.*

As if sensing he was in the room, she spun around, grabbed the T-shirt on the bed, and held it in front of her. "You startled me. I thought you left."

"I forgot something. Who the fuck hurt you?"

"No one. I mean, it wasn't punishment. It was a paid job."

"Did you want to do it?"

"I just told you I got paid."

"That doesn't answer my question. Is that what you wanted to do?"

"The money was good. I'm going to take a shower now. I'll meet you downstairs."

"Is that why you ran away?"

"No." She walked into the bathroom and closed the door.

Paco scrubbed his face. He was going to find out what the fuck was going on with her. Opening the dresser drawer, he grabbed his wallet, tucked it into the inner pocket of his cut, and walked out of the room.

"I thought I saw your bike in the lot. What the hell are you doing back so early?" Shotgun asked as Paco entered the main room.

"I didn't like the club being without a prez or VP for the whole weekend." He pulled out a chair and plopped down.

"How'd it go over there?" Skull picked up a strip of bacon.

"We got trouble with the assholes. The Fallen Slayers aren't really getting how serious it is. Los Malos is all over this. The West Avenue assholes think they're still in charge in Silverado. Steel's gonna call an emergency church when they all come back."

"How was the strip club? Army texted me some pics. It looked like something you'd see in Denver," Skull said.

"It was okay. Too many underage girls not wanting to be there. That's the first thing we gotta get rid of," Paco answered.

"Fuckers," Skull replied.

A low whistle from Cueball turned Paco's attention to the hallway, and he saw Misty coming into the main room. "Who the fuck's that? I didn't see her last night." He sat up straight in the chair.

"I would've remembered that one," Skull said.

"Back off. She's with me." Paco lifted his chin at her and she made her way over to his table.

Shotgun laughed. "That's why you came back early. Wanted some alone time with some new pussy you picked up in Silverado."

Paco bristled. "It's not like that. I'm just helping her out."

"And she's buying your crock of shit?" Cueball chuckled.

"Hi," Misty said softly as she stood by Paco.

"These are some of my brothers." He pointed at each of them. "Shotgun. Skull. Cueball. You want some grub?" The brothers smiled at her, then started talking among themselves. Since she was with him, they'd respect her.

"Sure. Did you eat?"

"I was waiting for you. Let's go in the kitchen and get something."

When they came back to the table, Cueball and Skull had joined four of the club women on the couch. Paco saw Lucy and she smiled at him, even though her eyes were fixed on Misty.

"I'll be right back," he told Misty, then went over to Lucy. "A friend of mine's in trouble, so I'm helping her out. Do you have any clothes she can wear until she gets some new ones? She needs a heavy jacket and maybe some other things."

Lucy looked over his shoulder at her and shrugged. "Send her to my room later on and I'll figure it out."

"Thanks." He squeezed her hand and went back to the table.

"Is that your girlfriend?" Misty asked.

"No. She's a friend."

"She's not acting like a friend. She's giving me all kinds of dirty looks. Reminds me of Crystal and Amber Jade." She took a bite out of her burrito.

"She's one of the club girls. They're territorial with the brothers. They live here with us, and they're not so accepting of a new girl staying in their space."

"So she's gonna give me some shit?"

"No. She knows you're with me. After we eat, she's gonna loan you some clothes. You know better what you need than I do."

"What's a club girl?"

"A woman who helps out around here and makes the guys' lives easier."

She glanced over at Lucy, then back at him. "I see. So they're whores. Are they here 'cause they wanna be?" She took a sip of orange juice.

"Of course. No woman's forced to do anything. We don't do that shit. And they're part of the family around here. If they don't wanna do something, they don't have to."

"How many you got living here?"

"Six."

"Not a bad deal. They get free room and board. Do you give them money, or do they work outside of the club?"

"We make sure they have what they need. Each of them gets a monthly stipend, but if they want to work outside of the club, it's cool as long as it doesn't interfere with club parties and such. If it does, then we ask them to either quit or leave."

"Makes sense. You need another club girl?"

At first he thought she was joking, but the earnest expression on her face told him otherwise. There was no way he'd ever let another brother touch her. "No."

"Too bad. It sounds like a good gig."

"What's your story, Misty? It doesn't seem to me that this life was your idea. Was Bobby forcing you to do it?" Her eyes narrowed, as if in confusion, and she pursed her lips. "You not answering tells me he was."

Her hands flew up in a defensive stance. "I didn't say that. You did."

He tilted his head and paused. *She doesn't trust me.* "I know you don't really know me, but there's no way I'd hurt you. I'm not gonna send you back to your fucking pimp—"

"Bobby's my boyfriend." She looked away.

"Fuck that. He's your pimp. I'm not stupid, sweetheart. I'm hoping in time you'll trust me enough to tell me how the fuck you ended up with that sonofabitch."

She pushed her plate away. "Well, you're right about one thing—I don't know you. And I'm not in the habit of spilling my guts to anyone, even if there was something to tell."

"You wanna go see about some clothes in Lucy's room?"

"So you're changing the subject?"

"No point in talking about it when I know you're lying. Are you ready or not?"

"Are you coming up with me too?"

"No. I have some club business I need to do."

"Oh," she said softly. Her shoulders slumped and she lowered her head.

Threads of empathy weaved through him, and he wanted to pull her to him and kiss her gently. He wanted to tell her that she didn't have to be afraid, that she could trust him with all her dark secrets, but he just got up and called out to Lucy.

I can't get too involved.

But he already was.

Chapter Ten

Lucy's room had two double beds, blue iridescent beads hanging down over the large window. Posters of fashion models, baby animals, and Harleys adorned the walls.

"What size are you?" Lucy asked as she stood in front of the closet, pushing the hangers across the clothes rod.

"A six or eight." Misty pressed her folded arms closer to her chest.

"So how long have you known Paco?" Lucy threw a few tops and some jeans on the bed.

"Not very long. He's just helping me out."

"With what?"

"Just some stuff."

"Where'd you meet?" She turned around and fixed her gaze on Misty.

"In Moab. Do you want me to try these on?"

"Just hold 'em up in front of you. I never saw Paco bring a woman to the club before. You must be a real good friend."

"I guess." She picked up a multicolored sweater in varying shades of purple and held it in front of her. "This'll probably fit okay. I'm not as busty as you are, but it should be good."

Lucy cocked her head to the side. "Paco loves my tits."

Her gut twisted. "Is he your boyfriend?"

"We have a special bond. Always have since I first got here."

Picking up a black pair of leggings and two more tops, Misty stepped toward the door.

"Wait. Paco wanted me to give you a jacket. I can't believe you don't have one. Were you running away from someone?" Lucy handed her a black winter jacket with brown faux fur cuffs and hood.

"Thanks. I'll return all these as soon as I can." Without waiting for a response, she slipped out the door and headed upstairs to Paco's room.

When she walked in, Paco wasn't there and emptiness filled her. After hearing Lucy talk about him, it made her feel even more like an intruder in his life. *I have to figure out what I'm going to do.* When Paco had asked her if she'd been forced into the life she had, she'd been tempted to tell him everything, but years of beatings, betrayals, and despair made even a sweet old lady who sang in the church choir suspect. It'd been so long since she'd trusted anyone, and when she had, she'd been dragged into a nightmare she couldn't wake up from. Even though Paco had been kind and caring so far, she didn't know if he'd turn on her and tell Bobby where she was—or even worse, Victor. She couldn't take the chance.

Misty locked the door, then grabbed the plastic bag she'd brought. She emptied it out on the bed, and among her toiletries and underwear, thousands of dollars in large bills spread out over the blanket. By now, Bobby would have known she escaped and took his money. *If he ever catches me, he'll torture me before he kills me.* She picked up several of the bills and wadded them up in her hand. *What am I going to do? Where am I going to go? What about Mom and Kate?* She hadn't called her mom and sister yet for fear that she'd cause more trouble for them if they knew she was still alive. If she didn't have contact with them, Bobby couldn't beat anything out of them. *But what if he kills them anyway just to spite me? He always told me he'd kill them. That's how he kept me.*

"What the fuck am I going to do?" she whispered under her breath. She could call the cops, but they'd help her for a while and then move on. That's when Bobby, and especially Victor, would strike. Victor wouldn't be too happy that he paid for nothing. He'd make it a point to find her. *He's a cold, cruel bastard.*

Maybe if I dye my hair and go to Europe. He'd never find me there. But she'd have to get a passport, and that was too risky. Her name was probably in every database in the criminal system. Anyway, she didn't even have any form of ID; it'd been taken away from her years before.

But I should warn Mom that she and Kate are in danger. Even Peter is in danger. She grimaced when she thought of her stepfather. They hadn't gotten along very well, especially when she got older and started dating Tyler Tarleton.

Stop! Don't think about any of that now. You have to do *something. Think.*

Adrenaline rushed through her veins when she heard Paco's and another man's voices outside the door. Scooping up the money, she stuffed it in the bag, then threw her personal stuff on top and shoved it under the bed right when the door opened. She perched on the edge of the bed, inhaling deeply to calm her racing heart.

"Did it work out with Lucy?" he asked.

Brushing away the stray hairs on her face, she looked up and nodded.

"Good. We can go shopping either tomorrow or the day after. It depends on what I have to do." He picked up the remote and turned on the television, keeping the sound muted.

She stared at him, but he didn't look her way. *I wonder if he only sees me as a pathetic woman in need of help.*

"If you have a bit of time, I'd like to pick up some personal things. I left in a hurry and didn't take everything I needed."

Without looking at her, he turned off the television and stood up. "Let's go." Taking the keys from the dresser, he walked out of the room.

"Wait up. I have to go to the bathroom."

"I'll meet you downstairs." His voice echoed in the hall as he disappeared down the stairs.

Throwing off her T-shirt, she picked up the cute lavender sweater Lucy had loaned her and slipped it on, then went into the bathroom and swept up her hair in a low messy bun, pulling out small strands of hair to fall around her neck. A swipe of glittering mauve gloss and a final look in the mirror and she was ready to join him. *You're being silly.* Maybe it was the giddiness of freedom that made her want to act like a normal woman who didn't have years of baggage in her past. She wasn't really sure what she wanted from Paco, but all she knew was she felt safe and protected with him.

When she entered the main room, Lucy stood close to Paco with her hand on his forearm and her mouth close to his ear. For a split second, a flash of anger tore through her. "Oh," she gasped under her breath, surprised at her reaction. The only thing she'd ever been jealous of was other people's freedom. Her day-to-day existence didn't allow for any emotions other than fear, shame, and anguish; anything else was a luxury she'd been rarely afforded.

Paco glanced at her and smiled, and it warmed her all over. In his black T-shirt that fit like a second skin and his tight jeans, he was all kinds of sexy. She'd noticed his tattoos before, but in the afternoon sun, they appeared more dangerous, fierce, and they enthralled her.

Pulling away from Lucy, he motioned to Misty. "Let's go." His silver earrings swayed with his movements, and she thought he must be the most perfect-looking man she'd ever seen. She dashed toward him, ignoring the stares from the other women, and went out into the brightness.

"Do you always ride your motorcycle?" she asked, walking toward it.

"Mostly. You gonna get a lot of shit, 'cause if you are, then we better take the truck."

"I thought we were going to go for clothes another day."

"Me too, but since we're going out, you might as well get everything you need."

"I didn't bring enough money. I'll have to go up and get some more." She turned around, but his strong arm held her back.

"I thought you said you didn't have any money." His brow wrinkled.

Blood rushed to her head. *Dammit. I fucked up.* "I meant I don't have a lot of money. I was able to take a few bucks."

"Don't bullshit me, sweetheart. A few bucks isn't gonna buy you squat." He laughed. "You think I want your money? I don't. What I want is for you to quit lying to me."

Chewing on a thumbnail, she gave a half shrug. "I'm not in the habit of sharing stuff with people. I do have some money I took when I left."

"First off, I'm not 'people,' and secondly, this lying shit stops now." He leaned back on the heels of his boots as his eyes tracked up her body. "Stealing from your pimp took guts. I like that."

"I have to go back up and get some more money for the clothes."

"No worries. I'll cover it. I told you I would."

"That was before you knew I had any money. I'm not into handouts." *I still have some fuckin' pride left, even though Bobby tried to beat it out of me.*

"I know that. You can pay me back later."

He opened the door for her and she slipped past him, the scent of black pepper, myrrh, and leather warming her senses like hot tea infused with spices. The aroma sent a current of electricity through her entire being, and she gripped his arm to steady herself as she settled on the passenger seat.

"You okay?" His deep voice made her tingle.

"Yeah." *You're acting real dumb. This gig is only temporary. You need to focus on what you're going to do, not on him. Besides, men just want to hurt you.* And she believed that wholeheartedly because the past had proven it to be true. *Given any power, men will cause great suffering.*

But Paco confused her. He was nice, caring, and the way he looked at her told her that he was attracted to her, yet he kept his distance. He hadn't forced her to do anything. Part of her wanted to believe he was different from Erik, Bobby, and all the men she'd serviced over the past eight years, but old thoughts and fears were hard to rewire.

"You good with going to Walmart? There's one about thirty miles from here."

"I love that store."

He switched on the radio and they drove in silence until he turned into the store's lot. She jumped out of the truck, secured a cart someone had haphazardly left in the middle of a parking space, and they went into the store.

For the next two hours, she tried on clothes, looked at makeup, sprayed on a variety of scents, and picked up some Cheetos, Hershey's Kisses, and peanut butter. Those were the items Bobby never let her have. He'd told her it was because she had to keep her body at a certain weight, but that wasn't it. The reason he wouldn't let her have them was out of sheer meanness. One night when she'd been rented out to a party, he'd torn through all her things, looking under the mattress, the bed, and every corner in her room, and he'd come across her journal. That night, he'd beaten her with a chain, and she was still surprised she'd survived it. In her journal she'd written her thoughts about him, Erik, her life, what had happened, and about her favorite snacks she missed the most: Cheetos, Hershey's Kisses, and peanut butter.

"Do you like this?" Paco picked up a bottle of eau de parfum.

"I do."

"I saw you kept sniffing your arm where you put it on."

She raised her arm. "Do you like it?"

He bent down and breathed in, then looked up at her. "That's you," he said hoarsely.

For a moment, she was mesmerized by his mahogany eyes that stared so intently into her own. The overhead intercom, the generic music playing throughout the store, and the customers' voices faded into the background as they stood in the perfume aisle, transfixed by one another.

"Did you want me to get you anything?" the saleslady asked.

Slowly dragging his gaze away from hers, he pointed to a clear crystal bottle filled with a light amber liquid. A big pink bow was wrapped around its neck. "That one."

"Good choice. It's Juicy Couture's best seller." She unlocked the glass container.

The price tag read forty-two dollars. "That's too expensive," she whispered to Paco. The saleslady frowned, the cellophane-wrapped box clutched in her hand.

"It's fine. I'll take it."

While Paco paid for it, she watched him, incredulous that he'd spent so much on her. No one had ever bought her something so nice, at least not since she'd been taken away from her home. She sniffed her arm again, the sweet scents of caramel, pralines, and honeysuckle filling her nostrils. Of all the perfumes and sprays she'd tried on, this one was her favorite, but she didn't dare hope to get it. And when Paco said it was her, a rush of surprise tingled through her.

When he handed her the bag, it was like he'd given her the world—and in a way he had. He was the first person to show any semblance of kindness since her whole ordeal had started.

As they waited in the checkout lane, guilt about not trusting him crept in. "Thank you for the perfume," she said softly. He lifted his chin and stroked the back of her neck with his fingers. As he paid for her purchases, she went over to the bulletin board of missing children. Again, she saw her smiling face from her sophomore school pictures, but that flyer had a computerized image of how she'd look now, and it was incredibly spot-on. A gripping feeling of fear and helplessness took hold, and her hands tingled while her heart pounded. She raised her hand to rip it off the board.

"What're you looking at?"

That's right. Bobby isn't around. I'm okay. She clutched her throat as she breathed in deeply.

"What's going on with you? Are you sick?" Concern laced his voice.

"No. I guess it was breathing in all those perfumes. I just got light-headed. I'm good."

"Why're you looking at these flyers?"

She pushed the cart, moving away from the board. "I don't know. I guess I think I may know someone up there and maybe help or save them."

"I never paid attention to these pictures." He stared at it and her stomach churned.

Grabbing his arm, she tugged him away. "I need to get to the car to sit down."

"Sorry. Let's go."

They walked out of the store, and she sat in the truck while he loaded the bags in the back. When he got in, he tossed her the bag of Cheetos.

She laughed. "You read my mind." Tearing them open, her mouth watered as she saw the crispy sticks. The first one she popped in her mouth was cheese heaven. Paco laughed and she glanced at him. "What?"

"It's just cute the way you're enjoying those. It's like you've never had them."

"That's almost true." She crunched down on another. "It's been a long time. You want some?" She pushed the bag toward him.

Shaking his head, he pushed it back. "I don't eat that stuff."

"You don't know what you're missing."

When they got back to the club, the guys and girls kept staring at them as they walked through the main room, each of them loaded down with plastic bags. After putting the bags on the bed, Paco took off his jacket and hung it in the closet, then slipped on a leather vest.

"I can give Lucy back the clothes you borrowed. I didn't know we were going to go shopping."

"I can give them back to her." For some reason, the thought of him in Lucy's bedroom bothered her.

"It's no big deal." He sat in the recliner and watched as she hung up all her new purchases.

"What're your plans for tonight?" she asked.

"Nothing much. We usually party big on Saturday nights."

"That sounds fun."

"Not for you. We have brothers coming in from other clubs, so it could be a problem for you. They may think you're a club woman or a hang-around. It's better if you stay in here for the night. I can bring dinner up to you."

"You're going to the party?" She wasn't sure she liked the idea of him being with the club girls and whoever the hang-arounds were.

"For a bit. I'll play some pool and have a few drinks. It's always a good time to see brothers I haven't seen in a while."

"Oh. I thought we could watch a movie and order a pizza. I haven't had pizza in forever."

He chuckled. "Are you on a mission to eat all the junk food you can in one day?"

"Pretty much." She folded the empty shopping bags. "So are you game for it?"

For a moment, he studied her intently, a gleam of desire in his eyes, but then he looked away. "I've already got plans, but I can pick up a pizza for you and you can order a movie on TV." He stood up. "What do you want on it?"

She cast her gaze downward. "That's okay. I changed my mind."

"Maybe another time," he said in a low voice.

"Maybe," she muttered.

The touch of his hand under her chin, tilting her head back, sent a warming shiver through her. She met his gaze and her heart turned over. The tip of his thumb swept over her bottom lip, sending her emotions whirling and skidding. Instinctively, she reached for him, but he stepped back.

"If you need anything, call me." He pointed to the cordless phone on the nightstand. "I wrote out my number and left it there earlier."

And then he was gone.

The scent of his cologne lingered in the room. His footsteps faded away, and loneliness pressed down on her like a steel weight. Her thoughts, jagged and painful, were her only companions. For a moment, she'd thought he was going to kiss her, but he walked away. *He probably doesn't want me because he knows what I am. A lot lizard. A whore. But not by choice.* Never *by choice.*

The windows rattled and a loud rumble filtered through them. Going to the window, she looked down and saw motorcycles galore filling the parking lot. It was an incredible sight: a sea of black leather and denim, the fading sunlight bouncing off the motorcycles' chrome, women in short skirts and stilettos cozying up to the men. In the midst of all that, she saw Paco, a beer in his hand, talking to one of the brothers. She searched the crowd for Lucy and found her wrapped around a tall, skinny man with a bushy beard. The lines in Misty's forehead relaxed.

As if sensing her, Paco glanced up. She held her breath as their gazes locked in an embrace. Then a big guy smacked Paco on the back and he turned away from her, the big guy drawing him into a bear hug. The moment had flitted away, and she was left again with her tortured thoughts. That day, she'd enjoyed pockets of time when she'd felt whole again, but then they blew away, replaced by the reality of who she was.

I'm broken, and I don't know how to fix me.

Misty wrapped the blanket around her and lay down, hugging the pillow close. It would be a long night. She could call Paco and tell him she was afraid, but she wouldn't. She had to face the demons and who she was on her own.

She owed it to herself.

Chapter Eleven

Bobby's face became rigid, jaw clamped tight, teeth grinding. *Where the fuck is she?* Looking at her phone on the dresser and her clothes hanging in the closet, he figured she couldn't have gone very far. "The fuckin' bitch!" He kicked the chair over, then threw the trash can at the wall. Bits of plaster rained down.

Opening the door between the connecting rooms, he looked at his two whores' sleeping forms. "Crystal, Amber Jade, get your lazy asses in here now!"

Crystal jumped up. "What's the matter?" She came into his room.

Amber Jade walked in slowly, rubbing her eyes. "What time is it?"

"Did you see Misty last night or this morning?" Both women shook their heads. "Fuck! Do you know where she is? And you fuckin' better tell me the truth or I'll kill you."

"I don't know anything about her. Last time I saw her, she was going into the room with you. That was about two thirty or so this morning," Crystal said.

"Same here," Amber Jade added.

"You bitches better not be lying to me." Bobby took out his gun and the women cried out.

"We're not BSing you. We'd tell you where the skank was if we knew." Crystal cringed in the corner.

"Even if she gave you some money? Did she do that? Did she pay you to lie to me?" He rushed over and pulled Crystal's hair. "Tell me, bitch. Where the fuck is she?"

Holding her hands up as if trying to shield herself from a possible bullet, tears spilled down her cheeks. "I don't know where the slut is. I'd tell you, Bobby. You know I love you."

Raising his arm, he slammed the gun down on her head, and blood started flowing down the side of her face.

"I swear, Bobby. I don't know nothin'. I'd tell you. I hate the fuckin' bitch. I wouldn't protect her. She's nothing but a fuckin' slave. Please don't hit me again. I didn't do nothin'."

Her nasally voice grated on his already taut nerves. "Shut the fuck up or I'll put a bullet through your stupid head!"

Bobbing her head over and over like a broken jack-in-the-box, she sank to the ground. "Okay, Bobby. I'm shutting up. I won't say another word." She put her hand in front of her mouth.

Whirling around, he glared at Amber Jade, who stood in the doorway, her face whiter than the sheets on the bed. "You know anything?"

"No. I swear. I love you too, Bobby. If I saw her leaving, I never would've let her."

"Get your worthless asses back to your room. I gotta think." He pointed the gun at them and they ran out.

The fuckin' cunt stole the money. I can't believe I didn't cuff her before I took the pills. I screwed this up bad. Fuck!

Anger weaved around him, choking him. He'd been too confident in his control over her and was sure she'd never run. A few times in the past, he'd done the same and she was always there in the morning, waiting for instructions. It used to make him feel smug as hell when he'd see her each morning. "I broke that fuckin' bitch," he muttered. But something had changed to make her take the chance and escape.

In the beginning she'd tried a few times, but after he punished her good, she stopped and life had been fine. Her ass gave him a good life, and he'd just struck a deal with Victor, but the bitch had gone and fucked it all up. Victor had paid him a load of money for her, and now she was gone. "Fuck!"

While he tapped numbers into his phone, he walked over to the window and looked down at the parking lot. Some johns were leaving from different rooms, each of them rushing down the stairs with hands in pockets and heads down. A couple of drug sales were going down in the corner of the lot near the dumpster.

"This is Bobby. Is she back home?"

"She's not with you?" the voice replied.

"If she were, I wouldn't be calling you. You made a deal with Erik and me eight years ago, and it still stands. Did the bitch call home?"

"No. How did she get away after all these years?"

"This cunt cost me a shitload of money, and I'm either gonna get it from her or from you. You call me the minute you hear from her. If you try and double-cross me, I'll kill everyone in your family before I get to you."

"I'll let you know. She's bound to come home."

A beep signaled an incoming call. "I gotta go. Don't fuck me over." Bobby clicked off and stiffened when he saw Victor's number. *What the fuck am I gonna tell him?*

"Yo," he said as smoothly as he could muster.

"Where's my fucktoy?" Victor asked.

"She's sick with the chills and a really bad sore throat. She woke me up around five this morning complaining about it. It may be strep. She's had it before."

"Why isn't she here as agreed?" Victor's voice was cold and detached.

"I just told you. She's really sick. She can hardly get out of bed. I'm gonna take her to the doctor and get her some antibiotics. You want her healthy and full of energy, don't you?"

"I want her. I fucking paid for her. Bring her to me now."

Sweat ran down the back of his neck and sides of his face, and it felt like his mouth was stuffed with a hundred cotton balls. He went over to the sink and poured a glass of water, drinking several large gulps.

Gripping the edge of the bathroom counter, he breathed heavily. "I just wanna make sure your merchandise is in first-class shape."

"I'll deal with her."

"It's not that. I've got a reputation to uphold. I can't be delivering a sick slave. She'll be ready to go in a day or two." He wiped his brow with a washcloth, then ran it over the back of his neck. "I'll send Crystal and Amber Jade over to your place to show you a good time. It's on the house. I'll bring Misty when she's better."

A long, strained pause. Bobby's heart pounded against his rib cage as he waited for Victor to say something. He wanted to keep talking, but he knew that was a sure sign of a nervous person, and he couldn't let Victor know his nerves were a tangled mess.

"I want my fucktoy by tomorrow morning no matter what shape she's in. It'll cost you ten thousand dollars for the delay. Make sure you bring it and her. I'll play with the other two sluts. Bring them to me."

Relief spread over him like a tidal wave. "That's fair. I'll have her to you in the morning with the money. I'll send the other bitches to you now."

Victor clicked off. Bobby had bought some time.

After sending Crystal and Amber Jade to Victor's mansion, he drove around the small town searching for Misty. *Where the hell is she?* As he played the events of the last twenty-four hours in his mind, he homed in on the asshole who'd broken his nose. He'd planned on going to the doctor that morning, but the bitch had fucked that up for him as well.

As he thought about the night before, he'd remembered that the jerk and Misty were talking when he'd gone out on the patio. *Maybe she knew him and they're in on this together.* But where would she have met him? Bobby always kept her on a tight leash.

A trucker? Maybe.

He turned into the driveway for Satin Dolls. He'd casually ask around to see if anyone knew who the fucker was.

It took a few minutes for his eyes to adjust to the dimness of the place. Two women danced on stage, and others were escorting men to the private lap dance rooms. One of the West Avenue Bandits, Chubby, came over to him and bumped fists. They chatted for a few minutes before Bobby asked if he remembered the guy from the night before. Chubby told him he didn't. Bobby knew it was a long shot that anyone would remember the jerk since the place had been packed, but he figured the women may since the guy had the looks females went crazy for.

Going behind the curtain, several dancers waved at him as they adjusted their costumes or put finishing touches on their faces and hair. He went over to a blonde who was dusting shimmering powder over her shoulders and cleavage.

"Hiya, Della."

"Bobby. I didn't think you'd be here today. How's your nose?"

"Okay. I wanted to ask you about a dude who was here last night. A tall guy with brown hair a little past his collar. Had some earrings on and a bunch of tats. He was back here."

"I remember him. He was gorgeous. I promised him a good time, but he was looking for your girlfriend, Misty."

His chest tightened. "Did he ask for her by name?"

"Yeah. He seemed to only want her. I told him I didn't know where she was but to stick around after my dance and I'd give him a better time, but he just left."

"Do you know who he was?"

"No. I've never seen him before."

"Are you sure?"

"Yeah. I'd definitely remember seeing someone that good-looking. Why all the questions?"

"He shortchanged me."

"That's not good. Tell Chubby or Gizmo."

"I'll take care of it myself. Don't tell anyone, okay?"

Darting her eyes around, she shook her head. "I won't."

But the way she said it told Bobby she'd be telling Chubby about their conversation before he even made it to his car. It was only a matter of time before Victor found out about it, and he'd know something was up. Bobby was sure that Misty and the asshole had planned all this, and chances were high she wasn't in Silverado anymore. Spending any more time looking for her would be futile and dangerous. He was a sitting duck waiting for Victor's thugs to shoot at him. He had to get out of town.

He rushed back to the motel.

Chapter Twelve

"I TOLD ROUGHNECK that we have to move on this quickly," Steel said.

Paco looked around the room and saw the members weighing what Steel had just said. Those words meant war with two gangs who probably didn't play by the same rules as bikers. It meant possible lockdowns, casualties, and death.

It'd been a while since the Night Rebels had engaged in an all-out war. The measures they took with the Skull Crushers and Satan's Pistons had been warnings but not declarations of war. This would be different. It wasn't just about the turf—it was about the lifestyle. There was no doubt in Paco's or any of his brothers' minds that women were being trafficked in the surrounding area, and the Night Rebels wouldn't tolerate that under any circumstances. They knew the Insurgents were on the same page with them when it came to sexual slavery, but Night Rebels preferred to handle the situation in the south on their own. As long as the Fallen Slayers were on board, they could manage it.

As the talk shifted from beating the asses of these gangs to the Insurgents' charity poker run, Paco's mind went to Misty. He had to admit that he'd been attracted to her since the first time he saw her. He shook his head. She was really playing havoc with his emotions. It'd been a long time since he'd had real feelings for a woman. After Cassie, he'd encased his heart in steel, and in all those years nothing had threatened its imprisonment until Misty. *But how can I even think about getting involved with her when all she's done is lie to me since I've met her?* Paco suspected she'd stolen money from Bobby when she took off. He wasn't sure what made her run when she had, but he knew she was keeping things from him.

The pounding gavel drew Paco back to the meeting. Members pushed their chairs back and headed out of the room, talking to one another in low voices.

"I knew we could count on all the brothers," Steel said as he put the gavel in its box.

"Can we count on all the Fallen Slayers members?" Paco asked.

Steel nodded. "From the way Roughhouse and Patriot were talking, I think we can. We gotta get together with Knuckles and Diablo and get a plan in motion. Chains is already doing the research on both gangs. We have to hit hard and fast. Surprise is the best defense."

"Agreed. I'll come up with some strategies. All that combat in Afghanistan will come in handy. I'll have Rooster help out. He did a tour in Iraq years ago. But Brick has to work with Diablo on the plan. Knuckles isn't the brightest and he'll drive Diablo fucking crazy."

Nodding, Steel sniggered. "I'll tell Roughhouse. One thing is for sure. We've got the arms and supplies. The fuckers won't forget this. We should add more security cameras around the place. Army's got a buddy who's gonna build a steel-enforced wall around the clubhouse. I've been thinking that while this is going on, we gotta have a lockdown."

Paco chuckled. "I can't see Breanna and Raven embracing that. Fallon's easygoing, though I'm not too sure about Hailey."

Steel jutted out his chin and narrowed his eyes. "Doesn't matter if the old ladies want it or not. It's for survival. Breanna will just have to deal with it. All of them will."

They walked down the hallway. "You sticking around?" Paco asked.

"Just for a drink. Then I've gotta get back to my woman and show her some loving. It's been too long."

Paco laughed. "I hear you. I'll have a drink with you before you take off. I've got some stuff to do, so I'm cutting out soon."

The members were already in full swing in the main room, drinking, laughing, and having fun with the club girls. Steel and Paco went over to the bar and picked up the shots the prospect had waiting for them.

"Why the hell did you leave Silverado early?" Army asked.

"I didn't want the club to be without a prez or VP the whole weekend," Steel answered for Paco. Army stared over Paco's shoulder and whistled.

As Paco turned around, he heard Sangre asking, "Isn't that the stripper from Satin Dolls? What the fuck's she doing here?"

Shotgun elbowed Paco. "You didn't tell us she was a stripper, bro."

"Way to go," Skulls said.

When Misty walked into the room, she took his breath away: her indigo knit top hugged her round breasts, her faded jeans fit snugly around her hips, her long hair spilled loosely about her shoulders, and her face had a rosy glow. She looked beautiful. Their eyes locked and a spark of desire flared in the pit of his stomach. As she came up to him, her lips parted, lips that were made for sinning, and he felt a tug in his jeans.

Steel spun around, then looked at Paco. "Why the hell is she here?"

"She was in a bad way. I'm just helping her out temporarily."

Misty stopped in her tracks, only a short reach from him. It was like she sensed the tension between the men.

Army shook his head. "You're bringing shit to the club because of a two-bit stripper? If Los Malos or the West Avenue fucks find out you took one of their strippers, it'll fuckin' jeopardize all of our plans."

"He's right," Steel said.

With his chin high, his legs planted wide, Paco shook his head. "She doesn't work for them."

"Maybe not, but we've found out some more stuff in the last couple of days about the prez of Los Malos. He's got the hots for her, so I'm sure he's not gonna like that you took her away," Sangre said.

"What the fuck were you thinking, dude? We got a whole bunch of strippers at Lust if you wanna fuck someone." Army picked up his beer bottle.

Paco ripped the bottle out of his hand and flung it against the wall behind the bar. Amber shards of glass flew everywhere, and dark brown liquid streaked down the wall. "I don't need you to fucking question my decisions. If you got a problem, let's go outside and settle it. And don't you talk shit about her."

Steel stepped between the two. "I'm with Army and the rest on this. You shouldn't have brought her to the club." Turning to Army, he said, "And I agree with Paco—show her respect."

Paco glanced over at Misty and she avoided his look. Pushing her hair over her face, it was like she was trying to make herself invisible. His insides pulled. "I said I fucking own this. If you want her gone, then I'll get a place and go with her until she gets back on her feet."

Surprise rolled over the brothers' faces. Steel cleared his throat. "You don't have to do that, bro. We're not against you helping her out or her staying. It's just we got a touchy situation in Silverado, and we don't want to start shit with these assholes sooner than we're ready."

"I get that," Paco said.

"Did anyone see you with her?" Steel asked.

"No. I just ran into her when I was riding through the town."

Steel motioned for Misty to come over. With ashen face and trembling lips, she came and stood next to Paco. He slipped her hand in his; it was clammy and cold. He squeezed it lightly and she leaned against him.

"Have you told anyone you're here?" Steel asked.

"No," she said in a voice barely above a whisper.

"Did you tell anyone you were leaving Silverado?" Steel said.

She shook her head. "I didn't plan any of this. Paco just saw me on the side of the road. Can I go now?"

Steel and the others stared at her for a couple of minutes, and Paco felt her body shaking. He bent down and whispered in her ear, "It's okay. Nothing's gonna happen to you. I'm here."

"Go on," Steel said.

Paco winked at her, and she smiled weakly and rushed out of the room. "Thanks," he said to the men.

"If we find out she's been lying, you'll have to step aside while we deal with her," Steel replied.

"What the fuck does that mean?" Paco asked.

"It means you're too involved with her not to be biased," Sangre answered.

"I'm not involved with her or anyone. I'm just helping her out, that's all."

"Yeah… keep telling yourself that shit." Army laughed but moved away as if anticipating Paco's fist on his jaw.

Anger curled around Paco's nerves. "If you don't shut the fuck up, asshole, I'm gonna make sure you do."

Before Army could react, Steel looked hard at Paco. "Just make sure the club isn't jeopardized in any way."

He stepped back, his fists clenched. "How the fuck could you think I'd put the club in jeopardy?" He slammed his fist down on the bar. "We're talking about the brotherhood. Fuck!"

"Chicks can mess up a guy," Sangre said.

"No chick's messing me up. Don't ever think that I'd endanger the brotherhood."

"You're overreacting. I meant to make sure she isn't lying to us. I'm not questioning your loyalty," Steel said.

Glancing at the brothers, he saw smirks on their faces, and he wanted to take them all on. He knew they thought he was hooked on Misty, but they were wrong. He was just helping her out. The fact that his cock wanted inside her pussy didn't mean squat. *I'm a man, for fuck's sake.* He'd feel that way about any pretty woman who was staying in his room. It didn't mean he was *involved* with her, or that he wanted to be.

"No one knows she's here. She isn't lying," he grumbled. Of that he was certain, but all the other load of crap she'd told him? *She's definitely lying about that shit.*

As he walked away, he heard Shotgun say, "Never seen him this hooked before," and the other men guffawed.

Fuck them. He went up to his room.

When he opened the door, he saw Misty stuffing her newly bought clothes in plastic bags. "You going someplace?"

"I don't want to be a bother to you anymore. I didn't mean to cause any problems with you and your club."

"You're not a bother, and the prez says you can stay, so take your shit outta those bags."

"Are they going to beat me?" Her voice quivered.

He jerked his head back. "Why the hell would they? Did you lie to them? Does anyone know you're here?"

"No. I'm trying to get away from Bobby and all that. Why would I tell him I'm here?"

"Just asking. We don't beat women, so you're good."

Misty sank down on the bed, her body shaking from her sobs. He watched her, rubbing his chin between his thumb and index finger, feeling helpless. He was the type of guy who came up with solutions and fixed problems, but if he wasn't able to, it made him impatient and annoyed. A crying woman always made him uncomfortable, but at that moment an ache throbbed inside him and it pissed him off. *I don't need any of this.*

She grabbed for the tissue box and took out a few, blowing her nose and wiping her cheeks. "Sorry for the mini meltdown," she said raggedly.

"Feel better?" An overall weighted feeling pressed down on him.

She rose from the bed. "Yeah." Picking up the plastic bags, she shoved some socks into them. "I think it's best if I go."

"Are you trying to get me to beg you to stay?"

Dropping the bag, her fingers flew to her chest. "What? No. Never. I don't want you to think that."

"Then stop packing. I told you it's all right for you to stay."

She kept shoving things inside those damn plastic bags. He came over and gripped her arm, but she jerked out of his hold. With both hands, he grabbed her and whirled her around. Her red-rimmed eyes stared at him, and her hair brushed over his hands. The skin on her arms was soft like satin, and the new perfume he'd bought her curled around him, sending all kinds of signals to his hardening dick. Holding her that close had fire roaring through his veins, confusing and angering him. He grabbed Misty by the shoulders and shook her hard. Tears spilled from her eyes as she whimpered.

"Now you listen to me! I don't want a girlfriend. I don't get involved with women. I'm only helping you. You understand that?"

Misty nodded, tears flowing down her face.

"I've got the club and my brothers. I have a lot of shit on my mind. I don't need a woman. I don't want one. Stop doing what you're doing."

"What am I doing?" she whispered, her gaze capturing his.

"Just that. You're… you're…." He pulled her in a fierce embrace. "Misty," he whispered in her hair.

"Paco." She pressed closer to him.

With his hand under her chin, he tipped her head back and his lips touched hers. She reached up into it, breathing out, her warm breath caressing his face. His wild eyes searched hers, and the flush of her cheeks pushed him over the edge. He gathered her hair, her face, all of her and claimed her mouth with a burning force. Hard. Full of heat. Uncontrolled. It was as if all the pent-up desire he'd been pushing down since he'd first laid eyes on her rushed out of him, and each kiss was a wild hunger for more. He swallowed her moans, and she clawed him frantically as he pressed her even closer to him. Tongues sliding in and out, panting, lips hard on hers, he craved her touch, her closeness, her essence.

He slid his hands down her arms and underneath her top. For a brief half second, she stiffened and pulled away. In that instant, a semblance of sense crept back into his head and he moved back.

"That shouldn't have happened," he said.

"I didn't mean to pull away. It's just… I don't know. I guess the past is always in my head."

"I wasn't talking about that. I shouldn't have kissed you."

"Why not? I wanted it just as much as you did."

Their gazes locked and he groaned internally, knowing he was totally fucked now that he'd tasted her sweet mouth, felt her soft lips against his, and held her in his arms.

"I gotta go. It's probably better if I crash in another room."

"You don't have to."

The memory of how she felt in his arms flitted through his mind. "Yeah, I do. Unpack your stuff 'cause you're staying. I've got some things to do. I'll come get you when it's time for dinner." The scent of her intoxicated him, and he didn't want to stay in the room any longer; he didn't trust himself to behave.

Without waiting for her reply, he left the room and headed downstairs, cursing his lack of control with each step he took.

Chapter Thirteen

MISTY JUMPED ON the bed, giggling like a silly schoolgirl. She leaned against the headboard and wrapped her arms around her bent knees, rocking slightly. *He kissed me.* Bubbles of happiness rose inside her and she closed her eyes, the kiss playing through her mind on repeat. Never mind that he apologized for kissing her and then rushed out; it didn't take away from the passion and desire that had sizzled between them. *If only I hadn't pulled away. Next time I won't.* And she was more than positive that there'd be a next time.

She looked at the bags on the bed and giggled again. *Paco wants me to stay.* For the first time in a very long time, she felt wanted. She got up and emptied them, then began to hang up her clothes. Folding her bras and panties, she decided to put them in one of the drawers instead of leaving them in the plastic bag where they'd been since she'd escaped from Bobby.

Bending down, she opened the bottom dresser drawer and moved some of the contents around to make room for her underthings. A large padded envelope came into view. Before pulling it out, she glanced around the room. She knew she shouldn't look inside, but one small peek wouldn't hurt anyone. Opening the envelope, she saw letters and photographs.

Maybe these are Paco's baby pictures. I bet he was cute as hell.

She padded over to the bed, sat on it cross-legged, and dumped out the contents next to her. Picking up a photo, she smiled when she saw a young Paco in a crew cut and Army combat uniform next to a tank. With her fingernail, she stroked the side of his face. He looked so different with short hair. Another photo showed him with his arms wrapped around a cute brunette. She turned the picture over and read the words "Cassie and me." Most of the pictures were of either Cassie alone or the two of them together.

Misty stared at one of the envelopes addressed to Paco with an Army post office address. *Do I dare read his letter?* It seemed like an awful invasion of his privacy, but she couldn't resist. He was such a hard person to read, and he always had his tough exterior on overdrive. She knew Paco the biker, but she wanted to see what lay behind all the leather, muscle, and tattoos.

The letter slid out of the envelope when she turned it upside down. Glancing at the door, she took a deep breath, then looked down and read the letter.

Hey, sexy,

I was so happy when I came home from work and found your letter waiting for me. My mom put it on my dresser, and I tore into it right away. Like you always do, you made me laugh, cry, and ache for you with your words of love and lust. (I loved all the dirty parts. ;))

I wish you were here. I miss you so fucking much. The days are dull without you, but I have work to pass the day. But the nights are awful. I miss your touch, the feel of your skin on mine, your awesome kisses (you ARE the best kisser ever), and the way you make love to me. Just thinking about you makes me wet. I wish you'd come home soon. I miss you too much!

I'm sending a picture of me in a new bikini I bought for the trip the family's going on next month. I wish you could be with me to walk on the beach, make love in the sand, and hold each other when the sun sets. California won't be as much fun without you.

Take care of yourself. Write me when you can. I hope you got the box of goodies I sent you. You didn't mention it in your letter, so maybe it hasn't gotten there yet.

Sending you a big kiss. I love you so much.

Cassie xxooxx ♥

Misty put the letter back in the envelope. *He was in love with her. That's a surprise. I never would've guessed it.*

She took out another letter. Again, it was addressed to him at the Army post office.

Hey, honey,

I've been thinking about you all the time. It makes me happy that you're doing the same. I know you told me not to worry, but sometimes I do when I hear news reports or talk to the other women in the group I go to. I just want you home. Now.

I was thinking about the first time we met three years ago at Rick's party. I've never told you this but I loved you from the moment I saw you. I told Cheryl and Lisa that you were the man I was going to spend the rest of my life with. So it makes me sooooo happy that you want to spend the rest of your life with me. I know you want to ask me properly when you get back, but just knowing you love me as much as I do you makes me warm and happy, but also sad. I'm sad because I want you here so I can show you how happy I am.

You know something? I sleep with one of your T-shirts every night. I doused your cologne on it right before you left last year and it still has your scent. I pretend it's you holding me. Just thinking about you now has me all horny. Dammit. I wish we could tear each other's clothes off and fuck hard and fast.

When are you coming home? I miss you terribly.
Love, love, LOVE YOU,
Cassie♥ xoxoxx

As the sun sank to the horizon, painting the sky in warm hues of copper, coral, and amethyst, Misty raised her arms above her and stretched. She moved her head from side to side, working out some of the kinks from sitting too long reading the letters and looking at the pictures. There were so many birthday cards, notes, funny sayings written on pink paper, and love letters from Cassie to Paco that she was surprised they weren't married with a bunch of kids.

Maybe they got divorced. Maybe that's why he's allergic to involvement. She picked up another letter, opened it, and read it.

Hey, Paco,

I'm not going to pretend that I'm not upset that your tour of duty in Afghanistan got extended four months. It seems that when I get all excited and hopeful to see you, something comes up to make it not happen.

It's been so long. It's hard to be this far apart for this long. I know you explained that you've been in combat and it's hard to call or connect with me as much as I'd like for you to, but it's not fun having you away. When you first joined, I thought it would be okay but it's difficult. I don't know.

Take care of yourself. Mom's calling me for dinner, so I have to go.

Hugs,
Cassie

She glanced at the door for the umpteenth time, knowing if he caught her going through his personal things, he'd be pissed.

Just one more. I swear. This time I mean it.

Opening the letter, she skimmed it, frowning. Then she read it again.

Dear Paco,

I want to tell you that you're a wonderful person. You made me believe in myself, and I'll always remember that. I'm sorry to tell you that I've met someone. I didn't want it to happen, but it just did. We just really clicked. It's like I've known Jeff for years. That's his name—Jeff. We're in love, and we're going to be married. I thought I could wait for you, but it was too hard. In the time you've been away, the distance came between us.

I hope this doesn't sound too callous, but I hope you'll be happy for me. It is possible to find the one. I did, and the way women always look at you, I know you'll find someone new in no time.

I guess that's it. I don't know what else to say except I hope you'll understand. I'll always value you as a friend.

With affection and best wishes always,
Cassie

The white piece of paper fell from Misty's hands and she blinked rapidly. *Poor Paco. While he was fighting for us, she was screwing behind his back. She wrote him a damn* Dear John *letter. How fucking cold.*

She stared at the scattered photographs, the envelopes, and all the silly notecards, the desire to hold him in her arms, his head pressed against her chest, overwhelming her. The past three hours had been emotionally draining.

The doorknob jiggling was like a firecracker under her butt. She leapt up, hurriedly gathering up the letters, cards, and photos and ramming them in the padded envelope. Blood rushed to her head and her temples pulsed as she shoved the envelope in the bottom drawer, straightening up just as he came into the room. He looked around, his gaze fixed on the heap of clothes on the bed.

"I was going to put things away, but I didn't get too far. I was so tired that I took a break." *Tired from hanging up clothes? He'll never believe that one.*

He threw a box on the desk. "I got you a burner phone."

"Oh… thanks. That's cool." *Why is he looking so pissed off at me? Is he still upset over the kiss?*

"I'm just gonna get a few things." He went to the closet and took out a duffel bag.

Please don't let him take anything from the bottom drawer. The manila envelope wasn't in the same place as when she'd found it. Not by a long shot. When he bypassed the drawer, she breathed an audible sigh of relief. He narrowed his gaze and stared at her as if he were studying her. She went over to the window.

"I love the colors in the sky at sunset." No answer. Glancing sideways, she saw he was still staring. Whirling around, she smiled. "Did you go out for a ride?"

"Yeah."

"You look like you did. I mean, you smell like the desert and the wind. Even the sunlight, if that makes any sense. And your hair's all messy. I like it."

He picked up his duffel bag and went to the door.

"Are you mad at me? Did I do something to upset you?"

"We gotta talk in the morning. I picked up a frozen pizza for you. It's in the freezer in the kitchen." He opened the door.

"Wait! What do you want to talk to me about? Did the guys change their minds about letting me stay here?"

"It's not that. The brothers will be partying when you go downstairs, but it's just them tonight, so you don't have to worry. They all know you're off-limits."

"You guys love to party." She laughed nervously. "Are you going to be there too?"

"I'll have some drinks and play pool." He gave her a hard look, and she took it to mean that he had no intention of hanging out with her that night.

"I'll just make my pizza and watch TV."

He lifted his chin and walked out, shutting the door behind him. She stared at the closed door for a long time as wild thoughts ran through her brain: he found out about the money she stole, he knew she'd snooped and found his envelope of memories, he *really* regretted the kiss and now couldn't stand the sight of her. That night, sleep would evade her.

As she watched the flickering screen, she wondered where the Paco in the photographs and letters had gone. *Is he gone forever, or is there a shred of him left deep inside him?* And if there was, how could she reach him?

Sighing, she grabbed the remote and changed the channel.

Chapter Fourteen

BOBBY CROUCHED IN the dark in someone's backyard, wishing the moon wasn't so bright. Like a statue, he stayed in the same position for what seemed like hours. One movement, one involuntary gasp or sigh and it was all over—Victor's people would find him.

Since early that morning, he'd been on the run, Victor's people making it impossible for him to leave town. When he'd told Victor that Misty was missing, he had the goddamn nerve to blame *him* for the cunt's insolence. And Victor expected him to give back the money he'd paid for Misty, but Bobby would never be able to do it. *How the fuck am I gonna be able to come up with that kind of dough just like that?* If he had some time, he could snatch another girl. Young ones went for big money; all he'd have to do was take some pictures and post an online ad, then let the money flow in, but Victor wasn't giving him any time. He never liked the sonofabitch. He always acted like he was the top honcho, but to Bobby he was nothing but a two-bit gangster.

One thing Bobby was certain of: he would find Misty and give her a painful end beyond measure before he snuffed the life out of her. *No one fuckin' double-crosses me. It's just a matter of time until we're reunited.*

Then he heard the high-strung barking of the dogs. *Victor's pulled out all the stops tonight.* It got louder and closer; he could almost hear their snapping jaws. Fear gripped him like an iron hand around his neck, and he bolted from his hiding place. Running wildly through the trees, branches clawed at him as he tried to escape before the dogs descended upon him and tore him up. The darkened sky pressed down on him as hopelessness gnawed at his insides. *If I can just get to the road.* Sweat poured down his neck, making his skin feel like a million insects were crawling over it, but he kept running toward the low rush of cars. Breathing heavily, his side was killing him but he didn't dare stop—not even for a second. The snarling and barking were closer with each step he took.

He could see the white glow of headlights as the highway came into view. *I'm almost there. I can do it.* Then he saw the yellow lights of a semitruck parked on the side of the road. Laughing hysterically, he rushed toward it, gasping for air, tripping on tree roots and brush, salty sweat stinging his eyes while the dogs came closer. For a split second, he turned around and thought he saw the gleaming white teeth of the snarling canines; he spun back around and pushed onward until he reached the truck.

Tears streamed down his cheeks when he saw the familiar face, one of the regular customers from the truck stops.

"Gus," he croaked.

The middle-aged man with a lived-in face looked startled, but then a smile split his lips. "Bobby. What the hell are you doing out here? I've been wondering where you and your gals have been."

"I need your help. Someone's trying to kill me. I need you to hide me." He looked behind him and saw the faint glimmer from flashlights filtering through the cluster of trees. "Please."

Gus looked over Bobby's shoulder. "Are all them yapping dogs coming for you?"

"Can you help me?"

"Get in. I was just getting ready to leave."

Bobby clung to the door handle like a drowning man grasps a life raft. Gus pulled him inside, then turned on the motor and pulled away from the side of the road. It wasn't until they were well past Silverado that Bobby's heart finally slowed down.

"So why were they after you?" Gus asked.

"I won the poker game."

He laughed. "Really? Damn, they were sore losers. So where're your women? I missed Misty the last time I came through Moab."

"We've gone our separate ways. I'm on my own now."

"Is that right?" He glanced at Bobby.

"Where're you headed?" Bobby relaxed back in the seat and stretched out his legs.

"Alina," Gus answered. "Does that work for you?"

"Sounds like as good a place as any." He watched the mile markers blur by as the truck drove down the highway.

Chapter Fifteen

CHAINS SWIVELED AROUND from the computer. "It's her. She comes from Findlay, Ohio. That's Twisted Warriors territory."

"That's right. We bumped into Sniper and Jacko on a poker run last fall."

"Yeah, that was a fuckin' good time. Anyway, she went missing in October eight years ago. It's been treated like an abduction from the beginning. You know her. What do you think? Was she a runaway or being held by force?"

Paco leaned back and stretched his legs in front of him. "This shows I don't know her, but I've suspected she was in some deep shit. Why the fuck didn't she tell me?"

"I don't know, dude, but if she escaped from her traffickers, then they'll be looking for her, and it's something the club needs to know about. You gotta find out who the fuckers are who are keeping her." Chains handed the flyer back to Paco. "I gotta tell Steel about this."

Paco nodded. "I was going to after I talked to her. Fuck, I can't believe she's been through all this." A deep sadness filled him as he stared at Misty's smiling photo from when she was fifteen years old. She looked so innocent, so trusting. He stood up. "Thanks, man. How're you doing with the layout of the West Avenue Bandits' clubhouse?"

"Good. The assholes have some crummy thousand-square-foot dump in the sketchy part of town. This is gonna be a cinch."

Paco laughed. "It makes our lives easier when dealing with dumb fucks. Let's get together with Rooster and put our plan of attack together."

"Sure thing."

Paco went into the main room and motioned for a double shot of Jack. Since he'd kissed Misty, his mind had been reeling. Instead of relieving the pent-up sexual tension that had been brewing since he'd met her, it made it worse. He wanted all of her.

He was prepared to tell her that when he came back from his ride, but he'd decided to buy her a phone and ended up back at Walmart. When he'd passed the bulletin board, he'd stopped, remembering how Misty had practically dragged him away when he'd come over to the board. It'd been like she didn't want him to see something, so he'd stopped and looked at the flyers.

Blood had rushed through him and he took a step back: a smiling girl in a poster looked like Misty. Then his gaze had drifted to the computerized image of a woman in her twenties who looked a lot like Misty. At first he'd chalked it up to a coincidence, but the harder he stared at the images, the more convinced he'd been that it was Misty.

The ride home had been fraught with battling thoughts and emotions. By the time he'd arrived at the clubhouse, he'd been pissed as hell at her for not telling him what the fuck was going on. He'd wondered if she was playing him like women did when they wanted something from a man. So when he'd gone into her room the night before, he'd been pissed and wanted to confront her, but figured he'd have Chains check on the details to make sure Misty was really Chelsea Sullivan. But the way she'd acted when he walked in had told him she'd been up to something, and she was lying to him again.

He brought the shot to his lips and drank, his mind going back to the afternoon before when they'd kissed. It was incredible, but now he suspected she was just acting because she wanted something from him. Women were that way—they played men until they got what they wanted, and then they walked away without a backward glance. Misty just reinforced his distrust in women. *Every fucking thing that's come out of her mouth has been a lie.*

He threw back the rest of the drink.

"You wanna get in on a poker game later on?" Eagle asked as he came over.

Paco shook his head. "I'll pass."

"How's it going with your hottie?"

"She's not *my* anything." He motioned for another shot.

Eagle chuckled. "She stays up in your room a lot."

Picking up his Jack, Paco threw it back and put the glass on the bar. "See you." He walked away and went up to his room.

When he went inside, Misty sat on the bed, her hair wrapped in a towel, wearing one of his T-shirts. The bright smile she gave him made him think she was happy to see him.

"I wondered if you were going to come by today. You seemed mad at me last night."

He sat at the edge of the bed. "I don't like it when people lie to me."

The bright smile faltered and then faded. "I don't mean to lie to you. It's just that I don't trust people."

"Am I *people* to you?" he asked softly. Lowering her head, she shook it. "Then what?"

She kept her head down, not meeting his gaze. An awkward silence filled the space between them. He reached out and grasped her hand, and she shivered.

"I'm not gonna betray you. You can open up to me." She looked quickly at him and then away. *She's scared to death. I'm gonna kill the fuckers who did this to her.* "I know. I saw the flyer when I went back to the store to buy your phone." Flinching, she jumped slightly and sucked in an audible breath. He squeezed her hand. "Do you wanna tell me about it? I have time."

"I don't really wanna talk about it," she whispered.

"You have to. It's important you trust me."

"Why?" She blinked rapidly then stared at him.

"Because I like you. A lot." And he did. He didn't understand it since they hadn't known each other very long, and he still wasn't sure if he could trust her, but he couldn't ignore the feelings building inside him. Denying it to his brothers was one thing, but he couldn't disregard the pull he felt toward her. They had a connection that was real.

"You do?"

"Yeah."

"I like you too," she said softly.

"That's good. We need to work on trusting each other." He leaned back against the headboard and watched her.

"I was kidnapped." She pulled her hand away from his and covered her face.

Gently, he tugged her to him and eased her head on his chest. "Tell me what happened. I'm not gonna judge you or say anything to hurt you. It's something you need to do."

She sat still in his arms for several minutes. The sunlight streaked into the room, casting thin gold stripes across the floor. In the distance, he could hear the drone of traffic on the old highway, and the low whirr of the club's heater as it kicked on.

"I grew up in Findlay, Ohio. My dad died when I was seven years old. He had a brain tumor and he was gone. It was my mom, my sister Kate, and me for a long time, and then my mom married Peter. I was about twelve when they got married, and I hated her for it. Peter and I didn't get along, and it just got worse as I got older. He was always telling me what to do, always mad if I went out with a boy, and always giving me weird looks. My mom usually sided with him, so I didn't feel like I had anyone I could turn to in the house."

Another pause. Paco didn't rush her, just held her and allowed her to let him into her past at her own pace.

"I was a sophomore at Roosevelt High when I first saw Tyler. He was the star quarterback on the team, and I was a cheerleader. I had the biggest crush on him and was so surprised when he asked me out. I mean, he was a senior and I was only a sophomore. We dated for about a month when he asked me to the homecoming dance. I was so happy." Bitterness crept into her voice.

"Did your mom like him?" he asked.

"Yeah, but my stepdad had a problem with any guy I dated. The plan was that Tyler would pick me up for the dance. When his dad picked me up, I was confused. He said that the coach had told the football players they had to be on some stupid float. I asked why Tyler hadn't called and told me that, and his dad said it was a last-minute deal. He said he'd take me to the dance and Tyler would be there. I got in and noticed another guy in the back seat who Mr. Tarleton said was Tyler's cousin. I got a weird feeling about it, but thought it was just nerves due to the dance. My mom and stepdad weren't home that night, or I would've had my mom take me."

She pulled away from him. "I need some water." She went over to the mini fridge and took out a bottle, then stared out the window.

"You doing okay?" he asked.

She shook her head and took another gulp. "When his dad turned in the opposite direction of the school, fear took over. I knew something was off. When I asked where we were going, he laughed, but his face and eyes were so damn mean and cold. I started to freak, and then all of a sudden, the cousin put a rag in front of my nose and mouth. Mr. Tarleton pulled over and pinned my arms down as I tried to fight. Then everything went black. That's the night I was sold."

Paco got up and stood behind her, snaking his arms around her waist and drawing her back against him. Bending down, he kissed the top of her head. "We can take a break if you need to."

She placed her hands on his, her body shaking as she took a deep breath. "When I woke up, I had no idea where I was except that I was in a small apartment. The man who said he was Tyler's cousin came into the room." She tilted her head back until it rested against him. "He beat me straight away, and then he… raped me."

Paco's jaw clenched and he breathed heavily.

"Afterward he blindfolded and gagged me, put a gun to my head and said he was going to kill me. He pulled the trigger but nothing came out. He kept doing that for hours. For weeks he beat and raped me. Sometimes he'd bring in friends and they'd… do a lot of nasty and… horrible things to me. It was awful." The words came haltingly, punctuated by a ragged sigh and cracking voice as she confided in him.

"Oh, baby." He kissed the top of her head and tightened his arms around her. Leading her to the recliner, he sat down with her curled in his lap, her head tucked under his chin.

"I heard other women in the next room. They were crying, screaming, and I knew he was doing the same thing to them as he was to me. I've always wondered why no one called the police. The neighbors must've heard all the crying. I later found out that the guy who held me wasn't Tyler's cousin. He'd bought me from Tyler's dad. His name was Erik, and he kept me for four years. He took pictures of me and placed ads online. I had sex with ten to fifteen men a day, every day. When I wasn't servicing the men who paid to have sex with me, I was handcuffed to the bed, or kept under lock and key in the bedroom. That small space became my prison. Erik also threatened to kill my mom and kidnap my little sister to sell her on the international auction block. He'd tell me young virgins were a hot commodity. Of course I believed him—I mean, he kidnapped me, after all. I couldn't have let my eleven-year old sister suffer the same fate as me, so I stopped thinking about escaping. I accepted that this would be my life. I couldn't let any harm come to my mom and sister because of me. I loved them so much." She wiped her cheeks.

"How'd you end up with Bobby?"

"After four years, Erik sold me to him. He said I was too old for his clients, that the money was in younger girls and my value had been dropping. Bobby beat me up just like Erik, and he was a master at playing mind games. Like Erik, he kept threatening to kill my mom and steal my sister, and I believed him. Even though he wasn't as cold as Erik, he was almost as controlling. He'd tell me what to wear, what color nail polish to put on, what to eat. He weighed me three times a week, and if I gained an ounce he'd beat me. For some reason, he picked me out as his favorite among his women. His other women loved Bobby and weren't slaves. I was the only one. He kept a close watch on me. He made me stay in the same bed with him, and sometimes he'd make me sleep at the foot of the bed like a dog just for the hell of it. If he wanted to screw Amber Jade or Crystal or some other woman, he'd lock me in the closet for the night. Bobby heard there was good money to be made at truck stops, so that's how I ended up there."

She moved her head away and tipped it back, her gaze locking on his. "You're probably wondering why I didn't tell someone or try to get some help. The truth is that I didn't trust anyone. Bobby was friends with the security guards at the lots, and he'd slip them money to keep the cops away. One time I went into a convenience store at a truck stop. An older woman who looked like she could be my grandmother got talking with me. She was so nice, so I told her that I was being held against my will and for her to call the police. She said she would, but she lied. The old bitch told Bobby, and he almost killed me that night. It seemed that each time I tried to get someone to help me, they didn't, and Bobby always found out and punished me severely, so I stopped trying. I just shut down. The night I met you, I couldn't believe how good you were being to me. I figured Bobby had planted you to check up on me. And when you let me sleep without fucking me, I thought you were too good to be true. I thought you had an angle, but you didn't. I felt something that night."

"Me too. I wish you would've told me what was going on. I would've killed the fucking bastard and taken you away, but I understand why you didn't. Your trust was gone, and when that happens, it's hard as hell to get it back. Why did the fucker take you to Silverado?"

"He said he got a good gig for us at a strip bar, but I found out that he took me there so Victor could see if he wanted to buy me. And he—"

"What the fuck? Victor Bustos from Los Malos?" The anger he'd been holding in abeyance shot through him like a wildfire.

"That's the pig. He paid Bobby $65,000 for me. When I found the money in his pocket after he'd passed out, I knew I had to escape. I knew everything I went through up to that point would pale in comparison to what Victor had in store for me. That bastard is one cold psychopath. I grabbed the money and took off. It was so easy that I thought for sure Bobby was testing me, but when you came riding by, I couldn't believe it."

I'm gonna kill those sonsofbitches. "You stole the money? You have it here?"

She went over to the bed, dropped to her knees, and pulled out a bag. "It's all in here."

"There's no way the fuckers aren't gonna come looking for you."

"I know, but I'm glad I did it. In some funny way, you indirectly gave me the courage to do it. Since the first time I saw you in the diner, I felt a connection to you. I never felt that way with a person I'd just met, even before all this shit started."

Paco went over to her, holding out his hand. She took it and he helped her to her feet, then hugged her tightly. "I felt it too. I'm sorry you had to go through all that shit. Fuckers who do this need to die. I can't change what's happened to you, but I'm promising you that I'll make sure these assholes pay for what they did. You gotta trust me. No more keeping shit from me, okay?"

She nodded. "A part of me trusted you from the beginning, but my fear held me back."

"I know. The important thing is that we're starting on a clean slate. No more lies or omissions, okay?"

"Promise." She pulled away slightly and looked up at him.

The pain and despair that had been in her eyes when he'd first met her were gone. How he wished he'd been there and saved her from all the pain, suffering, and humiliation she'd endured for all these years.

Warmth filled him as he placed two hands on her face. "You're a very strong, amazing woman," he said, staring deeply into her eyes. "I don't know how you have so much strength. You're very brave." Wet streaks ran down her face as he brushed his lips overs hers, her salty tears clinging to his mouth. "Chelsea. You're beautiful."

"I'm Misty," she whispered. "Chelsea died a long time ago."

"No she didn't. She's always been buried deep inside you. That's who you are. Misty is what you were forced to be." He traced the soft fullness of her lips with his tongue, then moved his mouth over hers, devouring it. Slick and full, her lips molded over his as she strained closer. *She feels so right in my arms.* He kissed her, breathing in each of her tiny moans and whimpers. He trailed his lips to her neck, licking and nipping just below the ear, then sank his mouth into the curve of her neck and shoulder.

"Paco," she cried out. Her fingers slipped under his shirt, gliding over the hard muscles straining under his tightened skin.

Her caramel scent swirled around him, landing on his throbbing cock. "I'm fucking going crazy here," he said as his lips brushed against the hollow at the base of her throat.

Then his damn phone rang.

Being in an outlaw club, a member always had to be available. He looked at it and saw it was Chains. "Fuck, babe. I gotta take this."

"This better be important," he growled into the phone.

Chains snorted. "Steel's looking for you. I also called Jacko and asked him to check on your woman's family. They're good."

"No one lurking around?"

"Nah. Jacko, Sniper, and Bull Dog said they're all alive and well. Hung around for a bit and didn't see anyone around checking out the house."

"I owe them. Thanks."

"No worries. Steel heard Victor's pissed as shit about losing $65,000. Seems like he bought a sex slave. Do you know anything about that?"

"Yeah. I'll be right down."

"You're gonna have to make a strong argument for her. And the fact that you didn't call me out on the 'your woman' comment tells me you got more than a boner for her."

Paco chuckled. "Fuck you." He put his phone in his pocket and looked at her. "Something's come up. I gotta go."

"Are you coming back?" she asked in a small voice.

"Yeah. We can go out to eat. You like steak?"

Her eyes brightened and she smiled. "I love it."

"Then we'll go to Flanigan's." He paused for a beat. "You should call your mom."

Fear crept into her face. "I can't risk it. I don't want to endanger her."

"Shouldn't you warn her? Anyway, some friends of mine live in your city. They checked on your family. They're fine. You need to call her." Tears welled up in her eyes as she nodded. "Don't tell her where you are. The club doesn't need the fucking badges coming around here. I'll take you back to see them."

"When? I can't believe I'm going to see my mom and sister again. I never thought I would." Her voice quivered.

He pulled her to him and kissed her tenderly. "We can leave in a week. I've got some club business to take care of, but we can go after that. Remember, don't tell your family anything about the club, me, or Alina. Got it?"

"I won't."

After kissing her once more, he looked back at her and winked before he left the room.

Chapter Sixteen

TELLING PACO ABOUT the kidnapping had been the best thing she'd ever done. She'd kept all the details of her harrowing ordeal in the recesses of her mind for so long, and now that she'd shared it with him, she felt an enormous albatross had been lifted from her.

Bringing her fingers to her lips, she touched them, remembering their kiss. *I'm crazy about him. He's been so good to me.* She was beginning to trust him, and she hoped he was beginning to trust her and let her into his life. Since she'd read the letter Cassie had written to him while he'd been deployed, she understood why he put up such a tough exterior with women. *He's afraid of getting hurt again. Just like me. But he's showing me that I can trust him. How do I show him he can do the same with me?* Sharing her life with him had been a gigantic step for her; she hoped he understood that and realized what it meant to her to do that.

Slowly she padded over to the dresser and grabbed the box he'd given her the night before. Taking the phone out, she clicked on the power button. With shaking fingers, she tapped in her old phone number. She waited with bated breath, her heart skipping a beat at each ring.

"Hello?"

Mom. After all these years, it's Mom. The lump in her throat pulsed.

"Hello? Is somebody there?"

"Mom," she croaked.

Dead silence.

"Chelsea? My God! Chelsea, is that you?" Her mother's voice rose in pitch and tears laced it.

"It's me, Mom. I'm finally free. I missed you so much. I thought about you every day. And Kate. How's Kate? Is she in college? Oh, Mommy, how I've missed you." Self-control crumbled and all the heartache, the longing, the fear came tumbling out like a dam breaking and releasing a tsunami of water. Her knees gave out and she sank to the floor.

"I love you, sweetheart. I always knew in my heart that you were alive. I never stopped searching for you," her mother sobbed.

In the background, Chelsea heard her stepfather ask, "What's the matter, Linda?"

"Nothing. It's all wonderful. Beautiful. Chelsea is alive. She's here on the phone. She's coming home. Where are you, honey? We'll come pick you up."

Before she could answer, her stepfather came on the phone. "Chelsea? Where are you?"

Past feelings and dislikes reared up. "Put Mom back on the phone."

"She's crying too much right now. Where are you?"

"I'm safe. Let me talk to Mom."

"Why won't you tell us where you are? Is this really Chelsea?"

"It's me. Give me Mom."

"Not until you tell us where you are."

"For God's sake, Peter. Leave her alone." Some slight noise in the background. "Sweetie, it's Mom. Are you safe?"

"I am. I'm with a friend. He's going to bring me home. I'll call you when I'm on my way."

"When are you coming? I can't wait to hug you. My baby."

"Soon. I'll call you again, Mom."

"Did she call the police?" she heard Peter yell.

"Tell him no. Mom, the kidnappers told me they'd hurt you and Kate. Please be safe. I'm scared they'll come after you. I'd die if that happened."

"I'll call the police and tell them."

"Don't call them until I get there, okay? Just watch out for anything suspicious, and if you see anyone around who's acting strange, call 911.

Promise me, okay, Mom?"

"I will."

"Who are these people?" Peter asked. She guessed he'd grabbed the phone from her mother again.

"I don't know. They're very mean and dangerous."

"How much money do you want?"

"What are you talking about?" Chelsea frowned.

"I don't believe you're our daughter. You're pretending to be because you want money. Why won't you tell us where you are? Why don't you want us to call the cops?"

"Peter, stop that!" her mother shrilled in the background.

"I'm Chelsea. Tell Mom I love her and will call again soon." She hung up and touched her forehead to her knees, trembling like a flame blown by the wind. She sat like that for hours until the sun sank lower in the sky, draining its blue hue and giving way to the inky dark of night.

Paco walked in and, all at once, the room was bathed in startling illumination. She jerked her head up and smiled at him, knowing she looked frightful with all the dried black streaks from her mascara.

"Are you okay?" he asked, kneeling beside her and running his fingers gently over her arm.

"Sorta. I called home. It was great to hear my mom's voice, but then Peter got on the phone and started asking me where I was and all sorts of other questions. He even said he didn't believe it was really me. My mom was crying and I just couldn't take it anymore. I hung up. I felt like I was in one of those dreams where everything is distorted and out of focus, and there's no way out no matter how fast you run."

He gathered her in his arms and rested her head against him. "Shhh. It's over now. You talked to your mom and that's good. She knows you're safe. You'll see her in no time."

He cradled and rocked her, and she was so touched by his tenderness that she curled her arm around his neck and brought his face close to hers, peppering it with kisses. In one fluid movement, she was on her back with Paco above her, lavishing kisses on her neck and shoulder as he pushed up her top and glided his hand over her belly. His kisses and touch sent a carnal tingle down her spine. The space between them was supercharged with the electricity of arousal and desire, and smooth sensation replaced words and thoughts. Her demons, her shame, everything she'd become were irrelevant. All that mattered was being in the moment with Paco, having him touching and kissing her while her body unfurled in ways it had never done before.

She slid her hand under his shirt and he bit lightly on her lip, dragging his tongue to her jaw and then trailing it to her earlobe, which he gently took between his teeth and sucked. She squirmed underneath him and her hand found his. He gripped her fingers, bone and ligament, easily broken. His tongue traveled down to her collarbone and then the tops of her breasts, her heart pounding as he licked and bit the delicate skin, craving his mouth on her aching nipples.

Pushing her top over her bra, he placed his hand on her breast and squeezed it. She moaned, arching her back and pressing closer to his warm body. In one movement, he unhooked her bra and licked her tits, and desire raced through her, searing her body. When he drew her pebbled rosy bud into his mouth, a jolt of heat burned right down to her aching sex. A deep sigh escaped her, like air rushing out of something. He looked up at her, his eyes smoldering, finding her mouth and kissing her hard, wet, deep.

"You stir crazy shit inside me, woman," he rasped as he unzipped her jeans and pushed them down.

Feeling his hard bulge against her thigh, she reached down and put her hand over it, playing with it. His low groan made her tingle all over, and she grasped his zipper and tugged it down. He rolled slightly to his side and kicked off his boots before yanking off his jeans and boxers. His cock was hard, smooth, and pulsing. On his knees, he slowly took her clothes off, piece by piece, kissing and caressing her skin as he revealed it. His actions stole her breath away and made her body tingle in anticipation of what was to come.

Catching her gaze, he dipped his head and swept his lips across hers. "You've got the most beautiful eyes I've ever seen."

"And you're gorgeous."

He ran his thumb under her lip. "I've never had a woman call me gorgeous. I like it." He kissed her again, then traced the curves of her body with feather-soft touches. "So fucking soft and beautiful," he said in a low voice.

He scooted down and bent his head over her quivering pussy. She reached out to touch his hair, but his fingers slipping between her thighs and teasing the slick folds of her sex stopped her. Instinctively, she spread her legs and moaned.

"Everything about you gets to me," he said hoarsely as he ran his finger from her engorged clit to her heated opening. His head between her legs, she felt the scratch of his stubble on the insides of her thighs. With one finger inside her heat, his lips and then his tongue teased the wet folds of her desire. Every lick, every flick caused an electric surge to flash through her body. And when he steadily stroked her swollen nub, he struck fire. She cried out in astonishment and closed her eyes as flashes of light burst in front of them. Her orgasm tore through her in waves of color—lemonade yellow, strawberry red, persimmon orange—wicked pleasure spreading to every corner of her body as she gripped his arms, crying out, "Paco!" Never had she experienced anything so intense, so magical.

He kissed her shoulders, his finger still buried deep inside her. Licking her lips, she grabbed his dick and squeezed it. A guttural groan echoed through her as she guided it toward her. He reached behind him and dragged his jeans over, taking out a condom. In no time, he had his cock sheathed and pushed her legs farther apart, his gaze still fixed on hers.

Taking his dick in his hand, he ran it up and down her glistening folds, then pushed it inside her. He filled her completely, and she loved the feel of him buried deep between her aching walls.

"Give it to me rough," she rasped.

Concern crossed his face. "Are you sure?"

"Don't you like it that way?"

"Yeah, but do you *really* want it rough?"

Skimming her top lip with the tip of her tongue, she fisted his hair and pulled it hard. "Yeah." Her heated gaze locked on his.

He kissed her, then pinched her nipples until she moaned. "Hold on, baby. I'm gonna fuck you good and hard."

His words were bolts of desire, lust, and excitement streaking through her. She lifted her legs and wrapped them around his waist, and he pulled out his cock and slammed it back into her—balls deep.

"Your pussy feels real good, baby," he panted as he pounded in and out of her. "I'm gonna make you come until you can't breathe." He slipped his hand between them and stroked her sweet spot as he kept pummeling in and out.

Her heated walls tightened with every thrust, and she knew she was about to come all over his dick. Faster. Harder. Deeper—his thrusts kept coming, driving her further up the ladder to ecstasy. A jolt of white-hot pleasure arced through her and she flung her arms over her head, grabbing the legs of the nightstand and twisting beneath him as euphoria pushed her over the top.

He stiffened, then held her gaze. "Chelsea," he rasped as he panted and then collapsed on top of her, his chest heaving. She draped her arms over his shoulders and lightly rubbed his upper back.

Her mind was whirling. She'd never experienced such an explosion of sensations in her life. She gave herself to him, and he treated her like she was a precious gift. He'd been hesitant to give it to her hard, but she needed him to. How could she explain that rough sex was her way of letting go, of putting all her trust in him, and in doing so she regained her confidence? Considering her past, she knew it had probably sounded fucked up to him, but she'd needed that trust in him to help her break out of the chains of distrust and fear.

She blinked rapidly. He'd done as she asked without ridicule or mistreatment, and in that moment, she felt closer to him than she'd ever felt to any man. *Is this what love is?* Her heart soared as she hugged him, kissing the top of his head.

He pulled up and smiled at her, stroking her jaw with the rough pads of his fingers. "Damn, woman." Dipping his head down, he kissed her gently.

As he looked at her, a low growl came from her stomach, and she cringed with embarrassment; she hadn't eaten since early that morning.

He laughed. "I promised you a steak." He pushed back and stood up, then helped her off the floor. Tossing the condom in the trash, he looked at his phone. "We better get going. Flanigan's closes early on weeknights."

With her insides bursting with joy, she kissed him quickly, then went to the bathroom to get ready.

THE CHERRY WOOD and red leather booths in Flanigan's reminded Chelsea of the Cotton Patch Steakhouse back home. She and her family had gone there at least two times a month for their Sunday night fixed menu.

Sitting across from Paco, sipping a glass of chardonnay, blew her mind. The previous week, she was forced to take off her clothes and shake her body in front of a bunch of men in Silverado. She never imagined she'd ever be free from that life.

"Did you find something you like?" Paco asked.

"Everything's so expensive here. What are you having?"

"Don't worry about the prices. I'm going with the porterhouse steak with cognac butter. The cognac butter fucking rules. You should try it. You like mushrooms?"

Nodding, she looked down at the menu. *The porterhouse is sixty fucking dollars.* She glanced up. "You make that much money owning a surplus store?"

Paco's face split into a wide grin. "The store makes a decent revenue. I also have money coming in from the club's businesses. All members share in that. Don't get hung up on the prices. Just order what you like." Grasping her hand, he brought it to his lips and kissed it, his gaze fixed on hers. "I'm glad you're having dinner with me."

She smiled. "Is this the standard restaurant that you take your dates to?"

"No fucking way. You're the only woman I've brought here."

Her body warmed. Looking at him in his leather cut and tats, he exuded toughness. She was sure he instilled fear in most people—they probably stepped out of his way when they encountered him—but to her, he had an inner beauty shining through, a sparkle nothing and no one could ever take away.

"Are you ready to place your order?" the waiter asked.

"Know what you want?" Paco asked her.

"Yeah. I'll have the filet mignon, princess size, with the cognac butter." She darted her eyes to him and he smiled. "I'll also have an order of asparagus. And please make my steak medium rare."

"Do you wanna share a Caesar salad with me?" Paco said. She nodded, and he placed his order.

Her dinner was delicious, the filet mignon melting in her mouth. When the waiter came by asking if they wanted any dessert, she shook her head and placed her hands on her belly. She was beyond full.

As they sipped an after-dinner drink—he a Jameson whiskey and she an Irish cream—his eyes never left hers for an instant.

She put her glass down and took a deep breath. "You know so much about me, but I don't know anything about you except that you're a gorgeous and sexy-as-hell biker, own a store, are a great kisser, have a kind and generous soul, and gave me my first orgasm."

"You've never had an orgasm before?"

She laughed. "How is it that you only homed in on that one?"

"I'm just surprised about it. I'm glad I'm your first."

"You're my first with so many things, like buying me perfume, treating me kindly, helping me out, respecting me during sex. I could go on and on, but the point I was trying to make before we got side-tracked about my orgasms was that I don't know much about your background. Do you have any brothers and sisters? Where do your parents live? Did you go to college? It's only fair you share with me since I shared my backstory with you."

"One sister, three nephews, no college, my mom's dead, and my dad is as good as dead to me." He picked up his glass and took a drink.

"Wait. I didn't want the condensed story of your life. Does your sister live in Alina?"

"Nope. She's married to a guy in the Army, and they live in Richfield, Utah. She's got three boys, just had the third a month ago. That's why I was driving through Utah when I stopped in Moab. I was coming back from my sister's. She's twenty-seven years old—three years younger than me. It's just the two of us."

"Are you from Alina?"

"Colorado Springs."

"So you don't get along with your dad?"

His face darkened and his jaw tightened. "He killed my mom, so I'd have to say that I don't." He lifted his hand and motioned for the waiter. "You want another drink?"

"Sure. Are you okay with me asking you these questions?"

"Yeah." He turned to the waiter. "Another whiskey and Irish cream."

"I'm so sorry about your mom… and dad. Why did he… kill her?" She gulped down the rest of her first drink.

"He wanted to marry his whore." She winced at the word and he frowned. "I guess I should've said mistress."

"Why didn't he just divorce your mom?"

"To him, my mom was worth more dead than alive. He took out a million-dollar life insurance policy a few months before he hacked her to death. Not only is he a fucking sonofabitch sociopath, but he's also a fucking dumbass. He really didn't think he'd be caught."

She reached for his hand and interlocked their fingers. "I'm really sorry. I don't know what to say. It must be awful for you. How old were you when it happened?"

"Fourteen. Kendra was only eleven. The bastard is dead to me." Picking up his newly delivered whiskey, he looked at her straight on. "I'm done talking about it."

Reflected in his eyes were pain and sadness. She leaned over the table and reached out for him to meet her halfway. He did, and she traced his bottom lip lightly with her fingertip. She lifted in her chair and pulled his lip in between her teeth, sucking and licking it. She had the urge to wrap her arms around him and pull him tight against her, cocooning him from his painful memories, from the horror that no son should ever have to deal with. His hand came behind her head, fisting her hair as his mouth pressed against hers, deepening the kiss.

"I'm sorry I made you conjure up the memories," she said against his lips, but he swallowed her words. The urgency and passion in the kiss spoke volumes, telling her that he needed her at that moment to feel something other than sadness, anger, and broken memories.

He pulled away, his gaze intense with desire and something else. *Admiration? Could it possibly be love? I don't think so. It's too soon, but then I feel something so wonderful for him, why can't he feel it for me?*

"What's going on in your head? I can see you're wrestling with something in there." He squeezed her hand.

"Nothing really. It's just that I'm glad you shared that about your family. I know it was hard."

"Only a few people know that part of my life. Not even all my brothers do. You're the only woman I've shared it with. I wanted you to know." He pressed her hand to his lips and kissed each finger.

A smile danced across her face as she slipped her hand away. "I have to go to the bathroom. I'll be right back."

On the way back to the table, she caught something from the corner of her eye. It was a form—familiar yet menacing. Slowly she turned toward the lobby, and all she saw was Bobby. Everything fell away: the low hum of conversation, the clink of glasses and dishes, the cars speeding down the street in front of the restaurant. She stopped dead; she couldn't move a single muscle, not even to scream. Her pulse banged in her ears and sweat dripped down her back. The absolute horror of seeing him in her space completely paralyzed her.

Bobby came toward her, his beady eyes flashing with rage. His thin lips were pulled back in a snarl, exposing his crooked teeth. Raising his hands, he clenched them into fists as if foreshadowing what he was going to do to her.

The more she thought about running away, or even moving a bit, the more terrified and discouraged she felt. It seemed as if this was the end of the road for her.

One. Two. Three. Each step brought her tormentor closer to her. The heels of the new shoes Paco had bought her dug deeper into the plush carpet, immobilizing her even more. *How is he here?* He was so close she swore she could smell the stench of his armpits and cheap aftershave.

A choked cry for help forced itself up her throat, and she felt a drop run down her cheek.

"May I help you with something, miss?" the waiter asked her. Simple words, but they were the ones she needed to ground her.

Forcing her legs to move, she stepped back and grabbed the waiter's arm. "I'm not feeling so well. Can you please escort me back to my table?"

"Of course." The waiter walked with her while other patrons filled in the gap between her and Bobby. She thought she could hear his frustration and feel his breath on her skin. Without looking back, she let the waiter take her to the table where Paco waited for her.

"Thank you," she said as the waiter helped push her chair in.

An inquisitive look spread over Paco's face. "Are you sick?"

"Bobby's here. I saw him in the lobby when I was—"

Paco leapt up with such force that his water glass fell over. He ran off and she watched him disappear, her heart racing and her mouth dry. The waiter hurriedly sopped up the water and in no time, he'd replaced the wet tablecloth with a clean, dry one. She played with the stem on her glass, trying to calm the thoughts that kept crashing into each other in her head. The only thing that mattered was that Bobby had found her.

Icy fingers gripped her insides and twisted them. *What if Victor is here to take what he paid for? I don't know what to do. What if this was a setup and they've hurt Paco? I don't know—*

"I couldn't find the fucker anywhere. Fuck!" Paco said as he sank in the chair.

She let out the breath she'd been holding. *He's safe.* "I can't believe he found me."

"Me neither. I don't see how he did unless he knows someone here in town, or it was just dumb luck. Alina's not too far from Silverado. If I were looking, I'd fan out over all the counties within a two or three hundred-mile radius." He looked at her then, holding her gaze with his fierce one. "You can't go anywhere without me, not until I find the sonofabitch and take care of him."

Take care of him? "What do you mean by that? Are you going to kill him?" she asked in a low voice, glancing all around.

"I'll just fix it so you don't have to worry about running into him anymore."

The way he said it, coupled with the hard look in his gaze, stopped her from asking any more questions. The truth was she didn't really want to know anything more about it. She hated Bobby, and it seemed right that his fate should be determined by a badass biker who probably never ran from a fight in his life. Bobby was the type of man who beat up women and cowered in front of men, but she suspected Victor wasn't that way. He was the type who loved hurting women *and* men—an all-around psycho.

"Let's go." Paco helped her up, then nestled her under his arm.

On the way back, he drove around town, through hotel, motel, and bar parking lots and up and down the streets looking for Bobby, but she didn't see him anywhere. He finally pulled onto the old highway and headed back to the clubhouse, constantly checking the rearview mirror.

When they'd gone up to his room, changed, and turned off the lights, he drew her into his arms and kissed her. "Don't worry about this. I've got your back."

"I know," she whispered against his chest.

After they slipped under the covers, he tucked her close, his strong arm tight around her. Paco fell asleep almost immediately, but rest evaded her for a long while. She hated what Bobby had done to her that night. He'd destroyed her safe world all over again. She could no longer pretend that all was good and normal in her life. He'd taken that away from her, and she hated him for it.

Chapter Seventeen

BOBBY STARED OUT the motel window into the parking lot. He'd seen the asshole driving around, slowing down and then coming back a few times.

I knew they were in this together. The bitch thought I was stupid. They planned this. I'm gonna kill his ass, then make sure I show the cunt who's boss before I turn her over to Victor.

He groaned. *Victor. What the fuck am I gonna do about him?* There was no way he could just waltz in and turn Misty over to him. Victor would take her and kill him for sure. He'd have to think of something else. He had to make this right so he could stop looking over his shoulder every time he heard a noise.

It was sheer luck that he'd noticed Misty at the steakhouse. He'd almost stayed in and ordered a pizza, but he was starting to get cabin fever, so he'd decided to venture out. A good steak dinner with a fine glass of wine always put him in a good mood. When he saw them kissing and holding hands like a bunch of fucking teenagers, it'd made his blood boil. *Is this trucker for real? Does he really want to hook up with a dirty whore like her?*

Shaking his head, he closed the curtains all the way and switched on the light. The jerk hadn't been back in over thirty minutes. Bobby had to be smart about how he was going to exact his revenge.

The buzzing phone pulled his mind away from his plotting.

"What do you have?"

"She called home tonight, told her mom that she'd call soon."

"Did she say if she's going to Ohio?"

"She said she was. Said she was staying with a friend and he was going to bring her, but she didn't say when exactly, only soon."

"What the fuck does 'soon' mean? I need more. Did she say where she's staying?"

"No."

"Did she contact the police?" Bobby grabbed a tissue and wiped his forehead.

"No. She told her mom not to call the police. Didn't say why."

"That's strange. Well, I found her. It was by accident, but she's in a southern Colorado town."

"What's the name?"

"I'd rather not say. You call me if you find out anything more. And if she comes home, you make sure you give her to me. I don't like double-crossers."

The phone clicked off. Things were definitely looking up. Much better than the way they'd been the past couple of days.

Bobby figured the trucker asshole must live in Alina. *He'll probably take her on the road with him. The cunt's used to truck stops.*

He laughed out loud, the sound bouncing off the dingy walls. All he had to do was get a plan together. Maybe he'd put the buzz in Victor's ear that his naughty fucktoy was headed back home. He was sure Victor would love the challenge of tracking her down, capturing her, and then punishing her.

Grabbing the pillow, he placed it against the headboard before stretching out on the bed. He switched on the TV and ordered one of the pornos the motel offered. With his hands behind his head, he waited for the movie to start.

Yeah… things are definitely looking up.

Chapter Eighteen

Paco pulled Chains aside as the members filed into the meeting room. "I need you to do something for me."

"What do you need?" Chains replied.

"Find out where Tyler Tarleton from Findlay, Ohio lives now. I need to know the whereabouts of his dad as well. I'll give you what I know about them after church."

"Did they do this shit to Chelsea?"

"Yeah, and they're gonna pay. I'm sure she's not the only one they did it to."

"Let's talk afterward, and I'll get workin' on it."

Paco clasped Chain's shoulder, shaking it lightly. "Thanks, bro." He walked to the front of the room and stood by Steel, who'd just hit the gavel signaling church was starting.

"How're the plans coming for the attack?" he asked Diablo.

Diablo stood up. "Good. Brick, Knuckles, and Tequila have been on surveillance with the strip joint and the fuckers' clubhouse. No one lives at the clubhouse, but they keep the women there in the basement. Some of the sonsofbitches have the women at their houses, and it seems those women are private slaves to the punks. The ones in the club's basement work at the strip bar and are sold for sex. Some are auctioned off. It looks—"

Angry voices drowned out the rest of what Diablo was saying.

Steel brought down the gavel and the brothers settled down.

"Do they have someone watching the club at night?" Paco asked.

"Just one or two. Sometimes no one is there. They got security cameras, but they're the cheap ones. I'd told Knuckles to start interfering with them intermittently so it looks like it's just an occasional problem. That way, when Chains scrambles them for us, it won't seem out of the ordinary. He's been doing that for the past week and the fuckers haven't done shit about it."

"Dumb shits are what makes this a whole lot easier for us," Eagle said, and the members rumbled their agreement.

Steel pushed away from the wall. "I already told Roughneck that we need to know where each of the members lives and the names and addresses of the ones who are keeping women captives. Chains has already found out where Victor Bustos lives." He gestured for Chains to pick up the discussion.

Chains rose to his feet. "The asshole lives in a big mansion in the ritzy part of town. Unlike the West Avenue Bandits, his residence is heavily guarded and has a top-of-the-line security system. If we're gonna attack it, we need to cripple the system beforehand."

"Does he live there alone?" Army asked.

"No. His wife and two young kids are with him."

"Fuck," Steel said.

"We gotta find a way to infiltrate without hurting 'em," Paco said.

"Do we gotta go after him? Isn't it the West Avenue Bandits who're the pain in the ass? We get rid of them and this Victor dude doesn't have his army in the county anymore," Cueball added.

"He'll just start shit up again. We gotta take him down." Paco replied.

"Do you want his balls because of the threat you think he poses, or is this about your stripper?" Army asked.

Burning anger hissed through him, consuming every inch of him. Picking up the chair in front of him, he hurled it at Army. Shotgun and Eagle leapt out of the way, and the chair crashed down on the table, its back clipping Army in the jaw. With clenched fists, nostrils flaring, and teeth bared, Army rushed toward Paco. He was waiting for him, picturing his fist shattering Army's jaw, splattering blood on the white walls. Then suddenly their fists were slamming into each other's face, chest, and stomach.

They stumbled apart for a brief second to catch their breaths, and Paco saw blood trickling down from the corner of Army's mouth; then he came at Paco, punching him hard on the side of his head. Streaks of light burst in Paco's vision, but he shook it off and kicked Army hard in the kneecap. He groaned and fell down, holding his leg.

"Have you had enough?" Paco asked as he stood over Army, anger and determination pumping through his veins.

Shotgun and Rooster went over and helped Army up. He glared at Paco, wiping the blood from his mouth with the back of his hand. Paco breathed heavily as he watched Army limp to the chair.

"I'm putting in a work order," Sangre said. "You planning on breaking any more chairs?" He was the treasurer for the club, and he watched the money like a hawk.

Muerto laughed. "You've broken some other shit over this chick. Fuck, dude. I've never seen you like this." The brothers chuckled and then mumbled among themselves.

Paco jabbed a finger in his direction. "You wanna start some shit?"

Muerto held up his hands. "I'm just saying. No one can say anything about this woman you brought into the club without you going ballistic."

"He's got a point," Goldie added.

"I gotta side with them," Shotgun said, and all the members nodded in agreement.

Paco ran his fingers through his hair. *They're fucking right. I'm outta control.*

"But I gotta say that you push too hard when a brother's interested in a woman. We took a few swings over the things you said about Hailey," Goldie said to Army, who sat glaring with his jaw tight.

"And Raven," Muerto added.

"And Breanna," Steel said.

"None of you can take some ribbing? You all turn into pussies when you got a woman?" Army leaned his chair back against the wall.

"It's the respect thing," Paco said in a low voice. "Chelsea isn't just 'some stripper,' she's someone I care about."

The brothers grew hushed, as if trying to comprehend what he'd just said.

After a long pause, Shotgun cleared his throat. "Do you really wanna get involved with a woman who's got all that emotional baggage?"

"And who's lied to you from the beginning?" Cueball added.

"Leave it the fuck alone. I don't question your decisions, and I sure as hell don't need to explain mine."

"We're just looking out for you, man," Shotgun said.

"Last time I looked, I did just fine on my own. Look after yourself."

Before Shotgun could reply, Steel rapped the gavel on the table. "We've gotten way off track here. Who Paco wants in his life is his own damn business. We need to figure out if we're going to take out Victor Bustos as well."

The anger in Paco still simmered; if another brother said *anything* about Chelsea, he'd lose it. He'd told Steel earlier about Bobby being back in town. He'd also told him about taking Chelsea home to see her family once the problem in Silverado was taken care of.

"I'm calling a lockdown in two days, so if your women or the club girls want anything, today and tomorrow are the days to get it. A few of the brothers and the prospects will stay here when we head to Silverado. We'll leave the day after tomorrow. Does anyone have anything else to add?" Steel waited for a few seconds. "Then church is over."

When the gavel hit the table, the brothers stood up, the scraping of chair legs on the concrete floor blended with the clink of chains and thud of boots as the members walked out of the room.

Paco stayed back, along with Diablo, Rooster, Steel, and Goldie. "The plan we've been devising prepares us for winning the attacks," he said.

Rooster nodded. "As they said often during my Iraq tours, 'Attack is the secret defense, and defense is the planning of an attack.'"

"You got that right, brother." Paco bumped fists with him.

"We'll go to Silverado and hide in plain sight. Paco and I agree that we gotta hit the members who have captives hard," Rooster said.

"Knuckles should have the addresses this afternoon. They're gonna scope out the places and fill us in on it when we get there." Diablo ran his hand over his shaven head.

"I've organized the weapons and vehicles on our end and coordinated it with Roughneck and Patriot," Goldie added.

"Good." Steel turned to Paco. "Is this Bobby fuck going to give us trouble?"

"Not with the West Avenue fucks. He's embroiled in that crazy shit with Bustos. He won't be a problem in Silverado, but he's aiming for Chelsea. I just have to make sure she's safe."

"Does he know you're a Night Rebel?" Goldie asked.

"I don't think so. He didn't know it that night at Satin Dolls or he wouldn't have gotten in my face," Paco answered. The other men chuckled. "Last night I didn't see him, and I didn't take my Harley. I think it was just a coincidence that he was in the restaurant at the same time we were."

"That's good. As long as he doesn't know, then there's no risk that he'll tell Bustos who we are. If that asshole knows, he's gonna figure something's up since we were all at the strip club," Diablo said.

Paco nodded. "Yeah. Bustos isn't stupid. He could be a real problem."

"Since you're here, your woman is safe. Once lockdown starts no one's leaving. He won't find out where she is," Steel said.

They spoke for another hour about the logistics of the upcoming attack. Afterward, Paco sought out Chains and filled him in on what he knew about Tyler Tarleton and his dad.

"I'll see what I can find, but it may not be until after we get back. I've got a shitload of stuff I'm monitoring in Silverado," Chains said.

"No worries. We have to focus on the upcoming mission. We can't make any mistakes. Thanks, bro."

Paco left the room and went upstairs, opening the door to find Chelsea lying on the bed, her back to him. The soft sunlight fell on her bare slender legs, across which a portion of the teal satin sheet shimmered. Her dark hair fanned around her, looking more like spilled ink in the late morning sun, and a sliver of purple lace peeked out from under one of his T-shirts he'd given her. Gentle snuffling noises came from her as she breathed, and he quietly walked over and sat in the chair, watching her sleep.

She's incredible. How had she sneaked in and cracked the ice around his heart? He never thought he'd ever feel anything more than lust and desire for another woman. He'd been vigilant in keeping his emotions buried, and it had worked—no woman even came close to challenging his decision.

When Cassie left him, he'd been devastated, angry, hurt, and bitter. For years, he never let a woman get close to him, only spending time with them for fun and carnal satisfaction. And he'd been just fine with that until he saw Chelsea at the diner. In that first connection between them, her captivating eyes pulling him in, his emotions were compromised. It was like hitting an ice patch while riding his bike: unexpected, out of control, intense.

He leaned his head back against the cushion. The way he felt for Chelsea was all-encompassing, allowing him to let his guard down, but it was also terrifying because he knew how trusting a woman with his heart could cut and hurt him deeply.

And she'll be going back home soon.

"Hey," she said in a soft voice.

He looked at her as she stretched, then sat up. "Hey."

"I got so sleepy waiting for you that I just laid down for a few minutes." She glanced at the phone. "And that was two hours ago." She chuckled. "How did your… what did you call it?"

"Church."

"That's it. How did it go?"

"Fine."

"What did you guys talk about?"

"Club business. I can't talk about it. You want to go out for a bit? Maybe we can go to Tula and have lunch."

"Tula? Where's that?"

"A town about thirty miles from here. It's better if you don't go around Alina since that fucker is here."

"Okay. What about your store?"

"My employees will take care of it. Jillian and Betsy are awesome." He went over to her and dipped his head. "Give me your lips." She tilted her head back and he covered her mouth with his, squeezing her tits softly. She locked her arms around his neck and arched her back, small noises escaping her.

"You feel good, babe," he said as he slipped his hand inside her T-shirt and swiped his fingers over her hardening nipples.

She tugged him down lower and soon he had her on all fours, his sheathed dick buried between her legs, her ass jerking against him as he banged the hell out of her. The more he shoved in, the more she told him to go harder. He pushed deeper and harder, and when her warm walls gripped and tightened around his cock, he thrust faster toward climax. Then the knot at the root of his dick dissolved in fire, melting. His shouts mingled with hers as he came, and then her knees gave out and she collapsed on her belly with him still twitching inside her. He fell half on top of her and nuzzled the back of her neck.

She giggled. "That tickles."

Paco rolled over and nudged her on her back, then propped himself up on his elbow and kissed her again. He couldn't stop kissing her. The taste of her mouth, the feeling of her lips cushioned against his, the warmth of her tongue twined around his got inside him and into the air all around him. She had become indispensable.

She lightly traced his tattoos. "How old were you when you got your first tattoo?"

"Seventeen."

"I always wanted one. I was planning to use my aunt Sandy's ID and get one, but then all that shit happened to me."

He glanced at her arm, at the crown tattoo. It was a simple design in black ink with initials underneath. "You got a tat." He ran his finger over it. "Who's EZR?"

She shook her head. "I don't count that one, or the one on the back of my neck. They were put on me to show other traffickers and pimps that I belong to someone. The one on my arm is Erik's brand—those are his initials, and the one on the back of my neck is Bobby's. Each of them marked me when they bought me. It's what they do to the women they own." She held his gaze. "They're my war wounds."

Anger lit inside him and his stomach tightened. He reached over and pulled up her hair. At first he didn't see it, but then he found a black bar code with some numbers under it. It looked like the bar codes on items in a store. *Fuck. Just like branding cattle. Like a fucking commodity to buy and sell.* He let her hair go and it cascaded down, covering the ugliness on her neck. With his hand on her back, he drew her closer, kissing the top of her head, her temples, and her nose.

A smile whispered across her lips. With a faraway look in her eyes, she ran her hand up and down his arm. "Every time I took a shower or tried to look at my body, I was reminded of the violence and exploitation that had become my new world. I figured that was going to be my life from then on. Then you came into my world, and you gave me hope. I bet you didn't know that." She paused for a second, eyes watering. "I'm so grateful to be alive, I really am, but having to look at those markings on my body every day just pulls me down, and the sadness can be overwhelming. I wonder whether I'll ever be anything but the person those tattoos say I am."

"Don't ever think that's who you are. You were forced to be something you weren't, but the real you was always there. You just had to bury her to survive. Now you're free and—"

"Am I? I couldn't even fuckin' run or scream or do *anything* when I saw Bobby last night. I stood there quivering, ready to do whatever he told me to." She buried her head against him.

"That's normal. You were beaten and raped into obedience for eight years. You can't erase it in a few days."

"But when I'm with you and we fuck, I'm just with *you*, not all the hundreds of men I was forced to have sex with."

Paco ran his hands over her back. "That's good, babe, but the shit you went through is still in your head. I can see it in your eyes sometimes, and in the way you thrash and moan in your sleep. You need to get some help to deal with it. You can talk to Breanna about it when I'm gone."

Her head jerked back. "You're leaving? Where are you going? How long will you be gone? Can I come with you? I don't want to be alone here. Bobby's in Alina."

"Whoa, calm down. First off, you'll stay in the clubhouse. Starting the day after tomorrow, the club's imposing a lockdown."

"That sounds like what they do in prison."

"It's along the same lines, I suppose. It just means everyone's confined to the club, and all kids, old ladies, girlfriends, and club women have to stay here."

"You mean no one can go outside?"

"No. It's just safer inside in case there's a sharpshooter waiting." He chuckled. "Don't look so horrified. We make sure no one's lurking around. We have a great security system, and the brothers know what they're doing. It's just until we think the situation has passed the danger zone. It'll be good for you since that fucking pimp won't be able to find you."

He took her hand and held it on his lap. "I gotta go out of town on club business. I can't tell you any more than that, but I'll try and call or text if and when I can. You'll like most of the old ladies. Breanna's nice, Raven can be blunt, Fallon's quiet but a great listener, Hailey is full of energy, Sam can be a pain in the ass, and Shannon will keep trying to find out your story—though you don't have to tell her or anyone jack shit. If Sam or Shannon get to be too much, tell Breanna. She's the head old lady since Steel's the prez and she's his woman. Sam and Shannon have been old ladies for a long time. Sam's married to Tattoo Mike, and

Shannon and Rooster have been hitched for over twelve years."

"Do the women know about me? I mean, about what I was?"

"The guys around here are worse than the club girls with all their talking and gossiping, so I'd have to guess that they probably do. The only ones who may make it an issue or get too personal with the questions are Sam and Shannon. Like I said, tell Breanna if they start shit with you. Better yet, tell Raven and she'll probably end up beating some ass. She's tough."

"I hope you come back soon. I'm not sure what to do. I'm not that good with mingling. I used to have a great group of friends, but for years I never talked to anyone except Bobby some of the time and the johns. I mostly asked them why they were with me when they had their wives and children at home, but they never answered. Most of the men were married."

"Not surprising. My fucking old man was like that."

"Would you be?"

"Whoa, baby. That's a helluva question. I don't have any plans on getting married."

"But if you did, would you be okay with cheating?"

"If I loved a woman, I'd never cheat on her. It wouldn't matter if I was married or not." *How did we get on marriage?* He sat up. "We should get going. We'll take the SUV."

"When are you leaving?"

"Day after tomorrow. No more questions. Get your cute ass in gear and get ready."

While she showered and got ready, Paco idly watched a boxing match on the television while his mind drifted to Chelsea. When he'd seen the two tattoos on her, he wanted to smash the walls with his fists, pretending they were the fuckers who created her hell. He couldn't stand knowing her traffickers' brands were on her, claiming her.

He placed a joint in his mouth and lit it. *I'm gonna kill that fucking Bobby. I don't know how I'm gonna find out shit on Erik, but if and when I do, he's done.* Chelsea had told him she only knew Erik's first name.

She'd said that he'd been brutal, and she was relieved when he sold her. All she'd wanted was to get away from his viciousness, his greed, and his stone-cold detachment. Paco had his poker face on when she'd told him about Erik, but inside an electric-hot rage seethed. Even though she left out the details, he knew what brutal was. He'd been accused of it on more than one occasion, but he'd never acted that way toward an innocent person. His fierceness was reserved for the betrayers of the club, the assholes who threatened to weaken the brotherhood, or the ones who preyed on the innocent. For those people, he didn't show any mercy, nor would he when he caught up to the men who were responsible for destroying Chelsea's innocence.

"All done," she said.

Looking over at her, he sucked in his breath. She was stunning with her damp hair falling around her and just a hint of makeup on her glowing skin. The tight-fitting jeans and form-hugging sweater made him reevaluate whether he wanted to leave the room at all until he headed to Silverado.

"Are you ready to go? I'm getting hungry."

"Me too, but it's not for food." He caught her gaze and winked.

She laughed. "You're so bad."

"I never told you I was good." He stood up.

"But you promised me lunch." She jutted her lower lip out in an exaggerated pout.

He laughed and went over to her, slipping her lip between his and sucking lightly. "So fucking tempting." He smacked her ass, then went into the bathroom to freshen up.

When they pulled in front of the tattoo parlor, Chelsea gave Paco a confused look. "What're we doing here?"

"I was thinking you should get rid of those fucking tats. We'll go in and have one of the brothers cover them up."

A pink flush swept her cheeks and she threw her arms around his neck, smothering his face with feathery kisses. "You're so good to me. You're the best. I love you." She buried her face in the crook of his neck, and he felt wetness on his skin.

He held her for what seemed like an eternity, and then he slowly pushed her away. "Let's go inside." She nodded, wiping her nose with the back of her hand. He chalked up the "I love you" statement to her being overcome with emotion, or just an exclamation without much thought behind it. He didn't want to think about her *being* in love with him.

She's going home. She needs a chance to live the life she was meant to. I'm not the one for her. I can't offer her anything smooth or ordinary. My world is chaos and violence, and that's the last thing she needs.

Liberty smiled when they walked in. "Hey, Paco. Long time no see. You here for a tat, or you want to see Goldie?"

With his hands on Chelsea's shoulders, he pushed her forward. "She needs some ink. Is Goldie busy?"

"He just finished. Go on back."

He lifted his chin, then headed back with Chelsea's hand firmly in his.

"Come on in," Goldie's voice boomed through the door.

Paco opened the door and let Chelsea go in first. From the way Goldie looked at her and then at him, Paco knew he was surprised to see them together, but Goldie didn't say anything.

"Chelsea needs a couple of tats covered up. She's been wanting a new one too, but that'll have to wait until I get back."

Goldie nodded and motioned for Chelsea to sit on a chair that resembled those in dentists' offices. "What're you trying to cover up?"

Chelsea pointed to her arm. "This one—" She swooped up her hair and turned sideways. "—and this one."

Goldie's gaze darted to Paco's when he saw the bar code tat. Paco gritted his teeth and jerked his head. Goldie touched the tattoo. "I can cover both up easily. Do you have any designs in mind?"

Without hesitation, she said, "For the one on the arm, I want the words 'free to be me' with a broken chain around the script and a few tiny birds flying out above it. And for my neck, I want a beautiful yellow rose with the stem and leaves. No thorns."

Goldie moved his stool over. "Been thinking about this for a long time?"

"You could say that." She latched on to Paco's gaze. "Thank you."

He came over to her and bent down, brushing his lips against hers. "You want me to stay?" She nodded. He kissed her, then went over to the black couch and sank down.

When the needle first went on her arm, she cried. "Do you want me to rub on a numbing cream? It'll take about forty-five minutes to do its thing," Goldie said.

She shook her head. "It doesn't hurt that much. I've felt dead inside for so long, but now I'm alive, beginning a new chapter in my life. It's just overwhelming, that's all. That this time I get to choose what goes on my body. That I'm free."

Goldie cleared his throat, and Paco came over and stroked her face. "You're free because of your strength and courage. You're a survivor, babe. Don't ever forget that."

She wiped her cheeks, then brought his hand to her lips and kissed it before releasing it. "Okay, I'm ready."

For the next two hours, over the whir of the needle and under Goldie's steady hand, the brandings on her arm and neck were replaced by colorful ethereal designs. Afterward, she moved her arm one way and then another as if admiring Goldie's handiwork. He turned the chair around and handed her a mirror.

"I can't believe how beautiful they are. I love them. You took marks that stripped me of my individuality, my humanity, and redesigned them, turning them into something beautiful. I just can't thank you enough. When I get a job, I swear I'll pay you for your work."

"Don't worry about it," Goldie said as he peeled off his gloves.

"Good job, dude. Thanks." Paco bumped fists with Goldie, then helped Chelsea out of the chair and wrapped his arm around her.

"Here you go. Follow the instructions, and if you have a problem, Paco can help you out with it. Be sure to cover the back of your neck real well when you shampoo your hair. Liberty will give you a kit."

"Paco's going out of town," she said softly.

"That's right. Well, if you have a problem, give the shop a call. Tattoo Mike will be here, and so will Jimmy."

"Thanks again," she said as Paco guided her out the door.

The rest of the evening was spent laughing and talking over a platter of ribs, coleslaw, mashed potatoes, and cornbread. As Paco drank his beer, warmth spread through him. Chelsea had been dancing on air since they'd left Get Inked. She was telling him a corny joke she'd heard from one of her cousins a long time ago. The more animated she became, the more turned on he got. At that moment, with her eyes sparkling, her hands flying every which way, and the peachy glow of her cheeks, he wished that he'd met her before her ordeal… and before Cassie. He probably would've fallen head over heels in love with her, and they could've been happy—maybe even have had a few kids.

If only our lives had intersected earlier.

He focused his attention back on her, ignoring the ache that throbbed deep in his heart.

Chapter Nineteen

CHELSEA AWOKE TO soft caresses as the morning light trickled in through the blinds. Snuggling deeper into the covers, her eyes remained closed as the remnants of a dream quickly slipped away. The scent of leather and myrrh enveloped her, and tiny bumps carpeted her skin as lips gently nibbled her ear. Slowly, she opened her eyes and smiled when Paco's face came into focus.

He brushed his lips across hers. "Morning, beautiful."

"Morning," Chelsea mumbled, propping herself up on her elbows. She sat up and rubbed her eyes with the insides of both palms, then stretched her arms toward the ceiling and yawned.

"I'm taking you somewhere," he said as he pushed off the bed.

"Where?"

"It's a surprise. We gotta get going, so drag your cute, little ass out of bed and get ready."

Excitement coursed through her, so she quickly swung her legs over the side and rose to her feet. As she rushed past Paco, he snagged her around the waist, pressed her close to him, and kissed her deeply. Then he turned her around so she faced the bathroom and smacked her lightly on the butt. "We're spending the night, so pack a few things," he added while he walked over to the closet, pulled out a small, black bag, and threw it on the bed. "I'll meet you downstairs."

"Where're we going?"

"Nice try. Now get moving." He winked at her and left the room.

When she entered the main room, she saw Paco propped against the bar talking with a couple of other guys. It looked like they were deep in conversation when she sidled up to him and swept her fingers across his forearm. "Hey," she said softly when he looked down at her.

His eyes slowly raked over her body before returning to her face. "Hey." His deep voice and piercing gaze made her a bit weak in the knees. "You ready to go?" She nodded and he took the duffle bag from her hands. "I'm outta here. See you tomorrow," he said to his brothers.

"We're not taking the Harley?" she asked when they walked past it in the lot.

"No. We'll take the SUV." He opened the door and helped her in.

Excitement bubbled inside her as she wondered where they were going. *It must be kinda far since we're staying the night.* He leaned over and kissed her tenderly on the lips and then started the engine. Soon they were on the highway heading east, the strains of bluesy rock from George Thorogood & The Destroyers filling the car.

Sage brush, cacti, and sandstone stretched out before them, and in the distance, jagged mountain peaks covered in snow were a stark contrast to the desert's reddish-brown rock formations. Birds flew gracefully in the air, jackrabbits hopped across the terrain, and lizards darted behind rocks.

"The landscape is beautiful," she murmured.

Paco placed his hand on her thigh and squeezed it lightly. "I love it here. The contrast between the desert and the mountains is awesome. Look at it. It's barren and dry with different shades of brown, and just at the edge of it, you have huge mountains." He slowly shook his head in awe as he pointed to one in particular. "Some are almost thirteen thousand feet or higher—filled with pine forests, open meadows, creeks, and waterfalls. It's a kickass mixture of fantastic landscapes. It doesn't get any better than this."

Placing her hand over his, she turned to him and smiled. "I keep learning new things about you."

He glanced at her. "What do you mean?"

"I can bet that most people who see you think you're a tough, badass biker who's one-dimensional, but you're so much more."

"You mean I'm not just a walking stereotype?" He threw her a teasing smile.

Chelsea shook her head. "Not at all. I mean, there's a definite badass vibe you've got going on, but you have so many layers, I'm guessing not too many get to see very often."

"You got me there. I normally don't hand out too much info about myself. Kinda like you."

"Yet, we've both opened up to each other. I find that you're easy to talk to."

"Yeah. I like talking to you. It's good to share, you know?"

"It's been so long since I did any of *that*. When Bobby used to drive us all around the country, I never paid attention to the scenery. All I could think about was keeping him happy so he wouldn't beat me. Sometimes, I'd wonder what the new truck stop was like, or how I could escape from him. Driving on the open road with you makes me see things in a new and wonderful light, and I like it. Thanks for that."

As he stroked the side of her face, she caught his hand and brought it to her lips and kissed it. "It's been a long time since I've let a woman get to know me."

I bet he's thinking of Cassie. Should I bring her up?

"I fucking love this song." He turned the radio's volume up and beat out the tune with his hands on the steering wheel as he sang along.

"What is it?"

He glanced at her. "It's 'Freewheel Burning.' Judas Priest fucking rules."

She laughed as he immersed himself in the song. When it came to music, she was so out of the loop. Before her life had changed, she loved pop rock and pop punk bands. Her favorites were Paramore, The Pretty Reckless, and All Time Low, but she hadn't been able to listen to anything she wanted. The music at the strip bars she'd been forced to work at over the years would forever conjure up bad memories.

Paco got off at the next exit, then made another right, and soon they were driving down tree-lined streets surrounded by two-story, stucco and wood houses on both sides. He continued meandering around several neighborhood streets until they ended up on a road that looked like it was a set in a western movie. Two-story, red brick buildings seemed to be the norm on Main Avenue, and the only five-story buildings were two hotels on each side of the road. As they drove down the street, Chelsea could actually feel the ghosts of the past clinging to the historic structures. Surrounding the small city were the craggy peaks of the San Juan Mountains.

After turning off Main Avenue, Paco stopped in front of a two-story brick building with green awnings over the windows, a large stagecoach wagon-wheel mounted on the left façade, two white columns framing a large front porch, and a metal sign above the porch which read "Palmer Hotel." Spruce, fir, and bare maple trees flanked the hotel, and a wooden fence curved around each side of it. A man dressed in jeans and a checkered shirt came out just as Paco got out of the car. He handed the man the keys then opened the back door and took out the two duffel bags.

Chelsea took Paco's hand and walked up the stairs to the large wooden and brass door. Inside, the lobby was decorated in an Old West motif, furnished with period antiques, handwoven rugs, and wall-hangings. A crackling fire in a stone fireplace lent an air of coziness and casualness. Several guests sat in over-stuffed couches and chairs near the fire, reading books and sipping drinks.

"We've got our key," Paco said, and she turned around and followed him up the stairs.

When Paco opened the door, the scent of cinnamon and crisp apples wafted through the air, and the first thing Chelsea saw was the view of the snow-capped mountain peaks from the large window. A fireplace was nestled in a corner, opposite a large bed covered in a colorful puff quilt, reminiscent of the ones her grandmother used to make. *I wonder if Grandma is still alive.* Turning away from Paco, she brushed her fingers over her eyelids, not wanting him to see the tears that threatened to escape.

"You like the room?" he asked as he placed the bags on top of a long, cherry wood dresser.

"It's beautiful, especially the quilt." She ran her hand over it, pressing her fingertips into the fiberfill of the eclectic squares. "My grandma taught me how to make these quilts. I wasn't as good as she was, but it was fun to sit together and quilt in the wintertime. She'd always make these awesome sugar cookies and the best cocoa I've ever had." She ran her hands through her hair. "I haven't thought about quilting in years."

He came up to her and curled his arms around her waist, drawing her against him. "You'll have to make one for my nephew. My sister would love it." He kissed the top of her head.

"I don't know if I'd remember how to do it. I guess I could watch some tutorials on YouTube. I'm sure they have them."

"Or you could ask your grandma to help out when you get home."

She inhaled deeply then slowly exhaled. "I don't know if my grandma is still living." Paco squeezed her tighter. Not wanting to let any sadness take over the joy she'd felt before they came into the room, she dipped her head back and looked up at him. "I'm going to have to check out some of the antique stores I saw on Main Avenue. My aunt Sandy, my mom, and I used to go antique shopping once a month. I love old stuff."

He skimmed her lips with his. "We'll go, but first we've got a train to catch."

"A train?"

"Yeah. I wanted you to see Cascade Canyon—it fucking rocks. It's one of my favorite places to go in the summer and fall. Since it's winter, I thought we'd take a train ride through the area. I didn't think you'd want to snowshoe through the canyon."

She laughed. "You thought *right*. Walking through the snow in freezing weather isn't exactly high on my list, but I'd love to see the canyon. When do we have to be at the station?"

"Pretty soon. Freshen up if you want, and then we'll head over. The depot is just a five minute walk from here."

She stroked Paco's face then tugged it down closer to hers. He met her lips with his, and they stood kissing in the middle of the room. Her body tingled; warmth, love, and happiness filled every inch of her. After so many years of degradation and anguish, Chelsea felt as though she was in the midst of a beautiful dream, one she never wanted to end. Paco made her feel happy that she was alive.

"I'll just be a few minutes, then we can go." She opened her bag, took out her makeup case, and went into the bathroom.

A coal-fired, steam powered locomotive pulled the train on the very same tracks that miners, cowboys, and settlers of the west traveled over a century ago. Paco had booked a private car for them, and now Chelsea was comfortably sitting in the plush, green velvet seat with her face mere inches away from the window, watching the spectacular and breathtaking scenery as the train wound around the bend of the San Juan National Forest. A gentle hush cloaked the land, and snow-dusted trees sparkled under the sun's rays. Towering pines and snowcapped peaks made the area feel mystical to her. She could imagine the burst of color from the wildflowers in the summer or the golden hues of the aspens in autumn, and she understood why Paco loved this place so much. It offered beauty and solitude and touched the soul. *And he's sharing it with me.*

A soft knock on the door had her turning toward it.

"Come in," Paco said, and a man in black attire stood in the doorway.

"Would you like anything to eat or drink?" he asked. His outfit looked like something out of a Hollywood western.

"I'll have a double shot of Jack." Paco swept her hair away from her neck and breathed into her ear. "What would you like?"

Warmth spread through her. "I'll have a Coke and a bottle of water. Oh, do you have any pretzels or nuts?"

"We have mixed nuts and pretzels. Would you like some?"

"Yes. Thank you."

When the waiter left, she turned back to the lovely scenery. "I can see why you love it here. I bet it's a great hike when the weather is warmer."

"It is. You can go deeper into the canyon. There're a lot of creeks, waterfalls, and open meadows. When I need to recharge shit in my life, I come here. It somehow puts everything in perspective."

"I bet it does. How long have you been coming here?"

"For about six years or so."

After Cassie broke up with him. Overcome with emotion, she turned toward him and kissed him deeply. "Thank you for sharing this with me."

He hugged her close to him. "I wanted to. You're the only person I've ever brought here. I'm glad I was able to do it before lockdown starts tomorrow."

"And you leave," she added softly.

The train ride was just under four hours, and when they arrived back at the station, Paco held her hand and guided her toward Main Avenue where they spent the next two hours exploring antique shops. Despite her protests, he bought her an antique amethyst crystal vase that she'd admired, along with a Navajo sand painting of a warrior atop his horse, several postcards circa 1870, and a small, framed watercolor of Cascade Canyon. As they walked out of the last antique store, thoughts of happiness, excitement, and even love had Chelsea's mind reeling. Love was the tricky one because she didn't want to frighten him away. Paco had shared many things with her, so she knew he liked her, but did his feelings go beyond that? *Can he ever love another woman the way he did Cassie? Is he just showing me a good time because of what I've been through?*

"I was thinking Mexican for dinner. Is that good with you?" he asked, cutting through her musings.

She nodded. "Sure. Can we go *now*? I'm pretty hungry."

He chuckled. "I was thinking the same thing. We can have an early dinner then go back to the room. I'll light a fire and show you a real good time."

Heat flushed through her. "Sounds like a great plan." She smiled and grasped his arm. Pressing against it, she kissed his cheek lightly. "Thanks for giving me one of the best days of my life." He lifted his chin at her and they walked down the street, his free hand holding the sacks from the store.

As she sipped her margarita, Paco's gaze bore into her.

"You're going to have to get some ID when you get back home," he said.

"I know. I was wondering if they were going to serve me this margarita."

"If I didn't know Francisco, they wouldn't have." Paco picked up a chip and dipped it in the tomatillo salsa.

"You must come here often. You seem to know a lot of people."

"Once in a while, I'll come to this town with a few of the brothers to hang out at some of the bars or play pool. It's a change of scenery from Alina." Then he added, "The hiking I do alone."

Taking a big gulp of her drink, she looked away. "Have you ever had a girlfriend?" The fluttering in her stomach made her hold her breath.

His face grew tight and his brows furrowed. He gripped the beer bottle and took a long drink. She didn't think he was going to answer, but then he caught her gaze. "Yeah." He motioned to the waitress for another beer and leaned back in the chair. "You must be looking forward to going home."

He changed the subject real fast. Don't push it. You don't want the demons from his past affecting this perfect day. "I am. I mean, I'm looking forward to seeing my mom and my sister, my grandma—hopefully—and Aunt Sandy, too. I'm not so anxious to see Peter."

"What's the deal with your stepdad?"

"We just never got along. In the beginning, I resented him for trying to act like he was my dad or my good friend. I got that my mom needed him to help her out financially and to keep her company, but I didn't care for him. When I started becoming interested in boys, he acted like a dictator or something. I don't know. Peter also had problems with alcohol. Once my mom married him, my growing years were chaotic and punctuated by fights. For my mom's sake, I hope he's sobered up."

"That's tough. It'll be an adjustment for you when you get back home. I know you'll be able to do it, but just know it won't be easy. Although, going to therapy should help you a lot."

I'm going to miss you so much, Paco. She blinked rapidly. "Do you ever see your aunt and uncle who you stayed with when your mom died?"

"Nah. After I was old enough to be on my own, I left. Kendra fared better with them and their fucking rules. Like I told you, they weren't thrilled that they got stuck with us after my old man went to prison. I can't say I blamed them. Money was tight, and they already had five kids. While I was with them, I worked after school at a drugstore, sweeping up and stocking shelves to help out."

"You didn't have any other relatives?"

"Nope. My old man was estranged from his family, so we never knew them, and my mom only had a sister. My maternal grandparents died when I was young."

"I bet you and your sister have a close bond." He nodded as he put some carnitas in a corn tortilla, rolled it, and took a big bite. "I'd like to meet her." *I still want to be a part of your life even when I go home.*

He wiped his hands on the napkin. "Someday. I think you two would hit it off. She's a friendly person."

Chelsea smiled. "And likes to chat?" He chuckled. "Maybe I could come back for a visit sometime." Her heart thrummed.

Lifting up his beer bottle, he locked gazes with her. "Maybe." He brought the bottle to his lips and took a drink.

Her stomach lurched. *He didn't say, 'For sure.' Just 'maybe.' I'll probably never see him again.*

"Anything else?" the waitress asked.

"Two flans," he replied.

All of a sudden, she'd lost her appetite. "I don't want any dessert," she said softly.

He gave a half shrug and smiled at the waitress. "Just one then."

When they came back to the hotel, Chelsea's mood had lightened, and she'd decided that she was going to enjoy every second that she spent with Paco. He was the only man who treated her like a person and not a pair of tits. Whenever they spoke, he talked to *her*, and when he held her in his arms, kissing her and fucking her, he didn't see her as an object. He saw *her*—Chelsea.

"Let me get a fire started. It's so damn cold out," he said as soon as they walked into the room.

"I'm sure my frozen feet have turned blue. I'm gonna go change." She grabbed the duffel bag and went into the bathroom. Taking out the T-shirt he gave her the night he picked her up in Silverado, she wondered if he'd let her keep it when she returned home. Just having his scent wrapped around her made her feel safe and fuzzy all over. She slipped it over her head, finger-combed her hair, then went back into the room.

Paco had his shirt up over his face as he tugged it over his head, then threw it on the chair by the window. Her eyes traveled over his body, drinking in his tangled hair, his rock-hard chest, and the trail of hair that slid under his waistband.

He walked up to her, his lips seizing her mouth as his tongue pressed against hers. His hand roamed down her body, slipping under the T-shirt and cupping her ass, squeezing it lightly. "I love that you're still wearing my T-shirt," he whispered over her lips.

"Can I keep it?" she whispered back.

"It's all yours, baby." He pinched her ass cheek and pulled away. "I'll be right back."

She watched as he ambled to the bathroom, admiring his tight ass and muscular legs before going over to the window. Outside, the street lights illuminated the roads in pools of yellow as several people milled around on the sidewalks. The mountains stood silhouetted against the darkened sky, and the wind weaved through the trees, shaking their bare branches.

She heard Paco's footfalls as they came behind her. His hands touched her shoulders, sweeping her hair over one of them, as he placed feathery kisses on the back of her neck. She relaxed into him, reveling in the way his kisses made her body tingle and quiver with desire. He pulled back a little and before she could react, something cool glided around her neck. Her fingers flew up, grasping a pendant that hung down from a chain.

"What's this?" she asked, craning her neck.

"I got something for you." He gently swiveled her around.

"When?" Her voice shook slightly.

"At one of the antique stores. As soon as I saw it, I thought it was perfect for you. I wanted to surprise you." He led her over to the mirror hanging on the bathroom door.

A silver necklace with an open heart pendant lay against her pale skin. Inside the pendant, a floating pink heart sparkled. She ran her fingertips over its smoothness. "It's lovely," she murmured.

"The stone is mined locally. It's rhodochrosite crystal. I wanted you to have something pretty to wipe out any ugly memories you have of Colorado."

It was the most beautiful necklace she'd ever seen, and he'd given it to her. She was overcome with emotions she couldn't tame. She whirled around and flung her arms around him, kissing him fiercely as she wrapped her leg around one of his.

"Fuck, baby." His words smothered against her lips.

"Paco." She loved saying his name. *Do you understand what I'm feeling?*

He lifted her up, folding her in his arms as he walked over to the bed and placed her on it. Her hair flowed across the pillow, and she licked her lips. "I want you to take me in every way you can."

He hovered over her, his dick pressing against her thigh. "You sure?"

"Yes… but only if you *want to*." She smiled mischievously.

He slowly pushed up the hem of the T-shirt, his heated gaze fixed on her sheer panties. "Oh, I want to, baby." He placed her hand on his erection, and she felt it through the fabric of his jeans. Finding the zipper, she pulled it down, and he helped her out by undoing his belt and the waistband. He jumped up, took off his belt, shrugged off his pants, socks, and boxers, then climbed back on the bed and lifted her shirt over her head. Dipping down, he nudged her chin with his and peppered kisses over her neck and beneath her ear. She moaned low in her throat.

"How does it feel?" he whispered.

"Amazing," she murmured.

He swept his tongue across her bottom lip, and she inhaled a ragged breath. Hovering over her supine body, he trailed his hand up her belly, over the ladder of her ribs to the soft underside of her breast. He covered one of her tits with the palm of his hand and squeezed gently. A shudder of raw passion coursed through her, and she arched her back, needing more, shifting restlessly beneath him as he palmed her other breast. He grazed her nipple with his thumb, and a surge of desire traveled from her hardened bud down to her throbbing pussy.

As he flicked, pinched, and pulled at her nipples, she rubbed her knee against his erection. He captured her lips while combined moans of pleasure swirled in their mouths as she lost herself in his touch, his scent—his everything.

Three hours later, naked, sated, and warm, they lay tangled together in each other's arms, a comfortable silence blanketing them. It seemed like they were the only two people in the world. She snuggled deeper into him, and he raked his fingers through her hair, kissing the top of her head softly. Realization that she affected him as much as he did her warmed her to the core. Feeling safe and cherished in his arms, she closed her eyes and fell asleep.

Chapter Twenty

"WE'LL STRIKE TONIGHT," Steel said, looking at Roughneck. "Chains tracked down all the homes of the members who have personal slaves. We don't want innocent people killed, but it may happen."

"The way I see it is that the only innocent people are the women being held against their will and the kids who have to live with these fucking gangsters. There's no way wives and girlfriends don't know a sex slave is in their house." Rage sizzled and electrified Paco's back, then spread down his spine, melting into his legs.

"Paco's right," Goldie said.

"Could be, but we're not here to pass judgment on anyone but the people who are bringing shit into this town and county, and usurping territory that isn't theirs. We know our goals, so let's not go off in a different direction. Scattering will bring defeat." Steel stared hard at Paco. "You need to put your personal feelings aside, bro, or you'll be useless," he said in a low voice.

Paco clenched his jaw, his eyes fixed straight ahead. Of course he'd put aside Chelsea's degradation by men very similar to the ones they were ready to annihilate that night. He'd let his rage bubble, but when it was time to move forward, he'd capture and squeeze it out of him until the mission was accomplished. He'd be spot-on. Cold. Calculating. A son of a bitch.

Chains passed around sheets of papers to the Night Rebels and Fallen Slayers members. The Night Rebels had come to Silverado the previous day, and the moment they'd been planning for and strategizing about had finally arrived.

Paco looked at the sheet of paper: *Chubby (aka Miguel Silva) 4579 Madison Ave.* The paper meant Chubby had a personal sex slave at his house. Paco would make sure it'd be his last. He folded the paper and shoved it in his pocket.

"We estimate there are six women being held in the basement. A couple of them will be shipped out tomorrow. We've learned they've been sold." Patriot leaned back against the wall. "We gotta move in fast, get the women, and blow up their fuckin' clubhouse. We got about five brothers on lookout. After some of the names on the sheets of paper Chains is handing out meet their demise, their wives will call and warn the others as to what's going on, so we gotta strike hard and fast. There're three fuckers with their own slaves. When you get them, get your asses to the fuckers' clubhouse and help us with the rest of the job."

Roughneck crossed his arms, his long hair falling past them. "Any questions?"

"What're we doing with the women?" Skull asked.

"We're going to take them over to Cortez and dump them at the hospital. No one wears their cuts tonight, and make sure your faces are covered. We got a bunch of ski masks and bandanas. It's whatever you want," Paco answered, looking at Cueball, Ironclad, and Jigger.

That night, the sky wasn't starlight and moonbeams—it was cracked asphalt blurred by storm-laden clouds moving silently like phantoms. No one was on the streets. An eerie quiet permeated the town. It was a weeknight, so children were tucked in their beds, bars were closed, houses were devoid of light. The night was perfect for people who worked in the shadows. Darkness brought the primal nature to the fore, a heady trance for men who craved dominance and power.

Paco stalked to the address on Madison Avenue. Goldie walked beside him, neither of them talking. When they came to the square house, it was quiet and dark like all the others on the block.

Paco took out a bag of ground beef and threw it over the fence. Two pit bulls ran over to it, their noisy breathing and flapping jaws making him smile. *They'll be out in no time.* He saw Goldie motion him to a large bush near the garage, and he went over. He crouched down and looked through the basement window, but it was too dark. Taking out his flashlight, he shone it through the window and saw an oblong box against the back wall underneath several hooks, rods, and straps hanging from the ceiling. He snapped his fingers at Goldie and he came over, bending down and looking in the direction Paco pointed with the light. Nodding at Paco, he stood up and took out a bump key.

As they started around back, they heard the garage open. They quickly took cover behind the bushes as a portly man of medium build with a shaved head came out into the driveway. The man popped open a beer and took a long pull.

Paco recognized him from the picture Chains had given him earlier in the day—it was Chubby. *This is too fucking easy.* When the man turned his back to them, Goldie rushed him, clamping his hand down hard over the man's mouth. Chubby's eyes bulged and he struggled, but before he could make any headway, Paco plunged a knife in the man's abdomen. A look of shock echoed in his eyes before they glassed over, unblinking. They dragged him into the garage and made their way into the house through the door.

It was as quiet as a tomb. Paco indicated through hand gestures that he was going downstairs, then watched as Goldie took out a 9mm from a holster decorated with a 1% sticker and stood watch at the top of the stairs. Shining his flashlight in front of him, he crept down the wooden steps, making sure to keep his feet apart so they touched the sides, thus lessening any creaks.

When he reached the bottom, he went immediately to the coffin-like box. On top of it was a small, square iron grid. He shone the light on it and two terrified blue eyes reflected the beam in them.

"Fuck," he said.

He pulled a crowbar out from his boot and broke open the locks— eight of them in all. Lifting the lid, he heard a muffled cry. A naked woman lay in the box, a gag around her mouth, her hands and feet cuffed. He took out a shim from his leather jacket and moved it around in the lock, freeing both handcuffs in no time. The woman's terror-filled gaze never left his face, and she flinched when he grasped her wrists and tugged her up.

"Come on. We gotta go. I'm not here to help you, not hurt you." Shining the light around the room, he spotted a fleece blanket and wrapped it around her, then put his fingers on his covered mouth. "Don't make any noise."

She nodded and they went upstairs, leaving the house through the front door. No one had stirred. Paco picked up the young woman, who cried out. "Shut the fuck up. I told you I'm helping you." He threw her over his shoulder, and he and Goldie walked the two blocks to the SUV in silence.

Paco sat in the back seat with the girl, who kept staring at him.

"Are you my new owner?" she asked in a halting voice.

"No. We're helping you. How old are you?"

"Sixteen." Her voice cracked.

"Where are your parents?"

"They live in Arizona. Are you *really* helping me?" She wiped her cheek.

Paco nodded. "How long did the fucker have you?"

"I was sold to him six months ago. Before that, I was with a man who kidnapped me. I was at a party, and a couple of my friends took off to another party. I just wanted to go home, so I started walking. This guy pulled up next to me in a BMW and asked if I needed a ride home." She cast her gaze downward. "I know. Stupid. Worst mistake I ever made." She sniffled.

"Yeah. When you get to Cortez, you call your parents."

"What's your name? Why are you guys helping me?"

"We don't fucking like sex traffickers. Let's leave it at that. No more questions or talking." He looked out the window and saw the van parked behind a closed warehouse. "I'm gonna blindfold you."

"No. Don't. Please." Panic laced her words.

"No one's gonna hurt you. It's to protect you from seeing too much." He slipped the black tie over her eyes and fastened it. "Don't take it off. We play nice, but we can also be ruthless."

Jigger came over to the SUV. "She's the last one. I'll see you at the target place." He grasped the girl's arms and led her into the van.

Goldie and Paco parked a block away from the West Avenue Bandits' clubhouse, carrying two gas cylinders each.

"There it is," Goldie said in a low voice.

The clubhouse was a one-story, free-standing cinder block building on a large lot. The next building was a block away. A chain link fence wrapped around the club, and numerous "Beware of Dog" signs were plastered on it. Without any sounds of barking, Paco surmised they were snoozing—courtesy of the brothers. Above the entrance, a makeshift sign read "West Avenue Bandits Clubhouse."

"Not for long," Paco said under his breath as he saw Muerto, Sangre, and Brick escorting several women, all of them draped in blankets or sheets. Chains came over to them and took two of the cylinders.

"We have to act fast. I'm not sure if they're going to come out and check why their security cameras are scrambled. Even though Knuckles and Brick have been doing it for the past few days, you never know."

"Let's go." Paco moved quickly inside.

"Are all the women out?" Goldie asked, placing the cylinders in different spots in the room.

"Yeah," Roughneck said as he came in behind them. "We're good to go. Let's blow up this motherfucking building."

Chains, Paco, Goldie, Roughneck, and Patriot placed the propane bombs in all the rooms while Diablo, Tequila, and Knuckles set a few pipe bombs around.

"Let's get the fuck outta here," Paco said. The timers on the bombs were set to go off in eight minutes.

"You know what to do," Paco said to Jigger, who was closing the van door. "Were all of them trafficked?"

"That's what Muerto and Sangre said. A couple of them are in their early twenties, but the rest are under eighteen. Fuckin' perverts." He stomped out his cigarette butt.

"Easy. You still got shit to do. I heard Diablo's going with you." Paco glanced at the time on his phone.

"Yeah, he's coming now." Jigger went around to the driver side. Cueball waited inside, scooting over when Diablo opened the passenger door. "See ya."

Paco nodded, then made his way to the SUV. There was enough force in there to demolish the clubhouse. The plan was that the Night Rebels would stay a couple of days to make sure there wasn't any retaliation the Fallen Slayers couldn't handle. If they were correct in their assessment of Los Malos and the West Avenue Bandits, the Bandits would think Los Malos double-crossed them, especially when they found the women missing. Trafficked women were worth a lot of money, and greed was what propelled the dark and tormented world of sex slavery.

"Let's take a spin by Bustos's house," Paco said to Goldie.

"Why? The pansy ass split. We were gonna hit him tonight too."

"I know. I just thought he may be hiding out in his house."

"Nah. Knuckles, Patriot, and Roughneck were pretty sure he left. They checked out the strip bar, and some of the women there said he'd taken off a couple of days ago."

"That seems strange. There's no way he even suspected what was going down. I wonder what made him take off."

"Maybe he's headed to Alina for Chelsea. You said her fuckin' pimp is there, and the fucker sold her to Bustos."

Ice ran in his veins as fear seized him. Not once so far that night had he felt fear. Adrenaline and hate pushed him through the mission, but fear never entered the picture. Now it crawled up his legs, poked at his brain, and splintered his heart. If Victor got a hold of Chelsea, he'd crush her, bone by broken bone. *I can't let it happen.* He was afraid for her, and for him. He cared deeply for her. He'd been lying to himself to protect his heart, but what he realized was that she'd had his heart ever since the truck stop.

Kaboom! Boosh! Kaboom!

"Right on time," Paco said as he looked over his shoulder. A rising ball of blackened orange-red flame shot up into the dark sky, billowing outward. As they pulled into the Fallen Slayers' compound, the wail of sirens echoed behind them.

Goldie got out of the car and looked at Paco. "Aren't you coming in?"

"Give me the keys. I'm gonna head back to Alina. I should be there in case the club is targeted. We got most of the brothers here."

Goldie threw him the keys. "I'd go too if I thought my woman was in danger."

Paco climbed into the driver seat, switched on the ignition, and drove away from the clubhouse, his heartbeat thrumming in his temples.

Chapter Twenty-One

CHELSEA BOLTED UP in bed, gasping for air; her insides quivering and sweat pouring down her back. *Where am I? Bobby's going to be mad that I'm not back yet.* Her eyes darted around the dark room. *I don't know where I am.* Fear slithered up her spine, sparking her nerves, tingling her skin, and threatening to send her over the edge into sheer panic.

A loud jingling noise at the door had her clawing the headboard, scrunching her body as much as she could. The pungent scent of fear enveloped her. It made her heart flutter, breath quicken, and legs itch to run, but where would she go? *I don't even know where I am.* Grasping the sheet until her knuckles turned white, she pulled it over her head and waited.

The door opened and she bit the inside of her cheek until she tasted metal, burying the whimpers back down her throat. *Thud, thud, thud.* The footfalls came closer. *No. Please don't hurt me.* She trembled under the cover. Her body was ready to explode. *He's standing by the bed. He's watching me. He's tormenting me. I know it. I can sense him.*

"Chelsea?" a deep voice said softly.

I know that voice.

"Are you having a bad dream?" A warm hand slowly tugged at the sheet balled up in her fists. A flip of a switch and then the muted glow of light from the lamp on the nightstand filled the room. Through the sheet, she saw the shadowy outline of a man. "Come on. It's me—Paco. I came home early. I was worried about you."

Paco! That's right, I'm in his room. I'm safe. She opened her fists and the cover fell. There was softness mixed with concern in his eyes.

Reaching out, she stroked his scruffy face. *I want to make sure you're real.* "I didn't think you'd come back at this late hour."

"I wanted to make sure you were safe. Did something happen?"

She shook her head. "It seemed so real. I was back with Bobby, and he was really mad because I didn't come home at the time he told me to. It was just all mixed up, you know. When I woke up, I was disoriented. I didn't know where I was. I thought he was coming to hurt me."

The mattress creaked and sank when he sat down and drew her into his arms. He stroked her hair and she nuzzled against him, the fear from earlier dissolving. The scent of leather and wind replaced the stench of terror.

"You just had a bad dream. I'm here now. You're safe. Did you miss me?"

Miss you? You're all I thought about. I wanted and needed you so badly. She nodded and pressed closer, snuggling against the firmness of his muscular chest.

"I missed you too," he whispered in her hair.

She tipped her head back and her stomach clenched with heat at the blistering want in his gaze. "Kiss me," she rasped, curling her arms around his neck. His mouth crashed down on hers, stealing her pain, chasing away the demons inside her head. He pushed her down, and his brawny build sandwiched her hard against the mattress. His hands roamed over her arms, her back, her hips, finally resting and then digging into her firm butt cheeks. His touch awoke every part of her, and her body hummed and tingled as she tugged his shirt up, pressing closer to him until they were skin to skin.

Pulling away slightly, he lowered his head and kissed between her breasts, slowly running his tongue up her neck and along her jawline. With ferocity, his mouth captured hers again and his tongue shot through her parted lips, pouring his heat down her throat. He tasted dark and delicious: espresso with a hint of cinnamon.

She wanted him. Her breasts ached and her stomach was tight with want, and the rush of arousal between her legs surged through her senses. Sliding his hand into her panties, he buried his finger deep inside her, pinning her legs down when she started to buck.

"Fuck," he groaned against her mouth.

"Don't stop," she whispered, heat surging through her with such intensity that she thought she would blow up right then and there.

He pulled up and fumbled with his jeans, tugging them and his boxers down past his knees. "Dammit," he said under his breath as he tried to push off his boots. He sat up and kicked them off, then lifted his T-shirt over his head. She watched as his muscles rippled and flexed with each movement, and then her eyes lowered and she licked her lips.

Bowing over her, he captured one of her nipples in his mouth, sucking and tugging it deep and hard. Her hands flew to his hair, pulling it and crushing his face against her breasts. He raised up and locked his gaze on hers while pinching her nipples painfully and deliciously.

"Feels so good," she murmured. The pain mixed with pleasure hit her deep in her core, and she craved more, more, *more*.

His gaze danced over her skin before he grabbed her green panties and ripped them off, then spread her legs wide. "You're so ready for me," he said thickly as he stroked her with skillful fingers, sending electric sparks through her.

She writhed beneath him, gasping, and he slid his finger into her. Deep moans escaped her throat and she arched her back.

"Look at me, baby," he said hoarsely.

She latched onto his smoky, dark gaze, sucking in a sharp breath when he plunged more fingers into her. She rocked her hips to meet his thrusts as every muscle coiled like a spring. Lowering his head between her legs, he kissed, licked, and teased while sliding in and out of her in a slow, even rhythm.

His heated gaze burned into hers as he raised his head. "You turn me inside out, woman. When I hold you close, kiss you, fuck you, I burn raw… deep down inside."

His words touched her deeply, and she craved him with a hunger that was insatiable, a passion that scorched every part of her. Not only did lust sizzle through her, but the desire to simply be taken, to have him master her, to take her hard and swiftly enough to make her forget herself overwhelmed her.

"I want to surrender to you." She dug her nails in his shoulders. *I need you to help me trust again. To feel without any thoughts. To see sex as something beautiful each and every time.* She threw her hands above her head.

Paco stared at her, his eyes dark with desire. "You like being tied up?"

"By you. Do you like it?" *Maybe he'll think I'm too damaged. A freak.*

A wicked smile spread over his lips. Slowly he withdrew his fingers from her heat, locking his gaze with hers. "Yeah, babe. I like it. A lot." Without breaking eye contact, he sucked her juices off his fingers, taking each one of them in his mouth. "You taste so fuckin' sweet." He leaned over and kissed her deeply, then jumped off the bed and went to the closet.

As she tasted herself on her lips, she watched how his firm ass rippled and his corded muscles strained against his taut skin. When he turned around, he held a black spreader bar with cuffs. She shivered as lust skittered up her spine.

The bed shifted under his weight, and he scanned her face. "You're sure about this?" She nodded. "If it gets too much, tell me. What word do you want to use?"

Without hesitation she said, "Freedom."

Holding up the bar, he nodded. Climbing over her body, he straddled her. "Give me your hand." She complied, and he secured it in one of the soft cuffs. "Raise your arms," he commanded.

She placed her arms over her head and he seized the bar, spreading it wide and hooking the middle of it to a ring on the headboard. He straddled her higher, his hard cock right next to her mouth. Swiping her tongue over his smoothness, she moaned.

He jerked away. "I'll give you permission when to touch me." The ominous tone of his voice made her throb and pulse with need.

He grabbed her other hand and fastened the cuff over her wrist, spread the bar out until her arms were outstretched and immovable, and locked it in the center. Her shoulders tightened and her sides felt as though they would tear open. She tried to move her arms, but he'd tightened it so there was no chance of any movement. Normally, when men had tied her up in the past, she'd been terrified, shutting her eyes and pretending to be in a different place until it was over, but with Paco, she found the experience incredibly empowering. She was submitting to him, and being unable to push him away allowed her to cross a limit—a boundary. Her trust in him enabled her to surrender and allow pleasure, while at the same time freeing herself from the chains of her past torments and demons.

"Keep your eyes open." Bending over her, he skimmed his fingertips slowly down her body, bringing heat and the caress of breath on her skin. Coming back up, he switched his fingers for lips, scorching featherlight kisses over her skin and leaving a trail of goose bumps in their wake. He fisted her hair, yanking her head to meet his mouth, then crushed his on hers. Rough. Wet. Deep. He pressed his body into hers and she felt his arousal against her thigh, mere inches from her sopping pussy.

"Fuck me," she whispered.

He froze, silence engulfing them for what seemed like an eternity to her.

"I call the shots. Not you," he said harshly. His words skated from her hardened nipples to her aching sex.

More kissing, touching, and teasing. The rip of the condom packet sent a sparking bolt of anticipation through her, and she moaned as she watched him slide the sheath over his pulsing dick.

"I'm going to fuck you." He spread her legs wider.

She sucked in her breath and quivered.

"You're mine." He pushed deep inside her, and a moan of pleasure escaped through her parted lips. She rocked her hips, taking in as much of him as she could. "You feel so fucking good," he grunted, pulling out and then pushing back in. His rhythm was slow, steady, and deep—so deep. He pulsed inside her as he dipped his head down and devoured her breasts. She writhed beneath him as he went in and out, her legs wrapped around his waist, connecting to his hot flesh, yearning to touch his chest and face but unable to in her restrained position.

Paco grabbed her ankles and flung them over his shoulders, then began jackhammering into her hard and fast. For each thrust, he would pull all the way out and then bury it to the hilt, his balls slapping her folds. The muskiness of his arousal curled around her, and she breathed him in as he pounded her with abandon while bolts of white-hot pleasure streaked through her.

"Fuck, Chelsea," he grunted before he leaned over and seized her mouth.

Every muscle began to tighten and her upper thighs quivered as a light sweat broke out over her body. She could feel the buildup as it went higher and higher, and then it burst. It was like melting and exploding at the same time—an intensity of sensation. She didn't have any control over it, and it was liberating.

Paco dug his fingernails into her hips as he came, groaning and grunting, his gaze fixed on hers before he collapsed over her, his warm breath fanning over her neck. They had both come hard, lost in the moment where there were no memories, only the two of them and pleasure.

He raised his head and swiped his lips across hers as he eased out of her. "I gotta get you out of this," he said, unfastening the cuffs.

When she lowered her arms, her muscles screamed. "That was incredible," she said, watching him as he massaged her arms lightly.

"We're good together. I haven't felt this good with a woman since… well… in a long time. Better?" He pointed at her arms.

She nodded. *He was going to say "Cassie." Do you still love her, Paco? Can you ever let your heart love another woman? Me?*

"You want something to drink?" He stood up and slipped his condom off.

"Some water would be good. You know, I'm clean. Bobby was always very careful about that. He didn't want a reduction in his price or, God forbid, a refund." She laughed dryly.

"The guy was a sonofabitch."

"I only brought him up to let you know that I'm good. I was checked the day before I ran away. I'm on the pill too."

He handed her a bottle of water and gently tugged her hair, tilting her head back. Kissing her tenderly, he stroked the side of her face. "I'll keep that in mind, babe." He threw back a shot of whiskey, then climbed on the bed. "I'm beat."

She took two more sips of water and switched off the lamp. He drew her to him and she cuddled close to him. Soon she heard his deep, steady breathing and knew he was asleep.

Tomorrow I have to call Mom. Her stomach twisted at the thought. She wanted to see her mother and sister desperately, but she was afraid that would be the end of her relationship with Paco. *Relationship? Is that what we have? I don't think so. I'm not sure how he feels about me. Can he just walk away from me? I know I'll miss him terribly.*

Sighing, she wrapped her arm tighter around him and closed her eyes.

THE CLASH OF thunder woke Chelsea up. It was dark and raining outside, and she tucked the covers under her chin. She reached over and felt the warmth of Paco's body, her nerves calming instantly. She was safe.

"Morning, beautiful," he said in a sleepy voice.

She turned around and faced him, loving the tenderness that shone in his eyes. Sweeping his hair off his forehead, she smiled. "Your hair's all messy." He caught her hand and kissed it, then dipped his head and kissed her softly.

Another clap of thunder shook the windows. She jumped. "I hate thunderstorms." She hugged his hand close to her as if it were a stuffed animal.

"I like them." His hot breath warmed her face. "That's how I met you."

She snuggled his hand harder as she lay there letting the happiness soak into her skin. Just being near him lit her up inside, giving her a peace she had never really felt in her life. "Being here with you, lying next to you like this, is the favorite part of the day for me. I just want you to know that."

The only sound in the room came from outside: raindrops pelleting the window, wind groaning through the trees, thunder crackling. She looked up at him through her lashes, and dread washed over her when she saw his clenched jaw and knitted brows.

I shouldn't have shared that. Me and my fuckin' big mouth! "I didn't mean anything too emotional by what I said. I mean… like, I didn't mean I love you or anything. It's just that I feel safe, and I'm grateful for that. That's all."

But I do love you, Paco.

A blown-out sigh. "I'm glad you feel safe. You've got a lot of years to catch up on. You have to promise me that you'll go to therapy when you go home." He curled a few strands of her hair around his finger.

Shivers skated down her spine at the intimacy of his action. "I will."

I don't want to think of never seeing you again.

"Did you call your mom? We can leave in a couple of days. I just have to wait for Steel to get back."

Two days is all the time we have left? A sliver of sadness pricked her. *I wish Mom and Kate could come here and stay with me. I know that's stupid, but I didn't plan on falling for Paco.* "I was going to call her this morning. I can't wait to see her and my sister." *And I can't.* Swirling inside her was an emotional storm that had no ending in sight.

"Why don't you give her a call while I'm washing up?" He kissed the top of her head.

"I was planning to."

He swatted her backside. "Come on, lazy girl, it's time to get on the phone. I have some business I need to discuss with Chains." He rolled away and rose to his feet, and she watched his naked body walking to the bathroom. He looked over his shoulder and winked at her, then closed the door.

She sat up, picked up her cell phone, and went over to the window. The rain came down in sheets, bouncing off the asphalt and erasing the sun. She tapped in the number.

"Mom?"

"Chelsea. Thank God you called. I was so worried. You need to come home now."

"I am. I'll be there in three days. A friend is taking me."

"I'll wire you the money. Just get on a plane and come home."

How could she explain to her mother that she needed Paco with her when she came home? She wasn't the girl her family remembered. She'd be changed in ways no girl ever should be. Everything would be the same… except for *her*. Paco met her when she was broken. He understood about the demons, the memories, the pain. He had his own hell, betrayed love and innocent blood on his hands.

"I can't take a plane. I don't have any ID, Mom. I'll be there in three days, I promise. I'll call you when I'm on my way. Will Kate be home?"

"She already is. She can't wait to see you. She's out with friends right now."

"Do you know these friends? You need to tell her to be careful. When we hang up, call her and make sure she's okay. She doesn't…." Her voice cracked.

"Oh, honey. Let's not talk about it. You'll be home soon. I left your room just like you had it. I never gave up hope."

"Has anyone threatened you or been around the house?"

"No. I think this guy was lying to you. That's what Peter thinks too. He used the love you have for your family to play mind games with you."

"I don't think so. Just be careful. Have you called the police?"

"Yes. They want to talk to you when you come home. Guess who's here? Aunt Sandy. She wants to talk to you."

Some shuffling sounds on the other end and then "Chelsea?"

"Hi, Aunt Sandy."

"It's so good to hear your voice. I couldn't believe it when your mother told me you were safe. After all these years, you're alive and safe."

"Yeah. Are you still with Uncle Dave?"

"Yes. He's here too. Hang on."

Paco came out of the bathroom, a towel wrapped around his trim waist and a few drops of water from his wet hair trailing down his chest. He smiled at her as he opened the top drawer and took out a pair of boxers.

"Chelsea? How're you doing, kid?"

"I'm okay, Uncle Dave."

"You sure?"

"Yeah."

"We're planning a big barbecue for when you get here."

"In the middle of winter?" She laughed.

"I'll grill the fucking steaks in twenty below if I have to. We're giving you a barbecue. You still like ribs, right?"

Tears filled her eyes as memories of family gatherings punched their way through the dark shadows of her mind. As if sensing her discomfort, Paco came over and tugged her against his warm body. He brushed her hair aside and kissed her neck gently. "You're okay."

Nodding, she swallowed the lump in her throat. "I still love ribs," she said.

"Where're you staying?"

"With a friend?"

"Are you in Ohio?"

"I have to go. Can you put Mom back on the phone? I'll see you and Aunt Sandy in a few days."

"Peter wants to talk to you."

"I'd rather not. Please put Mom back on the phone."

After she said her goodbyes, she put the phone down on the windowsill. Tremors invaded her and Paco guided her over to the chair, sank into it, and settled her on his lap. His arms cocooned around her, and all the emotions, the shame, the anxiety melted away in his embrace.

After several minutes, he rubbed her back in slow, soothing movements. "Your whole family's waiting for you. You'll get a hell of a homecoming."

She wiped her nose. "Yeah. I have a ton of cousins. My mom was the oldest of seven, and my dad the youngest of five. My aunt Sandy and uncle Dave are closer to my age than they are to my mom's. My aunt is the youngest." She softly tugged the hairs on his forearm, smiling when his skin pebbled. "I don't know if I can handle all this. I mean, they're expecting me to be the me from before, but I'm not."

"I'm not gonna lie to you—it'll be hard. When I got back from my final tour, I'd been through so much that I felt like a fish out of water. No one got me. They were all the same and I was fucking different. The old me had died when I killed a group of kids and their mothers. Even though the women had bombs strapped to them and used the kids as human shields, it still hit me hard. It's gonna be like that for you. You're going to be changed, but no one else will be. They'll expect you to act and do the same things you did before you disappeared, and it's gonna fucking suck."

"What did you do to get back on track?" she asked in a hushed voice.

"I joined the Night Rebels, and I never looked back. It was the best thing for me. Rooster, Army, and Scorpio had all done tours of duty. They understood, and the other brothers were there to lean on. We have a strong bond that no one and nothing can break. The brotherhood saved me."

"What's going to save me?" she whispered.

"You. You went through so much shit and you're still standing. You should be ranting and vowing vengeance, but you're not. You laugh, smile, and give me the true part of you when we're together. If I were you, I would be frothing at the mouth, buying a gun, and swearing to kill every fucker who ever touched me. You got gumption and a whole lot of inner strength."

"Or maybe I'm decaying inside and don't give a shit."

"That part *is* there, and that's what you need to work on with therapy. But the woman I see behind the decay, the abuse, the degradation, is a helluva woman who has a lot of living to do."

"I hope so. I'm glad you're taking me. I couldn't do this alone. How long are you staying?" Sadness crept through her, but she willed it away.

"Until I make sure you're not in any danger. I can guarantee that fucker knows where you live."

"How will I ever feel safe?"

"I'll make sure you do."

She looked up at him. "How?"

"By making sure the demon is destroyed. No more questions. I'm taking you for pizza, and not the frozen kind."

Joy shot through her and she kissed him. "I *love* pizza. What about the lockdown?"

"I'm VP and I can make exceptions. Me taking you to have a pizza is an exception."

She hugged him. "I'll be out in a sec."

She jumped off his lap and rushed into the bathroom. Looking in the mirror, she smiled at the sparkle in her eyes and the color in her cheeks. *I never thought I'd look like this again.* For years, the reflection that had stared back at her was devoid of joy, and hopelessness lived in its eyes.

Paco brought me back to life.

Refusing to think about their impending separation, she washed up and quickly applied her makeup.

That day would be just for them, and she would cherish every minute of it so she had something to hold onto when the nights were dark and he wasn't there to calm her fears.

She zipped up her jeans and came out of the bathroom.

"Ready?" he asked as his gaze traveled down her body.

With a big grin, she picked up her jacket and shrugged it on. "Ready," she answered, reaching out for him.

He took her hand and they walked out of the room.

Chapter Twenty-Two

PACO SAT IN front of Steel's desk, watching his president's face go from scowling to contemplative. He'd decided that if Steel wasn't gung ho about him escorting Chelsea to Ohio, he was going to do it anyway. There was no way he was going to send her off without making sure she made it home safely. It was killing him enough to see her go, but to not know if she arrived safely would eat at him. Besides, he wanted to be there to see if Bobby or Victor was lurking around. There was no way in hell either asshole was going to walk away from all that money. To them, Chelsea was property to be bought and sold.

"You have to take a couple of brothers with you to Ohio. I suspect this pimp of hers will try and get her back," Steel said.

"I'm good with that. I was gonna ask Chains to come with me anyway, since he's buddies with the guys in Twisted Warriors and I may need their help. I don't trust Victor Bustos one fucking bit."

"Neither do I. He ran his pussy ass out of Silverado. I'm not sure if he got wind of what was going down or if there was another reason he left."

"I think it had to do with Chelsea. He paid money for her and he doesn't have her. He's not going to let this go. I just don't know if that Bobby fucker told him she's in Alina or not."

Steel leaned back in his chair. "I doubt it. Bobby has to get the money first before he contacts Bustos."

"I think you're right about that. It's driving me fucking crazy not knowing where he is. I'm gonna check out all the motels today. I need to know if he's still in town."

Steel nodded. "I hear you. With the lockdown, Chelsea hasn't been around town. I bet he thinks she went back home." He picked up a can of Dr. Pepper and took a drink, then fixed his gaze on Paco. "After you drop her off, are you done with her?"

Paco wiped his hands on his jeans. "I'm gonna stick around and make sure she's safe."

"I meant after all that. I can see she's gotten to you. I've never seen you like this with a woman before."

Paco shifted positions. "I don't think I'll ever be done with her." He scrubbed his face. "She does something to me. Fuck… I don't know."

"Does she want to stay in Findlay?"

"We haven't talked about it. She's messed up from the shit that happened to her. It's real important that she sees her family and gets some therapy to deal with all of it. I guess I'll just see what happens." *I don't want to lose her.*

"Just let me know if you need anything."

"Thanks, bro. What's going on in Silverado?"

"Pandemonium with the badges and the fire department." He chuckled. "The West Avenue Bandits don't have a clue it was bikers. They think Los Malos double-crossed them, and with Bustos leaving, it cinched it with them. That asshole leaving made it easier for the Fallen Slayers. Chains talked to Hawk and he said no one suspects bikers, even the fucking Satan's Pistons."

"I guess the Pistons just got put outta business for a while. Cueball said the women followed the club's instructions about keeping quiet on where they were at. They're so damn scared of Los Malos and the other gangs that they're not going to give out too many details."

"I'm just glad we were able to free them," Steel said.

Paco stood up. "Me too. I need to talk to Chains."

"When are you leaving?"

"Tomorrow."

"I'll see you then. Lockdown ends tomorrow morning, so I'll be around."

"I bet Breanna's happy about that."

Steel laughed. "Yup. She did better than I thought she would."

"It'll be good to have the club back to normal. I'll see ya."

Paco saw Chains sitting at one of the tables with Lucy on his lap. He came up to them and tapped Lucy on the shoulder. She craned her neck and smiled widely when her gaze fell on him. "Hiya, stranger," she said.

"Hey." He pulled a chair out and plopped down.

"You've been hanging out a lot with your friend Misty." She uncurled her arm from around Chains's neck. "She still has to give me back my lavender sweater."

Paco chuckled. "She likes that one a lot. You want to sell it to her?"

Lucy's eyes widened. "For real? I mean, I like it, but if she wants to buy it, I'll sell it for forty bucks."

"Forty bucks?" Paco shook his head. "You know you only spent thirty on it."

"How do you know what I spend on my clothes?"

"Because I'm the one who usually takes you, Ruby, Alma, and Kelly shopping, and I collect the receipts to give to Sangre."

She rolled her eyes at him. "Whatever. Anyway, I changed my mind. I like the sweater, so have her give it back to me."

Paco nodded. "Now disappear. I got some business to talk about with Chains."

Pushing out her bottom lip, she slowly climbed out of Chains's lap and sauntered away.

"Hope you don't have a major boner, dude," Paco joked.

Chains laughed. "If I did, you'd be the one disappearing, not Lucy. I'll just catch up with her later. What did Steel say about Ohio?"

"He's cool with it, but he wants two brothers to come along in case there's trouble. I was gonna ask you to come because you're a wiz at computers and you know the Twisted Warriors. You up for the trip?"

"I don't have anything to do. I can work on writing code anywhere. How long are we gonna be gone?"

"Not sure. I'd say at least five days or a week. We leave tomorrow morning. That work for you?"

"Yeah." Chains was a freelance developer who specialized in real-time web applications and software. "I got that information you wanted."

"What did you find out?" Paco picked up the beer the prospect put in front of him.

"Tyler Tarleton died in a car crash the year after Chelsea was kidnapped by his dad. And his old man, Russ Tarleton, is doing a forty-year stint at Mansfield Prison. Seems like the fucker finally got caught for human trafficking, kidnapping, and a shitload of other charges."

"Too bad it's not here. I'd have a job for Scorpio if the fucker were in Canon City."

Chains laughed. "He'd like that."

"Thanks for the update. I'll let Chelsea know. It'll set her mind at ease."

"What time in the morning?"

"Around six. It's a little less than sixteen hundred miles. I figure with three of us driving, we can go straight through or crash overnight. We'll see how it goes. I already gave Sniper the heads-up that I'd be going. He's offering their clubhouse if we need to crash."

"That's cool."

"I'm gonna ask Army if he wants to join us," Paco said.

"Since he's always on the lookout for fresh pussy, I bet he'll be game."

Paco pushed his chair back. "You're right about that. I'm gonna see if I can find out if that fucker Bobby is still in Alina."

"You need some help with that?" Army asked as he came over.

Paco nodded. "If you don't have anything else to do. Do you want to go to Ohio with Chains and me? I'm taking Chelsea home."

"We're gonna crash at the Twisted Warriors' clubhouse. Hear they got some fine-looking club women," Chains added.

Army's eyes brightened. "Count me in. I've never been to Ohio, but those Warriors can party. Last year at Sturgis, they were off the charts."

"I know. We had some good times," Paco replied.

"Remember that cute brunette with hair past her ass? She was really into you, dude. You spent most of the trip with her. What was her name again?"

Paco shrugged. "I think it was Mandy."

"She was all over you. Fuck, those VP patches are chick magnets." Army laughed.

Paco chuckled. "I've noticed. Maybe you should put a temporary one on your cut when you go to rallies."

Army patted him on the back. "Don't think I haven't thought of it." Chains and Paco guffawed.

"I'll help you check out the motels. Let's see if we can find this asshole and beat his ass," Chains said, rising to his feet.

"More like kill his ass," Paco replied.

The three men went out into the chilly air, laughing and talking as they ambled to Paco's SUV.

"So Bobby's not in Alina anymore?" Chelsea asked. She sat facing him on the bed with shoulders hunched and legs crossed.

Paco leaned against the headboard, his legs stretched out. "Army found the motel he was staying in. The manager said he took off a couple of days ago. Probably thought I took you away right after you saw him at Flanigan's since neither of us has been around town."

Her face slackened and her pallor intensified. "Do you think he's in Findlay? I have to call my mom and warn her. And my sister." She clutched the base of her throat. "If something happens to Kate, I'll never forgive myself. I've got to call them." She reached for her phone and punched in the numbers.

While she spoke to her mom, he watched her, a feeling of loss punching his gut. He didn't want to dwell on her leaving, even though he knew it was for the best; she had to get her life back together, and he had a club to focus on. Whatever thing they had going on between them would go away once they were apart.

"My mom's super excited that I'm coming home, and my sister has a bunch of plans for us. I can't wait to see them." The color returned to her face and her eyes sparkled. "I feel better now that I described the asshole to my mom. She promised to call the police right away."

She's gonna be fine. What we had was a pause in our lives. I love seeing her happy. A slight thump on his leg broke in on his thoughts.

"You're a million miles away. Did you hear anything I just said?"

"Yeah. Your family's excited you're coming home and so are you. I'm happy for you. And don't worry about the fucker, the club's got you covered."

"What does that mean?"

"We got your back." A soft knock on the door stopped the next question he knew was coming. "Come in."

Lucy walked in, her eyes darting from Paco to Chelsea and back to him. "Hey." She stood by the door, shifting from one foot to the other.

"What do you want?" Paco asked.

"I know you're leaving tomorrow, so I came for my sweater."

"Fuck. I forgot about it, Lucy," he said.

Chelsea scrambled off the bed and hurried to the closet. "I'm so sorry. I've been meaning to give it back to you." She pulled out a hanger with the lavender sweater on it and handed it to the club girl. "Here you go. Thanks for letting me borrow it."

Lucy snatched it from her. "No worries." She ran her eyes over the bed, then locked gazes with Paco. "So you're going home for good?"

"Yeah." Chelsea closed the closet door.

Lucy smiled and the fine lines under her eyes crinkled. "That's cool. Have a good trip. See you later, Paco." She ran her tongue over her top lip and winked at him.

When the door shut, Chelsea came back to the bed and resumed her sitting position. "She's glad I'm going. Now you can go back to your old life." She pulled at a loose thread on the blanket.

"Lucy's got plenty of brothers to keep her happy." He waved his hand, pushing the idea way. "I bet you've got a few friends who can't wait to see you."

"I'm scared to see any of them," she said softly. "I know they're going to judge me, wonder why I didn't just run away. They won't say it to my face but they—my family included—will think I liked it and wanted to stay. They won't get that my whole identity was robbed, and unless they've been in that position, they can't understand. People's whole idea of prostitution is that the woman wants to be there. They think sex trafficking is about illegal immigrants smuggled into this country and forced to work in massage parlors to pay off a debt, or that it only happens in faraway countries." She shook her head. "They don't think it involves the teen next door or the college girl down the street. Before it happened to me ... I didn't either."

She locked gazes with him, her black eyes drilling into his. *Those eyes.* He'd never seen such darkness with so much light in them. They were the sweet silence before dawn and they pulled him in. But it wasn't just her eyes, it was every part of her, and he was falling... falling fast... falling in love with her. He brushed his hand over her knee. "As I told you before, it's gonna be tough."

Still holding his gaze, she grasped his hand. "You're the only one who hasn't judged me. Not even from the first time you saw me at the diner... before you knew. You thought I was just a lot lizard and you still treated me like a person. It was that night, with that small gift of normalcy and kindness, that you won my heart. I'm going to miss you so much." She blinked rapidly. "You don't have to say anything, but I want you to know that I love you. All my dealings with men have been horrible and I don't trust them at all, but you made me see that the men I came in contact with were the scum of society. You made me see that there are good men out there, and you're a good person. I'll never forget what you did for me." Before he had a chance to respond, she jumped off the bed and went to the bathroom, mumbling, "I have to pack up my stuff." From the steady stream of water in the sink, he figured she was trying to mask her sobs. *Fuck.*

"You got to me too, baby," he said under his breath. *But she has to go home and pick up the pieces. She hasn't dealt with all she's been through, and it's gonna bite her in the ass. I'm her rebound or her fucking stepping stone to regaining her life.* For a long time, he just sat there with his thoughts and the sound of cascading water. Nighttime had crept in, and long slivers from the moon provided the only light in the room. He pushed off the bed and switched on the lamp. He needed to hang with his brothers, get away from his thoughts and the ache he'd felt all day in his gut, so he pulled his boots on and went over to the door, knocking softly. "Are you okay?" he asked.

The doorknob jiggled and she opened the door a crack. "I'm good."

"I'm gonna go downstairs for a bit. Do you want something to eat?"

"I'm not hungry. Don't mind me. Just do what you'd normally do if I wasn't here."

"Text me if you want me to bring up some food, or you can come down and hang with me. The old ladies are still here, so you could talk with them. I'm sure Raven's gonna beat Brutus's ass at pool—that's a lot of fun to see."

"Thanks, but I think I'll just get things ready for tomorrow. We're leaving early, and I have a lot to do."

"Okay. If you want anything, text me or come down."

"Gotcha. And sorry for the meltdown. I'm just nervous about going home."

"I know. Don't sweat it. I won't be back too late."

"Have fun." She closed the door.

He stared at it for several minutes, then turned around and left.

Chapter Twenty-Three

CHELSEA SAT ON a faded couch in a room that looked more like a family room at her aunt's house than a biker clubhouse. When they'd arrived in Findlay, Paco had said that they needed to take a detour for a couple of hours, and they ended up parked in front of a ranch home with wood siding—the Twisted Warriors' clubhouse.

When they'd entered, a woman in a low-scooped T-shirt that showed off her more-than-ample cleavage guided her to the room she was now in while Paco, Chains, and Army went off with two guys who looked like they'd be on the FBI's Most Wanted list.

She glanced at her phone: Paco had been gone for almost a half hour. A few club women—from the way they were dressed she guessed that's who they were—sat on another large couch watching a reality show while giving her sideway glances. The club wasn't nearly as big as the Night Rebels' clubhouse, but it didn't seem like there were as many members who lived there.

While Chelsea waited, she tried hard not to think about Paco going back to Colorado. Every time she did, a surge of loneliness rushed through her, stabbing her heart. *It's only been a half hour since he left to talk with those guys and I already miss him terribly. How am I going to do this? I love him.* Heaviness filled her chest, and she pulled a tissue from her purse and wiped her runny nose. From the way he talked, it sounded like he wanted her to go back. *He's probably tired of babysitting me. But the way he kissed and touched me made me believe he cared about me as more than just a friend. I guess I can never compete with Cassie. I don't know how he feels about me.*

As she waited for him, she reflected on all the time they spent together, her emotions bouncing between jitteriness and sadness like a never-ending ping-pong game.

The familiar sound of his voice floated around her ears, and she looked over her shoulder and saw him walking into the room alongside Army, Chains, and the two scary-looking men. When he saw her, he winked, and a flutter of electricity ran through her body. Then he smiled at her, causing an instant warmth to radiate from within, and she smiled back. *He's so perfect. So awesome. So sweet.* She wanted to jump up, run into his arms, squeeze him tight, and never let him go.

"You ready?" he asked when he came over.

His words were like blows to her gut. "Yeah." She stood up and shuffled past him. From behind, she heard him say, "I'll be back later," and then his heavy footfalls followed her out the door.

He opened the car door for her and she slid inside. As they drove, she saw him looking at her from the corner of her eye.

"What's going on?" he asked.

"Nothing."

"Are you nervous about going home?"

She shrugged and stared out the window. The truth was she *was* nervous—it'd been so long since she was last home—but she was all mixed up about Paco. At that moment, she hated him for acting like it was no big deal that he was going to take off in a few days and be out of her life forever.

Snow-laden branches reaching up to the gray sky rushed past her, and memories of sledding with her cousins filled her mind. Craftsman houses dotted the landscape, and she smiled when they passed Riverside Park. *I used to go there all the time in the summer with my friends. Dad used to love to walk by Blanchard River. I'm really home! I'm going to see Mom and Kate and sleep in my own bed.*

"Memories?" Paco's deep voice pulled her back into the moment.

A big sigh. "Yeah. I can't believe I'm back home."

When he took the Forest Lake exit, her stomach churned. "I should call my mom and tell her I'm almost there."

"Do you live on a lake or something?"

"Yes, we live on the lake. We even have a dock. It's pretty nice. Peter used to take us fishing, though I never liked it. He always drank too much. I wonder if he still does."

Paco placed his hand over hers and a spark tingled through her. "It's going to be okay, babe."

"Is it?" Her belly fluttered, her heart banged, and her legs were like jelly.

He turned off the main road, pulled over, and set the car in Park. Locking eyes with her, he cradled her face and placed soft kisses from her temples down past her cheeks to her lips, licking the edges before nibbling them. Then he gripped her hair as he pulled her tighter to him, his mouth crashing down on hers as teeth, tongues, and lips tangled and meshed together. It was messy, passionate, and mind-blowing. It was like time had paused and all that mattered was how wonderful it felt to be in his arms. Sensation transcended all thoughts, and she lost herself in the moment.

A steady ringing sliced through the haze of arousal and love. Chelsea fumbled for her phone, and Paco pulled away. Instantly, her mouth missed the heat of his lips, and her body chilled from the absence of his warmth.

"It's my mom," she said as she put the phone to her ear.

"Why aren't you home yet?" Her mother's tear-filled voice was like a knife to her heart.

"I'm almost home. We just got off the exit. I'll be there in ten minutes. I love you, Mom."

"Just hurry home, honey."

By the time she hung up, Paco had already turned the car around. She glanced at him, but his gaze was fixed on the road. She took out her light pink lip gloss and swiped it on her lips. Soon they pulled in front of a two-story house with dove-gray wood siding on the second floor and brown brick on the first.

"They painted the shutters maroon," she said, unfastening her seat belt. "They used to be dark gray. I like the maroon better."

Paco opened the glove compartment and pulled out a key fob. "Take this and keep it with you always." He put it in her hand and pointed to a red button. "This is what you press if you're in trouble. It'll send an alert to my phone. Don't ever be without it, okay?"

"Okay." She slid the fob into her pocket.

Paco came over and helped her out. The front door opened and her mother, dark-haired and petite, ran down the porch steps.

"Chelsea!"

She ran up the sidewalk, meeting her mom halfway, and they embraced. Her mother squeezed her so tight she could hardly breathe. She laughed and cried at the same time.

"I missed you so much, Mom." Tears streamed down her cheeks, and she felt her mother's tears mix with hers.

A tall woman with sandy brown hair and chunky blonde highlights came out.

"Chelsea."

"Kate? You've grown. I can't believe it's you. You're beautiful." The last time she'd seen her sister, the girl had only been eleven years old. Kate came over and her mother pulled her into the hug, the three of them standing in the middle of the sidewalk embracing and crying.

Her mother wiped Chelsea's cheeks and looked over her shoulder at the street. "Is that your friend who brought you home?"

Chelsea turned around and saw Paco leaning against the SUV, his legs crossed at the ankle, his head cocked, and his silver earring shining through his brown hair. Happiness filled her. She nodded. "Paco, come over here."

He pushed away from the vehicle and swaggered up the walkway, coming beside her and putting his hand in the small of her back. His touch sent an electrical jolt through her.

Her mother held out her hand. "I'm Linda, Chelsea's mother. Thank you so much for bringing my daughter home." Her brown orbs brimmed, and she took a tissue from the pocket of her blouse and dabbed the corners of her eyes.

Paco shook her hand. "I'm Paco. You're welcome."

"I'm Kate. I'm Chelsea's sister."

"I can see the resemblance."

Chelsea smiled inwardly—she knew Paco hated all of this. He wasn't the type of man to engage in chitchat. She lowered her hand and pressed it against his thigh.

"Let's go inside," Linda said, tugging her jacket closer. "It's freezing out."

Chelsea started to follow her mom and sister, but Paco pulled her back. "I'll be there in a sec, Mom," she called over her shoulder.

"I'm gonna take off."

Her insides lurched. "So soon? Don't you want to come in and have a drink? You're going to miss seeing my room." She laughed dryly. *Don't you* dare *cry. I mean it.*

"You need some time alone with your family. You got my number. I'll give you a call later tonight."

"Am I going to see you again?"

"Of course." The whole time he talked, his gaze darted all around.

"What's wrong?"

"Just making sure no one's around. Take care of yourself. Don't go out. And when you talk to the badges, don't mention the club… or me."

"My mom just met you."

"You know what I mean."

"I won't say anything about the club or that you're a member. I'll say you just picked me up on the side of the road and gave me shelter until it was safe for me to come home."

"Good girl." He kissed her too quickly on the forehead. "Go on in. Your family keeps looking out the window."

"You're going to come to the barbecue, right?"

"Wouldn't miss it."

"So you're staying at the clubhouse?"

"I'll let you know where I'll be. It doesn't look like there's enough room for us, but we may crash there just for tonight and then get a motel."

"And party? I know how you bikers love a good party. The club women looked nice." *Why did I say that? He's going to think I'm jealous. I am, but I don't want him to think that. I should just go inside.*

"I'm not gonna fuck a club woman tonight if that's what you're implying." His gaze no longer darted around—it drilled into hers.

"Chelsea? Aren't you coming in? It's cold as hell outside. Tell your friend to come in too," a man shouted from the front door.

She rolled her eyes. "Peter, my stepdad."

"Go on in. I'll call you later." He walked around to the driver side and climbed into the car.

She waved at him and turned around. When she brushed past Peter, she heard Paco start the engine, and then Peter closed the door.

THE LOCK CLICKED on Chelsea's bedroom door, and she switched on the overhead light bathing the room in a soft glow. Leaning against the wall, she ran her gaze over the posters of teen heartthrobs from ten years ago that hung on the walls. It was as if her room had been tightly sealed in a time capsule; her mother had kept everything exactly the same as it'd been the day she was kidnapped.

On her desk, a picture of her and Tyler in a heart-shaped picture frame, taunted her. The day they'd taken that picture was clear in her mind: after school at Fruity Freeze sharing an almond mocha smoothie. *I was so happy that day.* She went over and picked up the frame, her gaze homing in on Tyler's lopsided grin. *There's no way you didn't know what your dad was going to do. You fucking set me up. How could you have done that?* Taking the picture out of the frame, she ripped it up in many pieces then threw them in the trash can. Sighing, she raked her fingers through her hair. *How am I going to do this?*

At dinner her family had talked about everything but what had happened to her. They kept glancing at her when they thought she wasn't looking. Afterward, she'd been in the kitchen putting the dishes in the dishwasher when Peter came in. The only questions he'd asked her were what she was made to do, and how many men she'd serviced. Not once had he asked her how she'd felt, or expressed sympathy of what she'd gone through. She couldn't get away fast enough, and she'd made her excuses and rushed up to her room.

She walked over to the window and stared at the lake; moonlight danced delicately across the water. *Will my life ever be normal again?* As she contemplated her present and her future, the phone vibrated on the nightstand. She dashed over and picked it up. *Paco!*

"Hiya."

"How's it going, babe?"

"Better now that you called."

"Did you hold up okay under all the questioning?"

"No one asked me anything except for Peter. I thought my sister and aunt and uncle would've wanted to talk to me about it since they're younger, but they all acted like nothing had happened. It was fuckin' weird. Peter just asked me about what I was forced to do and about the men. It was creepy."

"What the fuck's up with him?"

She could feel his anger emanating through the phone. "He's just an asshole… and he was drunk. I guess *that* hasn't changed since I've been gone."

"That can be tough."

"It's all so strange. I don't feel like I fit in with my own family anymore."

"I know it's hard, babe. It's just gonna take time. This is your first day home. No one wants to talk about it because they want to pretend it didn't happen… that everything is the way it used to be. I bet your mom's feeling some guilt over the whole thing."

"She shouldn't be. In no way was this her fault."

"Moms want to protect their kids so when something bad happens, they usually think they could've or should've done something to prevent it."

"I guess. The good news is that I'm going over to my grandma's next week to try my hand at quilting again. I swear I'll make a puff quilt for your new nephew."

Paco chuckled deep from the throat. "Kendra will love it. I'm glad you're doing something you used to do with your grandmother."

"Yeah, me too. What are you doing?"

"Just hanging with the Twisted Warriors. I stepped out back to give you a call. I wanted to make sure you're okay. It's fucking cold out here."

She laughed. "Welcome to Ohio in the winter."

"Have you talked to the police?"

"They're coming by tomorrow morning. I hope they can catch Bobby, Victor, and Erik."

"I wouldn't bank on it."

She walked back to the window. "The moonlight is pretty tonight. Do you see it?"

A pause. "Yeah."

"We're looking at the same thing right now. I miss you, Paco."

An audible sigh. "I miss you too, baby."

"How am I going to stand it when you leave?" she whispered.

"It'll get easier in time. You're strong."

"Sometimes I'm not so sure about that. Am I going to see you tomorrow?"

"Yeah. Call me when the badges leave."

"Can we spend some time away from the house?"

"Sure. Just let me know what you'd like to do and we'll do it."

I want to go back to Alina with you. "Okay."

A pause. "I gotta get going. If you have a hard time sleeping, give me a call, okay?"

"All right. Goodnight." She wanted to get off the phone because the lump in her throat was making it hard for her to talk. There was no way in hell she wanted him to know how lonely she was without him.

"Goodnight. I'll see you tomorrow."

Then the phone clicked and sadness enveloped her. She put the phone down and switched off the light then shuffled back to the window and stared at the moon-speckled darkness.

Chapter Twenty-Four

THE OVERPOWERING STENCH of mildew permeated the windowless room, and the dank coldness of the floor sent chills through Bobby's crumpled body. He could feel his abdomen distending rapidly, and his eyes were swollen shut. Every inch of his body ached, even his scalp. Bloody spit drooled from his slack jaws, and icy fear crept into his veins. *How the fuck did Victor find out the cunt was back home? Someone tipped him off. When I find out who did, I'm gonna kill—* His mind snapped shut. The irony of the situation stabbed at him: he'd never be able to exact revenge. *Victor's gonna kill me.* From the way his body felt, he knew there were internal injuries.

A rush of fresh air swirled around him, cooling his inflamed skin. A door shut. Footsteps approaching. A hard kick to his ribs. He grunted and groaned, and then a deep chuckle invaded his ears.

"I told you back in Silverado when you sold the cunt to me that the worst thing you could ever do is deceive me. And you fucking did it. *Cabrón!*" Another hard kick from Victor.

Bobby tried to speak but his throat was sandpaper, his tongue thick, and blood pooled in his mouth.

A hard laugh. "Not very talkative, are you?" The kick was harder than the last two; pain ripped through him, and he let out a choking gasp. "You underestimated me, and you forgot how powerful the lure of money is. Your contact here reached out to me. I put the feelers out and now you're a bloody mess. That's the way life works. You let the bitch throw you. You should've been straight with me."

I should've killed you first.

Another crashing kick. "No one." *Bam!* "Fucks." *Whack!* "Me."

Whack! "Over." *Bam, bam, whack!*

Bobby's groans turned into high-pitched nasally whines. *Just fuckin' kill me, you sonofabitch.*

But Victor didn't. His footfalls grew dimmer as he left the room.

Come back! Kill me, you fucker! Kill me!

Bobby Fenton—sex trafficker, pimp, cold-hearted bastard—was left to bleed out. It could be by the end of the day or after several days, but one thing was certain: he would die an agonizing death.

Darkness descended in the room, and he heard Victor laughing as he closed the door and turned the lock.

Chapter Twenty-Five

PACO LEANED AGAINST the counter in the enclosed porch, watching Peter grill the steaks in the backyard. Something about the big guy rubbed Paco the wrong way. Chelsea had told him he kept asking her about what she had to do to the men she'd been forced to be with, and the way he kept staring at her made Paco want to smash his fist into his face. He held back out of respect for Chelsea, but he was itching to rough up the asshole.

"I brought you another beer." Chelsea's uncle Dave handed him a Budweiser. Paco lifted his chin and took the can. "How long are you staying in Findlay?"

"Why?" Paco popped the top and took a long drink.

"Just wondering. It seems like you're watching over Chelsea. Do you think she's still in danger?" Paco took another sip and looked over at Peter, who waved. Paco turned back to Dave.

Her uncle scratched and rubbed his nose, laughing nervously. "I'm not trying to pry or anything. I think it's nice of you to stay. It's just that you're a long way from southern Colorado. Your family must miss you." Paco's gaze penetrated his. He laughed and wiped his hands on his jeans. "But you never know if those horrible men will come back. Chelsea told us there was more than one guy involved with all this."

Paco took another gulp of his beer.

"There you are," Sandy said as she came over and curled her arm around Dave. "Are you two getting to know each other?" Her gaze slid up and down Paco's body. "I can see why Chelsea's crazy about you." Her laugh was too shrill, grating on his nerves.

"Paco's not much of a talker," Dave said, his gaze darting away from the biker's.

Paco crushed the can and tossed it in the trash can. "Later."

As he walked out of the room, their voices grew hushed. When he entered the kitchen, Chelsea was pouring 7-Up into a large punch bowl, her nose wrinkled in a funny little way as her face tightened with concentration. *She's so damn adorable.* Her long hair draped around her, and her tight jeans showed off her curves just right. His dick twitched and he adjusted his pants. She set down the two-liter bottle and closed her eyes, inhaling deeply, and then a smile spread over her soft, glossy lips.

"Paco," she murmured as she turned toward him.

"Hey, beautiful. What're you making?"

"Punch. Where have you been hiding?" She padded over to him.

"Been having a smoke and a beer on the back porch. Your aunt and uncle came out to chat." He slinked an arm around her waist and drew her to him.

She chuckled. "And how did the chatting go?"

"What do you think?" He nuzzled the soft spot on her neck right below her ear.

"Oh, Paco," she moaned, running her nails up and down his back. "I miss you… miss *us*."

"I miss your warm body next to mine when I wake up. I got a burning for you real bad, baby," he whispered in her ear before gently sucking her earlobe between his lips.

"Chelsea?" Sandy said as she and Dave came into the kitchen.

Paco pulled back but kept his arm around her waist.

Chelsea blushed. "I made some more punch. Can you take it out to the dining room, Aunt Sandy?"

"Since we already set up this whole homecoming party, I think you could help out and do it yourself," Dave said, a frown deepening the lines around his brows and mouth.

"You're right. I'm sorry." She tried to tug away from Paco but he held her firmly.

"Why don't you be a nice auntie and take the fucking punch to the dining room? I'm talking to Chelsea right now."

His hard scowl didn't go unnoticed, and Sandy's eyes widened while Dave picked up the punch bowl and walked out of the kitchen with his wife following.

After they were out of earshot, Chelsea kissed Paco. "You're such a badass," she said against his mouth.

"I've missed your lips," he murmured, his hand pressing against the small of her back.

She looked over his shoulder. "Peter's going to be coming in. I see him putting the steaks on the platter."

"Give me your lips." He crushed his mouth on hers and kissed her deeply. She melded into him, and he dropped his hands lower and placed them on her ass.

She pulled away, straightening her hair and smoothing down her top. "I don't want Peter to see us kissing. He's weird enough as it is, and he's had too much to drink."

"You didn't care about your aunt and uncle."

"Aunt Sandy's cool, and so is Uncle Dave. They're more modern. They're just a couple of years older than you."

"Does your uncle snort coke?" he asked.

"What made you ask that?"

"Just the way his eyes looked and how he kept rubbing his nose."

Looking around, she said in a low voice, "Yeah, and so does Aunt Sandy, but my mom and Peter don't know. I'm not sure if Kate knows about it now. They've been doing it since I was in middle school."

"Did you tell anyone about the money?"

"No. I've decided to donate it to Street's Hope. It's a nonprofit that helps women who are victims of sex trafficking."

A crazy mix of emotions tore through him and, in a single flashing moment, he wanted nothing else but to spend his life with her. She was like the sun giving him heat and light when for years he'd only had cold and darkness. His feelings for her were an alchemy of possessiveness, tenderness, and something else that made him uncomfortable, but at the same time made him feel alive.

"What? Do you think it's a bad idea?" Her soft voice washed over him.

Pressing her to him, he cupped her chin and tilted her head back. "I think you're wonderful." He crushed his lips to hers, ignoring Peter's loud footsteps and the floating laughter and conversation from the dining room. Everything was suspended—it was just him and Chelsea and their passion for each other. It was a heady mix, and he wanted it to go on forever.

"What the hell's going on here?" Peter stormed in, anger molding his features.

Paco winked at Chelsea, then glanced over at her stepdad's blotchy red face. "We're kissing."

"Are you lovers?"

Paco sneered. "That's none of your fucking business."

Peter slammed down the platter of steaks. "Let go of my daughter and get out of my house. Now. You're just as bad as all the men who abused her. You're nothing but—"

Paco had him flat against the wall, his hand tight around his neck, his face barely a breath away from the shocked man's. "Don't you ever compare me to those fuckers again." He squeezed tighter, and Peter's eyes bulged as he choked and sputtered. "And no one tells me what the fuck to do."

"Paco, please." Chelsea's small voice and soft hands on his arm focused him.

With one last squeeze, he let go and backed away. Peter stood against the wall, coughing and gulping for air. His gaze fell on Chelsea's. "He's crazy," he stammered.

"You disrespected him. He's nothing like those horrible men. How could you have said that? If it weren't for Paco, I don't know where I'd be."

"What's all the yelling about?" Chelsea's mother asked as she stood in the doorway looking at all of them.

Peter pointed at Paco. "He tried to kill me. He's crazy. He was kissing Chelsea."

Linda stared at Paco. "Is this true?"

With narrowed eyes, he zipped up his leather jacket. "I didn't try to kill him."

"Yes you did. I'm going to call the police."

"If I wanted to kill you, you'd be dead."

Linda gasped and ran over to Peter, running her hand over his forehead. "Are you okay?" she asked softly.

"No, I'm not." He pushed her hand away from him.

"Mom, Peter accused Paco of being like the men who kidnapped me."

Linda clutched the top button of her red blouse. "Why would you ever say such a thing to the man who helped Chelsea?"

"He was kissing her."

Linda shook her head. "They like each other. He's been the only bright spot in Chelsea's life. I'm grateful to him for bringing her back home, and for making her glow with happiness amid all the horror she's had to endure. Leave them alone. You always did this when she was a teenager and I never said anything, but I will now. Leave her alone. I mean it." Linda walked away and went over to the sink. "And stop drinking so much," she added in a low voice.

"Is everything okay in here?" Sandy asked as she came into the room and went over to Linda.

Pushing her shoulders back, her chin lifted, Linda grabbed her sister's hand. "Everything's perfect. Peter's finished with the steaks and it's time to eat." Glancing at Peter, she pointed to the platter. "Bring those to the dining room. Chelsea, Paco, come on. The food's going to get cold." She waited until Peter left, and then she and Sandy followed him out.

For several seconds, silence descended on them. Then Paco hugged her close to him. "I can see where you get your strength from, babe." He kissed her quickly. "Let's get some food."

PACO SAT IN the SUV across the street at the end of the block, watching Chelsea's house. Ever since Bull Dog and Jacko had told him they saw a man matching Bobby's description lurking around the house and neighborhood a few days before he and Chelsea had arrived in Findlay, he'd been living on adrenaline. The night before, when Bull Dog had come over to the motel for Chains to relieve him, he'd told Paco that he hadn't seen the Bobby guy in a couple of days. The news hadn't comforted Paco, it just lit up all his red flags. And so he sat watching her house.

Several of Chelsea's cousins filed out the door, waving their good-byes. Sandy and Dave left next along with a few friends. Soon everyone was gone. The sky had turned from gray to black, and the stars twinkled and shone in the frigid night air. Opening a thermos, he poured a cup of coffee and sipped it slowly; he was there for the night.

I'd rather be in your warm bed with you in my arms. I gotta find Bobby and Victor and get rid of them. How can I go back to Alina with them still out there? He took another sip of hot coffee. *How can I go back without Chelsea? Fuck.* She got to him. The way she smiled, talked, smelled, and felt in his arms had seriously melted the steel surrounding his heart.

Her shadowed outline danced from behind the curtain, and he watched her while his body heated from want.

The light went off and Chelsea's house was encased in darkness. He leaned back and kept his gaze steady.

Chapter Twenty-Six

CHELSEA STOOD AT the edge of the lake, watching the water flow over the frozen chunks. She picked up a rock and threw it onto a thin piece of ice, watching it crack before sinking down into the cold water. She crossed her arms tighter around her as the chilly wind kicked up. Chelsea loved looking at the lake, watching the constant movement of the water. Standing at the bank had always given her comfort since she'd been a child. That day, she needed its movement, its strength, and its mesmerizing effects. Her emotions were scattered, skipping and bouncing like a kite in a windstorm.

I feel like a fish out of water around here. I don't fit in anymore. Mom, Kate, Aunt Sandy, Uncle Dave, and all the others are trying so hard, but I can see the unasked questions and the impatience behind their eyes. The only one who makes me feel comfortable and who sees me for who I am is Paco, and he's leaving.

Whenever she thought about him going and her staying, it was like her heart snapped in two.

"Chelsea, come here for a minute."

She spun around and saw her aunt Sandy holding the back-door's screen wide open.

"Coming." With a quick look at the water, she headed back to the house. Her mother was terrified to leave her alone, so Linda had called Aunt Sandy to come over while she went to her doctor's appointment.

A rush of heat enveloped her when she entered the mudroom. She latched the back door and went into the family room. Her uncle sat on the couch, watching her as she came in.

"I didn't know you were coming over. Do you have the day off?" she asked.

He nodded and motioned for her to sit down. She sank into the couch and glanced at the fire spitting in the brick fireplace. "What did you want?" she asked her aunt.

Sandy cleared her throat. "Your friend stopped by to see you."

A surge of joy zinged through her. "Paco?" She tore her gaze away from the fireplace and craned her neck, trying to locate him.

"No. His name is Victor."

Her blood turned to icicles, her ears pounded, and her heart beat so wildly that she thought it would tear through her chest cavity. *Victor? No!*

She leapt up from the couch. "He's not my friend. He's a trafficker. He's the one who bought me. Call the police!" She rushed to the kitchen phone and picked it up.

Firm fingers gripped her shoulder painfully and she froze.

"Put the phone down."

It's him. It's his voice.

Taking the phone from her, he put it back in its cradle. "That's a good girl." His mouth was right next to her ear. The tension in her stomach congealed into a frozen ball of fear. "You've been such a naughty girl, making me come to this freezing fuckin' town just to bring you back. Your punishment will be sweet, fucktoy."

She broke away and ran into the family room. Rushing to her aunt, she threw herself into Sandy's arms. "You've got to call the police. He's going to hurt all of us. He's evil."

"Stop acting like a brat," Sandy snapped, pushing her away. She fell backward and Dave caught her.

"What are you saying?" Chelsea asked.

Dave grabbed her arms and pulled them behind her. *What's going on here?* Something cool wrapped around her wrists and he yanked hard until the plastic dug into her tender flesh.

"What are you doing?" She looked over her shoulder and met her uncle's cold, flat eyes. "No. This can't be happening."

"It's nothing personal, Chelsea. It's just business," Sandy said.

Her mind whirled as she tried to comprehend what was going on. It was like she'd stumbled into a bad B-rated movie. *This can't be happening. Aunt Sandy and Uncle Dave can't be doing this to me.*

"We needed the money, and when Bobby called and told me you'd run away, he wanted us to pay him what you stole from him." Sandy clucked her tongue. "You should've just accepted your life. You put us in a bad way."

"You know Bobby? What the fuck are you talking about?"

Dave came over and shoved her toward the couch. "We sold you to Erik, who sold you to Bobby."

"You? I thought it was Mr. Tarleton."

"He was the delivery man. He got his money too. We had no choice. We needed to pay our drug debts to Erik and then to Bobby. As I said, it wasn't anything personal."

"Aunt Sandy, I love you. How could you've betrayed me? And Mom? What's wrong with you?"

"I needed the money. They threatened to kill us if we didn't pay our debts. And now we need the money again."

"Speaking of money, where's mine?" Victor came over to her, digging his fingers cruelly into her cheek even as she cried out. His panting echoed in her ears as he rubbed against her like an animal in heat.

"I don't have your money. I just ran that night. Ask Bobby where it is," she said in a strained voice.

"He's not talking, but it doesn't matter. You'll pay me every fuckin' penny back with your body." He leaned in close. "And when I tire of you, I'll sell you overseas for tiger meat," he whispered in her ear. From the way he acted, he wasn't stealing her but rather claiming what he believed was rightfully his. "Enough of this. It's time to go home."

Victor threw her on the couch and she landed on her side. Her aunt avoided Chelsea's gaze as she held out her hand for the envelope he gave her.

I can't let him take me away. I can't go back to that life. Then she remembered the key fob Paco had given her. He'd told her that tapping it once would send an alert to his phone.

If only I can reach it before Victor finds it on me.

As her aunt and uncle counted the money Victor paid them for leading him to her, she tried to slip her fingers into her back pocket. The zip ties dug into her skin, and she bit the inside of her cheek to keep from making any noises. *I have to reach it. Please let me.*

Victor bent over her, his cold hands stroking her face. "How obedient and quiet you are. Not one sound out of you. No fighting. And that's how you're going to remain—silent." He bent lower and she could feel the vibration of his lips on her ear. "When I beat you, you'll be silent. When I rape you, you'll be silent. And if I decide to kill you, you'll be silent. You're in my fuckin' world with my goddamn rules." He kissed her and nausea poked her stomach.

"You promised us ten baggies of coke," Dave said.

"We're going to have a lot of time together, fucktoy." He straightened up and walked away.

Chelsea resumed fumbling for the key fob. And then her finger found it. Adrenaline shot through her. *I can do this. I just need to go in a little bit more.* From the conversation behind her, she surmised that they were wrapping up the sale of her. The fact that her beloved aunt and uncle were the ones who sold her eight years before was incomprehensible.

I can't think about that now. I just need to push the button. I can't let him take me. I'll never be found.

"You need help getting her in the SUV?" Dave asked.

"I can manage. I have two men with me."

I almost have it. I can feel it.

Then he grabbed her shoulders. *No! I almost had it!* Her insides quivered and screamed silently as tears slipped from the corners of her eyes. Victor took out a sack. *No!* He jerked her up and put it over her head, cutting out all light, then fastened it around her neck. The musty scent of the sack filled her nostrils, and bile rose up her throat. She offered no resistance as he propped her straight on the couch, her finger sliding into her pocket. Resignation turned to hope as she pushed the button right before Victor jerked her onto her feet.

Heavy footsteps thudded into the foyer. She cocked her head, trying to see something through the sack. Nothing. Several hands grabbed her and forced her into something cold. When they pushed her down on her side, she realized they were putting her in a trunk.

"No! Aunt Sandy, please don't let them do this to me. Please!"

"Shut the fuck up. Your disobedience will cost you," Victor gritted.

Someone pushed her head down, and the snap of the lid sealed her fate. She rocked back and forth and knew they were carrying her. Her teeth chattered when they threw her on the ground. The revving engine and the shifting motion from side to side told her she was in a vehicle. At first she hit her feet against the walls and cried out, but the only reply was her own echo from the metal walls. Cruel laughter filtered in and she willed herself to stay calm.

Please come find me, Paco. He's taking me away. I love you.

She concentrated on remembering how it felt to be with Paco. Over and over she replayed each of their moments as the car drove farther and farther away.

Chapter Twenty-Seven

PACO RAN TO the SUV and jumped in when the alert signal came from Chelsea. He took out his phone and called Chains and Army, telling them to meet him at her house. Hanging up, he tapped in War's phone number, cursing the Twisted Warrior member under his breath.

"Yo," said War in a gravelly voice.

"Are you at Chelsea's house?" Paco asked.

"I'm just heading there now, dude. I took a break and went to grab some snacks at the convenience store."

"Haul ass over there now. I'm on my way."

"What's going on?"

"I got an alert signal from her. She's in trouble. I'm checking the GPS on her phone and she's on the move. Fuck!"

"I'm there. I'll call for backup," War replied.

He called Army back. "Change of plans. The fuckers have Chelsea. Her GPS tells me they're hitting the interstate. It's just a matter of time before they find her phone. War's going to her house now. Something doesn't feel right. She was in her fucking house."

"War didn't see anything?" Army asked.

"He took a break to get some food. They nabbed her then. She's been betrayed by someone close to her, I know it."

"You think it's her stepdad?"

"I gotta admit I thought Peter was involved, but it hit me not too long ago that her uncle Dave asked if I was going back to Colorado. How the fuck did he know that's where I lived? Chelsea never told him. I got a bad feeling here. I'm gonna follow the GPS."

"We're with you. Where are you?"

"I just made a U-turn on Springfield."

"Meet us at the motel. Chains is on the phone with Jacko and Sniper. They're heading over to the house."

"Tell them to keep us posted. I'm just turning into the motel lot. Where the fuck are you?"

"Right behind you. Bull Dog, Blue, and Dime Bag are behind us. Let's go get your woman."

As Paco waited for Chains and Army to get in, Bull Dog came over to the driver's side. Paco rolled down the window and bumped fists with him.

"We know this area inside out. What direction are they going?" Paco handed him his phone and he looked at the map. "We'll take the backroads and cut them off. You guys follow them from behind. You got enough guns and shit?"

Paco nodded. "Enough to blow up half this fucking town. We brought some assault rifles and grenades. Take what you need. The only ones getting hurt are those fuckers."

Bull Dog chuckled. "I like the attitude, brother."

Chains set it up so they shared the GPS screen, and Bull Dog jumped into his vehicle with his brothers and sped away. With jaw clenched, hands gripping the steering wheel, and eyes fixed ahead, Paco made a sharp turn and screeched out of the parking lot.

When they were ten minutes into their drive, Chains's phone rang. "It's Jacko," he muttered, putting the phone to his ear. Silence filled the SUV, and then Chains's voice broke through it. "He said there're two people at your woman's house—a Sandy and a Dave."

"Tell him to blindfold them, take the fuckers to their clubhouse, and keep them on ice until we get back. I've got some business with them. Remind him not to mention any of their names, our names, or the clubs."

Chains nodded and relayed the information, then put the phone down and chuckled. "The brothers are loving this. They don't get this much action. They're mostly into riding, partying, and stealing cars and bikes."

"Let's hope they know what the fuck they're doing," Army said as he lit a joint.

"They do." Chains snapped his fingers and Army gave him two joints. He handed one to Paco. "Don't worry. We'll get Chelsea back okay. There's no way we're gonna let any fuckers slip from our fingers."

Paco inhaled deeply and glanced at Chains. In that one glance, all the love, loyalty, and pride of the brotherhood were conveyed. They drove in a comfortable silence, Army messing with his phone, Chains watching the GPS map, and Paco staring at the road. *I can't lose her. She means everything to me. Chelsea, baby, hang on.*

"They're five miles ahead of us and just took Exit 281," Chains said. "Wait. Bull Dog's saying that the exit is where some abandoned warehouses are. There's also an old quasi-airport in the area that was used for agriculture and small planes."

"The fuckers have a plane waiting." He pressed down on the accelerator. *I have to get there in time.*

"Bull Dog's coming in on the side. He's gonna park behind one of the warehouses. He said we should come in from the west."

Paco nodded. "Army, start taking the guns out, and a couple of grenades." From the rearview mirror, Paco saw Army bending over the seat and bringing guns over it.

"Once we get there, we'll kill the engine and walk in. We'll come in strong. Since they're only in one car, I don't think there are too many of them. Chains, get Jacko on the phone. Ask him to *persuade* the traitors to tell him where Chelsea is and who took her."

Chains called Jacko and after a minute, he laughed loudly. "The fuckin' pussies gave everything up. It's Victor who's got her. Him and two guys. They put her in a metal box in the back of their SUV. Bustos's taking her to Pueblo on a private plane."

Veering to the west, Paco parked behind an abandoned barn, killed the motor, and jumped out of the car. He took several deep breaths to calm down and focus, pushing all emotions far away and replacing them with ice cold detachment. He slung a semiautomatic rifle over his shoulder and carried a Mag sniper rifle while Chains and Army carried assault rifles. As much as he wanted to capture Victor and torture him, Steel had told him to do away with him and Bobby in a fast and efficient way. The brothers weren't in their territory, and they didn't want to mess with the badges or have too much scrutiny on them and the Twisted Warriors.

They came in from the back, giving the thumbs-up to Bull Dog, Dime Bag, and Blue. Victor stood behind two large men dressed in black suits, a small aircraft about three hundred yards away. He watched as Victor opened the back and motioned for the two men to come over. They took out a large square metal box. Paco's heart splintered, but he pushed away the image of a terrified Chelsea folded inside.

"I have a perfect view of the fucker," Army said in a low voice.

"I don't want them to shoot Chelsea. Let's wait until they start toward the plane." He turned to Chains. "Tell Bull Dog that when the fuckers clear the vehicle and start toward the plane, I'll give the signal and we'll kill them. Tell them not to shoot at the box." With the precision of their weapons, they could pinpoint exactly where the bullets would go. The guns they'd bought from Liam were Army issued and had cost a fortune on the black market.

As if sensing something, Victor turned and looked around the area. He stood staring for several minutes, then slowly turned away, bending down and unlocking the box before dragging a tied Chelsea out. When Paco saw the sack over her head, he wanted to kill the fucker right then and there. Victor placed her in front of him and slowly walked backward.

"He senses us," Paco said. "I'm going to go around closer to the plane. He's using Chelsea as a shield."

"I'll go with you," Army said.

The two men went behind the buildings and dropped to their bellies, slithering across the ground as they had done numerous times overseas in Afghanistan. As Victor dragged Chelsea, she started screaming and struggling to break away from him. He punched her several times in the head and stomach, but she kept pushing away from him. He took out his gun and put it to her head. His mouth was moving, but Paco couldn't hear what he was saying.

Stay cool, babe. I'm here. Feel me. I'm here.

Chelsea stopped and moved her head around as if trying to see if he were there. At that moment, he felt her. He couldn't explain it, but a connection as strong as a current of electricity passed from her to him. The way she stiffened and turned her body in his direction told him that she'd felt it too. It was something he'd never experienced in his life.

Victor shoved her forward, and she stumbled and fell on the ground. Paco beamed. "That's my girl," he said under his breath. By falling, she'd opened Victor up like a bull's-eye at the shooting range. Paco lifted his weapon, looked through the scope, and aimed at Victor's head.

"I hate like fuck that the sonofabitch's death's gonna be quick," he whispered to Army.

"I hear you. When you fire the shot, the others know to take out the other two goons and the pilot." The pilot was a casualty that couldn't be helped. In the outlaw world, they never left any witnesses.

Paco pulled the trigger. The bullet flew out of the rifle and into the air, piercing the asshole's skin, and he jerked back. Another bullet. Then another. Victor's eyes bulged and he looked shocked, like he hadn't expected to end his life that way on that day. Then he fell on the ground with a thump. More bullets whizzed through the air, and Paco slithered over to where Chelsea was on the ground. Her whimpering touched him deeply, and he reached out and yanked her to him, dragging her behind him to safety.

He pulled off the sack and her wild eyes searched his face; then recognition settled in, and she leaned against his chest and sobbed. He took out a knife from his boot and cut the zip ties. Her arms flopped down by her side and he embraced her tight, rubbing her back and whispering in her ear over and over again, "It's all over. You're safe. I'm here."

Chains came up to him. "They're all down. We're gonna get rid of them. Bull Dog says they can take the plane to sell the parts. He says Blue's a pilot and he's gonna fly it to a nearby strip a friend of his has. Why don't you go back to the SUV and take care of her. Army and I will take care of everything."

"You sure?"

"Yeah." Chains gripped his shoulder, then took off.

Paco carried Chelsea back to the SUV and slipped into the back seat with her. He took out the first aid kit and cleaned the blood and dirt from her wrists and face, then kissed her gently and pressed her close to him. "I'm so sorry this shit happened to you. It killed me when the alert signal came through. One of the guys dropped the fucking ball."

"All that matters is you came. I knew you would. I felt you out there. Is that crazy?"

"It is, but I felt a charge pass between us. You did too. That's why you fell down, isn't it?"

She nodded. "I never felt something so strong in all my life." She looked up at him through her lashes. "Aunt Sandy and Uncle Dave were the ones who sold me all those years ago. They arranged the whole thing, and Mr. Tarleton was the delivery person. They sold me to pay off drug debts they owed to Erik and Bobby. And they told Victor I was home. I can't believe they did that to me. How could they? What's wrong with people that makes them do that? I loved her." She clung tighter to him.

"They're fucked in the head. They don't have a soul. To betray someone who loves you is the worst."

"You have experience with that. First your dad killing your mom, and then Cassie leaving you for someone else."

His hand stopped in the middle of her back. "How do you know about Cassie?"

"I snooped, but not on purpose. I was trying to make room for my underwear when I found the envelope. I'm sorry, but I couldn't resist. I read some of the letters. Don't hate me."

Years of memories flooded into his head, bumping into each other:

his mother's butchered body, Cassie's hair glowing in the sunlight, his father's crocodile tears, him and Cassie riding on his Harley, his sister's gut-wrenching sobs when their father was convicted, Cassie's betrayal. As the snippets from the past tangled around each other, other memories pushed them away: images of Chelsea, sick and vulnerable, sipping hot tea in the diner on a rainy night; her beautiful eyes boring into his; her soft lips; her laughter; her kindness amid so much suffering; and her strength.

"Are you mad at me for reading them?"

He bent down and kissed her gently. "No, I'm not mad. That was a long time ago. It was because of her that I decided women couldn't be trusted."

"Do you still feel that way?"

"Not since I met you. You've touched me in ways I can't explain. You've brought out so many emotions that I thought I'd buried a long time ago."

"You did the same for me. Before I met you, I thought that all men did was cause great suffering, that they couldn't be trusted. For years I thought my gender was a curse, and I would never enjoy sex and be normal again. You changed all that for me."

He kissed the top of her head. "I've only told one woman that I loved her, but since you came into my life, I've realized that the love I had for Cassie was not sustainable. Yeah, I loved her, but you're the first woman I've ever been in love with. I'm crazy about you, baby. For a long time I fought it because I didn't want to give up the bitterness, and I thought it would be better for you to try and build your life with your family. I didn't want to be your rebound relationship. I didn't want to get hurt again."

"I'd never hurt you. I'm in love with you, and it feels wonderful. I think I've loved you from that very first night you let me sleep in your room because I was sick. I'm so dreadfully sad that you're leaving. I don't feel whole without you. You fill in the cracks that keep the darkness out."

"It's gonna be hard to let you go. It took almost losing you to kick some fucking sense into me."

She pulled his face closer to hers and kissed him passionately. "If you love me then why are you letting me go?" she asked against his lips.

"Because you need to live your life. You need to be independent, meet new people, and fulfill your life without me for a while. You have to get to know yourself again and your family."

"But I don't want to be without you," she said softly.

He stroked her cheek, his eyes boring into hers. "I know, but I need to let you spread your wings. If we truly love each other then we can be apart for a while and come back together and still have the same feelings."

Her lips trembled and he embraced her to him, his resolve melting with every breath he took. He wanted nothing more than to take her back to Alina and make her his old lady, but he knew she had to make sure what they had was real. For the past eight years her life had been suspended, and she needed time for reflection, for healing before they could come together."

"I love you, Paco." Her voice hitched.

"And I love you, Chelsea. Don't ever forget that." Warmth spread through him as he held her close and listened to her light breathing. "You should call your mom and let her know you're okay." She pulled away and he wiped the tears from her cheeks.

"What am I going to tell her about Aunt Sandy and Uncle Dave? Will she believe me? I have to call the police."

"I'll take care of them. You just let your mom know you're okay."

"How will you take care of them?" She glanced up at him. He didn't answer. "I don't want them hurt. I know what they did to me was despicable, and I still can't believe it. I hate them for it, but I don't want their suffering to be on my conscience. Promise me you won't hurt them."

"I can't promise shit like that."

"Paco, please. Let the law handle this. I'm sure I wasn't the only one they did this to."

He sat rigid, looking out the window. *I can't let them go. They betrayed my woman, and they know too much.* "Did you tell them I was a Night Rebel?"

"No. I didn't say anything about you. They kept thinking you were a trucker. They knew you lived in Colorado and I was surprised about that, but I never confirmed that either. They told me today that Bobby had told them I was in Alina. I think Bobby thought you were a trucker."

"Where is the fucker? I'm surprised he wasn't here."

"I think Victor killed him. He didn't say it, but he hinted at it."

"Call your mom now."

She nodded, and a tacit understanding evolved between them. Then she picked up the phone and dialed while Paco pulled her back into his embrace and held her close.

Chapter Twenty-Eight

PACO STARED AT Sandy as she sat tied to a metal chair, her eyes bulging. Dave sat slumped over in the chair next to her, his face cut and bleeding.

"Let's try this again," Paco gritted as he pushed away from the concrete wall. Chains and Army leaned against a long, metal table while War, Bull Dog, and Sniper smoked joints in the corner of the basement room. "What the fuck is Erik's last name, and how do I get a hold of him?"

"If I tell you, will you let us go?" Sandy asked feebly.

"You got a better chance of leaving this room if you talk." Paco took out a hunting knife and ran the flat side of the blade over the side of her face.

"Don't tell him shit," Dave growled. "He's not going to let us go."

Like lightning, Paco's fist punched his face, and Dave's head tipped back.

"I thought you were a trucker. That's what Bobby told us," Sandy said as she looked at her husband.

"Shouldn't believe what that fucking scumbag tells you. How do I get a hold of Erik?"

"He has a cell phone, but he won't pick up unless he recognizes the number."

"How does he get *johns* for the women?"

"He puts ads in an internet newspaper—*Backstreet*."

Paco looked at Chains who was already tapping the name into his iPad.

"Found it. The site is for employment, houses for rent and sale, and… here it is—the adult section." He handed Paco the tablet.

Reading the section given to him, numerous names and phone numbers appeared on the left side, and very suggestive photos with names and phone numbers were on the right. Shoving the screen in front of Sandy's face, he asked her if she recognized Erik's ads. She looked at them and nodded.

"Which ones?"

Sandy glanced over at her husband again, who still had his head back with his eyes shut. "He made me do this," she said in a low voice. "I never would've done this to Chelsea or any woman, but he threatened and beat me. He got me hooked on coke. I love Chelsea. I never would've done this to her. I swear."

"I'm not gonna repeat myself again. Which ones?"

"You'll let me go, right? I mean, I'm cooperating with you. I didn't argue or anything. Not like Dave did. I swear he forced me. Bobby and Erik threatened to kill me if I didn't do what they wanted. Erik had seen Chelsea at a high school basketball game. She was a cheerleader, and he wanted her real bad. He told Tyler to make a play for her. He did." Sandy kept rambling on, "Did you know that was the only reason he went out with her? He knew what was going to happen to her. I had no choice."

Paco grabbed her hair and pulled it hard, making her cry out. He slammed the tablet into her face. "I told you I don't like repeating myself."

"Okay… okay," she sniveled. "The sixth one down on the page. The one that says, 'Ready to play… are you? Looking for the girl next door?' That's his ad. And the next two under it."

Paco looked at the ad and saw the woman's age listed at twenty-three. He looked at her pictures and shook his head. "She's not more than fifteen or sixteen," he gritted, showing the screen to Chains and Army. They grumbled in agreement.

"That's fucked," Sniper said as he came over to take a look. "You want us to take care of these two?"

"No! Please. I helped you out. You promised."

"I didn't promise shit!" Paco yelled as he walked toward the stairs.

"Show some mercy. Please," she sobbed.

Paco turned around and in four long strides he was back in front of her. Again, he yanked her head back by her hair and leaned over real close. "I'll show you the same fucking mercy you showed Chelsea. She was your blood for fuck's sake! How the hell do you do that to your family? She loved and trusted you. You're nothing but a selfish, cold-hearted cunt." He kicked the chair out from under her and she toppled onto the concrete floor, the metal legs crashing down on her.

"Gut them like the pigs they are," he said as he left the room. Army followed after him as Paco ascended the stairs.

"You want me to go with you when you snuff out this fucker?"

"Yeah. I want to make sure he gets what's coming to him. I'll give him a call and tell him we want two girls for us. Let's buy a burner phone and get this shit over with."

On the way back from the store, Army opened up the box and took out the phone. "Is Chelsea coming back with us?"

Paco gripped the steering wheel, his gaze fixed on the road. "No."

"Really? I thought you guys had something going there."

"Her life was interrupted. She needs to find out who she is."

"She seemed like she had her head on straight. Are you sure you're not going to regret this?"

I already do. "I'm doing this for her. Did you get the phone to work?"

"Yeah."

"Then call the asshole and make the arrangements for tonight. Tell him we want three hours with the women at a motel."

"Here we go," Army said, tapping in the number then bringing the phone to his ear.

The Ambassador Motel sat off the freeway and was one of several motels that lined the frontage road. Paco and Army had arrived a few hours before and sat across the street waiting for Erik to show up with the two girls. They didn't want to take any chances with the security cameras, so they parked the car by the curb. At nine thirty, a yellow mustang rolled into the lot and parked in front of the third building. A stocky man of medium height got out of the car then pulled two women out. One of them looked like she was resisting him, and Paco saw him backhand her before pulling her hair and dragging her to the metal stairs. The three of them disappeared into one of the rooms. It was torture for Paco to sit and wait in the car before confronting Erik, but he knew if he let his emotions get the better of him, costly mistakes could very well be made.

A little before ten o'clock, he and Army got out of the car, pulled their hoodies down low over their faces, crossed the street, and walked upstairs. They knocked on the door, and a deep voice told them to come in.

When they entered the room, the same stocky man they'd seen earlier stood near the dresser, a black briefcase in his hand. A blonde girl of about fifteen, dressed in skimpy lingerie, sat in one of the chairs next to the window while another blonde of about the same age, wearing a skirt that showed the underside of her butt cheeks and a too small top, sat on the bed. Both girls had their eyes cast downward.

He glanced quickly at their gloved hands then took a step back. "Gentlemen. This is Sasha"—he pointed to the teen in the chair, then directed their attention to the girl on the bed—"and this is Gemini." He snapped open the briefcase and took out a ledger. "You want three hours of … anything goes … with the two women. That'll cost you three hundred sixty dollars. Credit card?"

"Cash," Paco said.

A broad smile spread over his face. "Even better." As he took out a receipt book, Paco pictured a terrified Chelsea cowering in the corner as the dirtbag in front of her beat her. Rage seared his nerves, and he clenched his fists and took a couple of steps toward him.

"Have the chicks take a shower," Army said.

Erik looked up, surprise etched on his face. "They're clean. I made sure they took one before they came."

"If they don't do it, the deal's off." Army crossed his arms and his biceps bulged.

Erik shook his head. "You're the customers. If you want them to take a shower, they can." He turned to them. "Get in the shower. Now." Fear laced the girls' eyes as they hurried into the bathroom, never once looking at Paco or Army. "Once you pay, I'll leave you alone with your dates."

"Only a pussy forces a girl to have sex for money," Army said.

Erik closed the briefcase and his hand began to slip inside his leather jacket. Paco jumped forward and grabbed his hand, bending it back until the sex trafficker cried out. "Don't even think it, fucker. Go ahead and hit me, or do you just like hitting women?"

"Are you guys cops?"

"You're gonna wish we were." Paco slammed his fist full force into his face. Erik cried out. "That's for the two women in the bathroom." Paco jerked his head toward the TV and Army switched it on, turning the volume up. Paco bent Erik's head down then brought his knee up, smashing Erik's face.

The man groaned. "Do you want money? Take it."

"I want retribution for what you did to Chelsea and all the other women, you sick motherfucker." Another punch, that time to the belly.

"I don't even know a Chelsea. This is a misunderstanding," he sputtered.

"Misty, you asshole. You fucking stole her dignity! You forced her to do things she *did* not want to do—fucked up things that she was scared, ashamed, and appalled to be doing. You made her live in hell twenty-four seven. You fucking raped her!"

Army and Paco jumped on him like animals attacking prey. Paco hit his head into the wall so hard the cheap paintings shook. They pulverized him, leaving him in a heap on the beige carpet in his own blood and excrement.

Paco went over to the bathroom door and knocked softly. There was no answer. He knocked again. "Open up. We're not gonna hurt you," he said. Once again, he pulled the hoodie low over his head, shadowing his face. Army had done the same and walked over to switch off all the lights but one dim lamp.

The door slowly opened, and the two girls glanced over to Erik's body then back to him. "Please don't hurt us. He forced us to be here. We just want to go home." Sasha's voice hitched.

Paco handed them two hundred dollars each. "Go call your families and get out of here." The women opened the closet, grabbed their jackets, and dashed out of the room. "Let's get the fuck outta here."

Paco and Army left the room and crossed the street to their waiting SUV. They drove in silence until they reached the Twisted Warrior's clubhouse. Chains, Sniper, and Jacko were waiting out front. Chains slipped into the back seat, and Sniper and Jacko came over to the driver's side.

Paco bumped fists with them. "Thanks for your help. Whenever you're in Alina, you've got a place to crash. If you have trouble with all this, let me know."

"There won't be any trouble. Everything's been taken care of. Have a safe ride back, and we'll see you at Sturgis this summer."

"Fuck, yeah," Chains said.

"Can't wait for August to get here," Army added.

"It's time to get home. See you at Sturgis," Paco said, putting the car in Drive.

As he left the city limits, emptiness filled him but he pushed it down. Chelsea's captivating eyes invaded his mind, her soft laughter filled his ears, her quiet strength pulled at his heart, and he almost turned around. But he didn't.

He merged onto the highway and headed back to Alina, leaving his heart in Findlay.

Chapter Twenty-Nine

WHEN THEY ENTERED the Night Rebels' clubhouse, Lucy rushed over and gave Paco a big hug. The look in her eyes showed just how glad she was that Chelsea wasn't among the trio. Paco gently pushed her away, went up to the bar and downed the shot of whiskey Rusty had waiting for him.

Lucy stood next to him, her gaze on his. "Your friend didn't come back with you?"

Paco motioned for another shot. "No."

"I guess it makes sense that she'd want to stay in her home town and be with her family."

"Yeah." He threw back the second shot then picked up his bag.

"You're not disappearing so soon, are you? I thought we could talk, or I can give you a nice massage. I bet your shoulders and back are sore from the long drive."

Smiling weakly, he shook his head. "I'm good. Army's always in the mood for a massage. I'm beat." He ignored Lucy's crestfallen face and trudged up the stairs to his room.

The whole ride back, Chelsea filled his mind, and he kept wrestling with his decision to leave without her. He went over to the window and opened the blinds and stared at the bluish-tinted mountains in the distance. All of a sudden, he was back in the train car with Chelsea, winding through the snowy canyon. *That was an awesome day.* Then the images of the two of them riding his Harley, dining at Flanigan's, talking in his room—along with a myriad of other snippets of time they shared together, filled his mind. *All the time we spent together was awesome. Fuck, babe. I miss you.*

Turning away from the window, he went over to the dresser and opened the bottom drawer. Moving aside some clothing, he pulled out the padded envelope that held past memories. He'd been surprised when Chelsea had told him that she read the letters Cassie had sent him so many years before. He dumped the contents of the envelope on the desk and sifted through them. Photographs of his mother with him and Kendra made his insides tighten; he was transported back in time to when his mother was alive and life had seemed perfect. "You didn't deserve what the fucker did to you, Mom," he muttered under his breath. For as long as he lived, he'd never be able to forgive his dad for taking the life of such a beautiful, loving, and vibrant woman. When he really wanted to drive himself crazy, he'd think about how his mother must have felt knowing that the man she loved and promised her future to, was stabbing the life out of her. "The fear must have been incredible, but it was the betrayal that must have hit you the hardest, Mom."

He sighed as he put the photographs down, and his gaze landed on a pink envelope with blue writing—the *Dear John* letter. He took it out and skimmed it, remembering how his insides had turned to ice when he read her letter explaining how she no longer loved him. Her words had been a double whammy: not only had he felt abandoned, but he had also been replaced. Amid the stifling heat, the bombs, the boredom, and the awfulness of war, he'd been stuck with the harrowing and lonely feeling of knowing that the woman he loved was loving another.

Paco leaned back in the chair and closed his eyes, the ghosts of the past flitting through his brain. Since Cassie had smashed his heart, he'd been more than careful to let any feelings of love into his life. Over the years, he'd blamed her for his bitterness, but now he wasn't so sure it was all her fault. When he'd been in Afghanistan, getting killed was a daily concern, and he didn't want to bring the war to Cassie, so he'd made the decision not to share his "adventures" with her. She accused him many times of being lousy at communicating. She told him she wanted to hear about everything—the good and the bad, but the time he'd spent writing to her and thinking about her was his refuge amid the loss and destruction all around him. "You never understood that," he said aloud. *How the fuck could I explain to her that I'd just spent the night sitting in a bomb crater, ducking AK rounds, or that I just killed a pack of kids who had bombs strapped to them, courtesy of their fucking mothers?* So he'd shut her out. He kept the day-to-day existence at bay, and in doing that, he'd put a distance between them. Because he wanted to spare her from worrying, he ended up losing her. *If I'd been more open, maybe she wouldn't have felt so disconnected. But if we stayed together, I never would've met Chelsea.*

The love he had for Chelsea was off the fucking charts, and it made him realize that Cassie had never been *the one*. With Cassie, he'd never felt the deep connection he had with Chelsea. She was the person he lost track of time with, the one he confided in, and the one he missed after saying goodbye. She'd slipped into his life quietly on a rainy night, and a series of events kept bringing them together. Each moment he shared with her chipped away at the shield around his heart, letting new light in until he fell completely in love with her.

The tune on his phone rang out, echoing in the quiet room. He glanced at the screen and put his phone to his ear.

"Hey, Kendra. How's the little man?"

A small giggle. "Tommy's doing great. Vicky just left, so I'll be flying solo."

"I told you to move to Alina, then I could help you out and so could the old ladies. Besides, I know a lot of people with daughters who could also lend you a hand."

"I'm seriously thinking about it. I spoke to Jesse yesterday by Skype and told him I missed having you around, so he suggested I move there. He also mentioned that once his contract is up in five years, he wasn't going to reenlist. He wants to start a business in Alina or in one of the neighboring towns."

Warmth spread through him. "Is this for real, or are you just talking out of your ass?"

"This is for real. I've really missed you. We've been apart for too long, and the boys adore you. Anyway, I want to meet the woman who's captured your heart so I can give her a big hug."

"What're you talking about?"

"Don't play dumb with me. The last few times we spoke, I knew something was different with you, but I never imagined it was a woman. When Goldie and Cueball stopped by over the weekend, Goldie let it slip out that you were interested in a woman."

Paco shook his head. *That fucking blabbermouth.* "Chelsea's cool. I met her when her life was in transition."

"You're talking like it's over."

"She's back home… in Ohio. She's got a lot going on. How much did Goldie tell you about her?"

"Nothing about her per se. He just said you had a woman in your life, and he never thought he'd see the day when you'd be hooked on someone. I have to agree with him. Is she coming back to Alina?"

"I don't know. It's kinda complicated. That's great news about you moving here. When you're ready, I'll get some brothers to come with me to help you out. How much time do you have left on your lease?"

"You're changing the subject, and I know when *you* don't want to talk about something, it's *not* going to happen. I just want to say one last thing about Chelsea. Don't let her get away from you. When you find happiness and true love, you have to go after it at all costs. That's all I'm going to say about it. I have two months left on the lease, so I was thinking to give notice at the end of the month."

"That's fucking awesome. It'll rock to have you and the kids living here. If you want me to check out any places for you, say the word."

"I will."

"And if you want to come sooner, break the lease and I'll pay for the two months you have left."

"You're too good to me."

"You're my sister. We only have each other."

"You're the best brother. I may take you up on that offer." A loud cry in the background. "I have to run. Tommy just woke up. We'll talk soon. Love you."

"Later."

He put the phone down, a huge grin spreading over his face. Having Kendra and his nephews in Alina was something he'd wanted for a long time. Since Jesse was away so much, Paco didn't feel comfortable with his sister living alone. Now, with her and the boys nearby, he'd be able to make sure they were safe, and he'd be able to spend more time with all of them.

The letters, notecards, birthday cards, and photographs were spread over his desk. He took out all pictures of his mom, his sister, and of him alone, then put all the photos of Cassie back into the envelope along with the letters and other writings. He picked up the envelope, shrugged on his leather jacket and left the room.

Pink, orange, and mauve streaks painted the sky as a few stars twinkled against the impending darkness to the east. His boots crunched under the frost covered ground as he made his way to the ash pit in the backyard. The chilled wind tugged at his open jacket and whipped loose hairs about his face. He threw the envelope into the pit then doused it with lighter fluid. Cupping his hand around a match, he struck it repeatedly until it lit then threw it on top of the envelope. A bluish-orange flame shot up, and he took a step back. Tiny black cinders danced above the flames as he watched his anger and bitterness burn away alongside the memories of Cassie.

After all this time, it's finally over.

He turned away and sauntered back to the clubhouse.

Chapter Thirty

Six weeks later

CHELSEA WAITED UNTIL the garage door closed all the way before she got out of the car. Since her ordeal, she hated being exposed to any open spaces where someone could sneak in and attack her, especially at night. Her therapist had told her that the nightmares and paranoid feelings would dissipate in time, and she already felt better since she'd started intensive therapy three times a week.

Her schedule was full with therapy, GED classes, and her job at Street's Hope, helping other women and children who were the victims of sex trafficking. At first she didn't think she could do it, but she found that the women there helped her as much as she helped them.

Chelsea still felt out of sorts at home even though her mother and Peter tried to treat her as if nothing had happened. When she'd told her mother about Aunt Sandy and Uncle Dave, she refused to believe that her beloved sister had done such a horrendous thing to Chelsea, so she put all the blame on Dave. Her mom blamed him for getting Sandy into drugs, putting them into horrible debt, and forcing her sister to go along with him in selling Chelsea. It was incredible that her mom couldn't see the truth, but Chelsea supposed her mother needed to believe that Sandy was also a victim and that Dave was the master manipulator in order to keep her life in balance.

However, Chelsea knew the truth, and when the police had come over to question her, she hadn't been surprised that Sandy and Dave had sold at least four other women over the years. The police had found a lot of incriminating evidence when they'd conducted a search of their home.

It seemed that Aunt Sandy and Uncle Dave had disappeared. The police thought they may have changed their identities and slipped into Canada or Mexico. Her mom thought they went to Australia since Sandy had always wanted to go there, but Chelsea suspected that Paco and his buddies had made sure they'd never destroy another person's life again. She really didn't want to think too much about it; she was just happy that she'd never have to see them again.

Being away from Paco got harder as time went on. Sometimes, she thought her heart would literally break from sadness or her eyes would run out of tears. She missed him terribly and loved him more than ever. Each time they spoke on the phone, he'd tell her that he loved her, but he never asked her to come back to Alina. Whenever their call would end, loneliness filled her, and the ache of him not wanting her was unbearable at times.

She walked into the kitchen, grabbed an apple from the fruit bowl and an iced tea from the fridge, and then headed up to her room to start her online class. She hoped to take the GED test at the end of the next month. After changing into sweats and a fleece top, she settled down on the desk chair and switched on the computer. Thirty minutes into her class, her phone rang and an adrenaline rush flooded her body when she saw Paco's name on the screen.

"Hi, Paco," she said, propping her elbows on the desk.

"Hey, babe. Whatcha doing?"

"Studying."

"How was work?"

"Good. I've been working on getting sponsors to donate money so the women can go to tattoo parlors and have their branding removed. I remember how liberating it felt when you made that happen for me." She took a large gulp of iced tea. "I miss you so much. Sometimes, I think I'll go crazy if I spend another day, another minute, or another second without you."

A long pause. "I feel the same way. You've gotten into my blood, and my heart and soul, woman."

She wanted to scream out, "Then why are we apart?" but she knew that he'd been right about giving her some space to get her life back on track. In her mind, the GED represented a huge milestone because once she had it, she could apply to colleges and jobs. *Passing the test and therapy are the necessary steps I have to take in order to make my life more normal.*

"Did your sister move to Alina?"

"Yeah. A bunch of the brothers and I helped her move a few days ago. She's already settling in real good, and I'm enjoying being a full time uncle." He chuckled.

His voice washed over her and inside her, sending shivers along her spine. *How I miss him!* "That's good. Are you still going to club parties?" *Are you fucking anyone? I can't ask him that, but I want to know. I need to know. Each time we talk, I want to ask him.*

"It's all the same—like it's been for years. What about you? Last time we talked you said you were thinking about going out with your friends. Have you gone out with them?"

"A couple of times. It wasn't that much fun. All my old friends treat me like I'm some attraction at a freak show, and I'm so busy right now that I don't have much time to make any new friends. It's okay, but I wish I was with you."

A long sigh. "Me too. I miss your kisses, your soft skin, and the way we fuck."

"This totally sucks. Are you with anybody?" *I couldn't help it. I have to know.*

"Yeah—you. If you're asking if I'm fucking anyone, the answer is no. I hope it's the same for you."

"It totally is. I don't want anyone but you. I love you. Nothing has changed."

"Not for me either."

A soft rap on the door made her jump. "Hang on," she said to Paco as she padded over and opened it. Her mother smiled at her. "Hey, Mom."

"I just came up to tell you dinner is ready. I picked something up from Luigi's."

She pointed to her phone. "I'll be down in a sec."

"Okay. Don't be too long or the food will be cold." Her mother turned away and walked down the hall.

"Sorry about that," she said as she stood by the window watching the snowflakes twirl and spin in the evening air.

"No worries. I'll let you have your dinner. I gotta get over to Kendra's. I promised to take her and the boys to Woodhouse Pizza."

"I wish I was with you," she whispered.

"Me too. I love you, babe."

"I love you. Bye."

Emptiness filled all the nooks and crannies inside her, shutting out the light, pushing her down, choking her. She turned off the computer, switched off the lamp, and lay on the bed, tugging the covers over her head. Shrouded in silence and darkness, she let the memories of Paco fill her mind and ease her pain.

I miss you too much. If you asked me to come back, I'd be there in a heartbeat. Oh… Paco.

Chapter Thirty-One

Two months later

EVER SINCE CHELSEA had received notification that she'd passed the GED test, she'd been walking on air. She pulled into the driveway and turned off the engine, smiling when she looked at all the shopping bags sprawled out in the back seat. As a gift, her mom and Peter gave her five hundred dollars to spend however she liked. At first, she thought about saving it for a car, but she'd decided that morning to go on a shopping spree at the mall.

As she bent over to collect her bags, a crunch on the gravel behind her made her stop. Her senses went into high alert, her heart raced, and the hair on her nape lifted. *Someone's behind me. What am I going to do? Think!*

"Need some help with that?" a deep voice said.

She cried out and bumped her head on the car door's frame as she tried to spin around.

"I didn't mean to scare you."

That voice. It's Paco! She dropped the bags from her hands and turned around. Paco, dressed in black jeans, a T-shirt, and leather jacket, stood behind her. She flung herself into his open arms. "How… what are you doing here?"

Bringing his hand to her chin, he tilted her face upwards and looked into her eyes. Then he lowered his head and kissed her hard, deep, and hungry, sucking her bottom lip, then nibbling it. As he continued to kiss her, her pulse raced, her skin tingled, and she sagged in his strong arms that kept her from falling. She savored his warmth and proximity; safe in his arms, nothing could hurt her.

"I missed you so much," he whispered into her soft skin before returning to her lips. His hard dick pressed against her belly as his hand slid under her sweater and cupped her breast.

Paco's scent—fresh air, leather, and myrrh, swirled around her in a heady combination of love and lust. Desire surged through her as a dull ache between her thighs pulsed.

"I can't believe you're here. I've dreamt of this moment for so long," she whispered against his lips.

"Me too, baby," he said, his tone deep with arousal as his hands ran up and down her back.

"How long are you staying?" she rasped as she rubbed against his hardness.

"Just until you pack and get things in order." His lips trailed down her neck.

She drew back. "What do you mean?"

Gathering her in his arms again, he nuzzled her neck. "I can't live without you so I came to take you back with me. I'm addicted to everything about you, baby. I crave your sweetness, your laugh, your warm body next to mine. You're the fucking blood in my veins." He bent down and crushed his lips against hers.

A million butterflies fluttered inside of her as she sank into his embrace. *He came for me.* All she wanted was to freeze time and stay forever in his arms, clinging to him, kissing him deeply.

"You're so beautiful," he murmured. For the first time in years, she believed she was.

The sound of the garage door opening cut through their sexual fog as he drew back slightly, looking over his shoulder. Her mother's car pulled into the garage, and Chelsea grasped Paco's hand and tugged him beside her.

"Paco. What a pleasant surprise," Linda said as she got out of the car. She went around back and opened the hatch where bags of groceries filled the space.

"Hey. Let me help you with those," he said, rushing over to take the bags from her hands.

"Did you know he was coming?" she asked Chelsea.

"No. I was shocked … but in a great way." She took out a couple of bags and followed her mother into the kitchen.

"I thought I'd come by and congratulate Chelsea on getting her GED." Paco placed the sacks on the island. "I also came to take her back to Alina with me."

Her mother placed three cans of beans in the pantry, and from the way her eyebrows furrowed, Chelsea knew she wasn't pleased by what Paco had said.

He looked fixedly at her. "I love Chelsea and she loves me. I want her with me, and I'm pretty sure she feels the same way. I gave her some space, but now it's time for my woman to be with me."

"Chelsea?" Linda stared at her.

"I love being home with you, Mom, but I was ready to leave with Paco three months ago. He was the one who told me to enjoy more time with you and to concentrate on myself as well, and he was right. I got my GED, I've been in therapy, and I've been working—but none of it means anything if I can't share it with Paco. I love him. When I'm with him, it feels like I'm with someone I've known my whole life, someone who sees me for who I am and loves me for the things I don't even love about myself."

"We love you, honey. You must know that." Linda wrung her hands.

"I do, and I love you, but it's not the same. I don't feel like I fit in. People stare at me like I'm a freak, and you, Kate, Peter, and Grandma act like nothing has happened to me … and so much has. I'm not the same person I once was, Mom."

"I hate that the news on TV showed so much coverage on your kidnapping and escape, and that you lost your sense of privacy with all the fanfare that surrounded it, but you'll always be the same person to me."

Chelsea went over and hugged her mother. "I need to move on with my life. I'm not fifteen anymore, and so much has happened to me. Paco met me when I was at my lowest, and he still reached out to me and gave me his heart."

"What if it doesn't work out?"

"What if what doesn't work out?" Peter asked, coming into the kitchen.

Chelsea groaned inwardly. The last thing she wanted was for Peter to throw his two cents in.

"Paco has come to take Chelsea with him to Alina, and she wants to go."

Peter narrowed his gaze, highlighting the nets of wrinkles at the corners of his eyes. "What the hell are you thinking? What do you have to offer her?"

Linda came over to Peter and leaned against him. "He's right. Chelsea wants to go to college."

Paco gripped Chelsea's arm and drew her to him. "I love your daughter."

Peter shook his head and exhaled loudly. "That's it?"

"I'll always have her back," Paco draped his arm around her shoulder.

"What the fuck does that mean?" Peter said.

"Everything."

Chelsea felt Paco stiffen next to her. The last thing she wanted was a big blowup between him and Peter, and from the way they were both glaring at each other, it seemed like it was inevitable. She cleared her throat. "I love Paco very much. I can still go to college and be with him."

"I don't know, honey. You've just been home for such a short time. Again, what if it doesn't work out?" her mother replied.

Paco held her tighter. "It will. I promise to take good care of your daughter. She trusts me with her forever, and, as I said, I'll always have her back. *Always.*"

"Aren't you in a motorcycle gang? We don't really know you. She's been through enough heartache and disappointment. I don't think it's a good idea," Peter said.

"I would never hurt Chelsea. And I'm not in a gang—I'm in a club. Chelsea is old enough to decide what she wants to do."

"She hasn't grown up normally, so I don't think she's capable of making this type of decision," Peter said.

From the way Paco clenched his jaw, Chelsea knew he was holding his anger at bay. She pulled away from him slightly. "I'm capable of a lot of things. You have no idea what I went through, yet I survived. I've decided to go back with Paco and, as far as I'm concerned, the discussion is closed on this subject. I'd love for you and Mom to visit us in Colorado. You guys have been talking about going there ever since you got married. The San Juan Mountains are spectacular, and we'd be more than happy to show you all around. Paco knows the area so well. Please be happy for me, Mom. I never thought I'd ever be happy… but then Paco happened."

Silence engulfed the kitchen, and after what seemed like hours, her mother nodded. "For the past three months, my heart broke whenever I saw the sadness in your eyes, and I knew it was because you missed Paco. I'm not going to tell you that I'm happy to lose you so soon after all the years you've been gone, but for the first time since he left, I see the light back in your eyes. I just hope you're not planning to leave tonight."

"This is fucking unbelievable! You've always given in to Chelsea, Linda." Peter stormed out of the kitchen, slamming the back door behind him.

Chelsea picked at her cuticles. "I'm sorry if I caused a problem between you and Peter."

Linda smiled weakly. "He'll be fine. You know his bark is worse than his bite. So are you leaving tonight?"

Paco shook his head. "We'll leave after Chelsea gets things in order with her job and makes sure everything is how she'd like it to be between all of you. It's up to her when we leave."

"I have to give two weeks notice at work, and I want to finish the quilt I'm making for your nephew. So, I suppose we can leave in two weeks." She brought his hand to her lips and kissed it then glanced back at her mother. "I want to take you, Kate, Peter, and Grandma out for dinner before we leave, Mom."

"Okay." Linda went over to Chelsea and pulled her into a loving embrace. "All I ever wanted for you and Kate was to be happy. When you disappeared I blamed myself for it."

"Mom, stop. You did nothing wrong. Things happen. I refuse to see myself as a victim. The important thing is that I'm beyond happy."

"Just plan on a visit from me and Peter real soon." She kissed her on the cheek while smoothing down her hair.

"I'm counting on it."

She helped her mother put away the rest of the groceries while Paco sat at the table and watched her. Each time she caught his gaze, her heart turned over. *I'm finally going home.*

One month later

CHELSEA RANG UP the last sale of the day, then went over to the front door and locked it. "We're officially closed," she said to Jillian.

"I'll be ready to go in a few minutes. I just want to freshen up."

Chelsea watched her disappear among the Army surplus items, leather jackets, and biker boots. She and Jillian were meeting Paco at Cuervos for dinner and drinks. Since she'd come back to Alina, she'd started working at Paco's surplus store. She and Jillian hit it off right away, and Chelsea was thrilled to have a good friend after so many years.

When the two entered Cuervos, her eyes caught Paco's and her stomach fluttered. He came over to her and kissed her deeply. "You look hot, babe," he said.

The rest of the night was spent eating, drinking, laughing, and dancing, not to mention fooling around in the back room down the hall where they kissed and groped each other. It was like Chelsea could never get enough of Paco. She was addicted to him and wouldn't have it any other way.

Later that night, as they lay together in bed in their new house, he played with her hair. "Did you have a good time tonight?"

"Yes, but then I always have a good time with you. I'm so happy now. Sometimes, I can't believe how I've come such a long way since that night you told me to get on the back of your bike and you rode me to freedom. You brought me back to life." She stroked the side of his face. "You make me feel safe and protected."

"Baby, you'll never be alone. I'll always have your back. You're a survivor, and I love that about you. A VP needs a strong, kickass old lady."

"I'm your old lady?"

"Yeah. Hang on." Paco jumped out of bed and walked over to his closet. She watched his toned, corded body as he moved. *He's simply magnificent.* He came back with a leather vest and handed it to her, then switched on the lamp. "Chelsea, will you be my old lady?"

The leather was soft and cool between her fingers. "Yes. I'd love to be your old lady." She ran her hand over the vest. "It's beautiful," she murmured and turned it around and read the white embroidery: "Property of Paco." She smiled. Normally, the "property of" phrase would've freaked her out, but she was stronger now, and she trusted Paco implicitly. For her, belonging to Paco meant a relationship full of trust, love, and understanding. They accepted each other for who they were—with their own limitations, demons, and all. Her heart belonged to him, and his did to her. They were the property of each other.

She leaned over and kissed him. "I love it. I can't wait to wear it."

"I like hearing that."

"I love you so much."

"I can't wait to see you wearing my cut and nothing else."

She chuckled as she stripped off her nightshirt and put on the cut. It felt soft against her skin. The lust in his eyes sent shivers down her spine.

"Get over here," he gritted.

She came over and he swung her on top of him, the cut falling open and exposing her breasts. He grabbed them and squeezed them hard. The sweet pain made her tingle and throb everywhere. She bent down low and kissed him while wiggling her butt over his hardening dick. With a wicked glint in her eye, she pulled up and opened the nightstand drawer, pulling out soft cuffs and a feather teaser.

A devilish grin spread across his face, and he grabbed her arms and pulled her down on him. "First we're gonna fuck, and then we're gonna make love."

She rubbed her nipples against his smooth chest. "I'm not going anywhere. I have all the time in the world."

She licked his lips, then trailed her tongue down his chin, past his Adam's apple, and around his nipples. With her heated gaze latched onto his, she slowly licked her way downward as anticipation in pleasing her man shivered through her.

My man. I like the sound of that.

Epilogue

One month later

THE WHISKEY SPILLED on the granite counter as Paco poured another shot for Sangre and Muerto.

"Sorry," Chelsea said, brushing past him. She grabbed two potholders and opened the top oven. Steam billowed out of it and the sweet and peppery scent of hot wings filled the kitchen. She placed the large sheet pan on the stovetop and opened the bottom oven. Garlic and onions mingled with the chile sauce of the buffalo wings as she pulled out a bubbling dish and placed it next to the wings.

Paco wiped down the counter. "Need some help, babe?"

She looked over her shoulder, her face flushed red from the heat. "I'm good. Just make sure there's room on the table for the wings and artichoke dip," she replied as she walked toward the dining room, the brown cast iron pot in her hands.

He shoved some casserole dishes and bowls aside, and she placed the dip on the table. "It smells real good," he said, drawing her close to him. "And so do you." He nuzzled her neck. She laughed and smacked his arm lightly with the potholder.

"Can I have some of these wings on the stove?" Goldie asked.

Chelsea pulled away from Paco and ambled into the kitchen. "Go ahead and take some. I'll put the rest in a bowl and put it on the buffet table."

"Let me help you," Breanna said, coming into the room.

Chelsea handed her a platter of deviled eggs. "You can put that on the table. I want to thank you again for recommending Dr. Jagow. She's the best. I feel so comfortable with her, and I actually look forward to our sessions."

Breanna beamed as she took the platter from her and headed to the buffet table. "I'm happy it's working out. I thought it would be a good fit." She placed the deviled eggs down and picked up a slice of French bread, spreading dip on it then taking a bite. "You have to give me the recipe for your artichoke dip. It's so good."

"It's my grandma's recipe. I'll e-mail it to you."

Paco smiled as he listened to Chelsea and Breanna, happy that she'd found friendship among the old ladies. Since she'd been back in Alina, she'd blossomed, and her confidence and independence had grown so much. He loved that she had girlfriends who accepted her without judgment.

"Your house looks real good," Steel said as he came up to Paco. "Are you finished remodeling?"

"Yeah… finally. Talk about a pain in the ass. It would've been easier if we would've just built the damn house from the ground up. Chelsea kept changing her mind on what she wanted, it was driving me fucking nuts."

Steel nodded and brought his beer to his lips. After taking a drink, he looked around the room. "Your woman makes a nice home for you, and she can fucking cook."

Pride surged through him at Steel's words. "Chelsea's awesome, that's for sure."

"Are you taking her to Sturgis this year?"

"Who's going to Sturgis?" Army asked as he came over with Shotgun and Cueball.

"Chelsea and I. She can't wait to see what it's all about. And she's chomping at the bit to ride all the way to South Dakota. She loves riding on my Harley." He chuckled. "She's definitely the right woman for me."

Sangre walked over, a plate of food in his hand. "I can't wait for the summer. It means a ton of riding well into the fall."

"How's your security business going?" Cueball asked as he picked up a buffalo wing.

"Good. I signed several contracts over the last week."

"Do you want me to fix you a plate?" Chelsea asked, looping her arm around Paco's waist.

"I'd love to eat you," he whispered into her ear.

"You're so bad,—" she said softly. "—and that's one of many things I love about you."

Tilting her chin back, he kissed her gently on the lips. "I can't wait for everyone to leave," he said against her mouth.

"Chelsea," Breanna said, putting a large bowl of potato salad on the table. "How's it working out with your classes?"

"Great." She drew back from Paco then ambled over to Breanna. Chelsea was studying online for her bachelor's in sociology; she wanted to become a counselor.

She came back over to Paco and handed him a plate filled with a sampling of everything. Laughing and talking with Breanna, she made her way to the large family room and sat down next to Kendra.

"We're having such a wonderful time," Chelsea's mother said to him as she went over to the buffet table. "You've been a wonderful tour guide during our stay."

Paco lifted his chin, a smile twitching on his lips. Linda and Peter had been in Alina for the past ten days and they were leaving the following day to explore the Rocky Mountains and Grand Lake in the western part of the state. Chelsea had been more than ecstatic when her mother told her they were coming for a visit. At first, Paco had dreaded the visit, knowing that Peter would most probably piss him off, but since Chelsea's stepdad had given up drinking, he was a much nicer person, and Linda seemed much more relaxed.

"It's been wonderful seeing Chelsea. I love seeing her so happy." Linda put her hand on his forearm. "Thank you for making her shine. I'm no longer worried about her. I can see that she has everything she needs with you."

Paco glanced at Chelsea who was holding Tommy close to her. "You raised a strong, kickass woman. We both have everything we need in each other." He slugged down his shot of Jack, sucking his teeth as it burned into his system.

"Hey, dude. What is it with women and babies? I mean your nephew has all the women around him and we're standing here like we're at a damn stag party," Army said before he shoved a bacon wrapped scallop in his mouth.

Paco laughed. "I gotta admit we can never beat that type of competition."

"Even the club girls were all around him when you brought him by last week. Fuck."

As the party went on, Paco leaned against the kitchen counter watching all the guests as they mingled, ate, and drank, and then his gaze focused on Chelsea. He watched her as she held Tommy in outstretched arms, making faces at him as the rest of the room chuckled. A tingling warmth coursed through him, and as he watched her, he longed for her. Her lazy smiles and the way her nose crinkled when she concentrated were some of the things he loved about her. And… her eyes. *Fuck.* They had pulled him in, but who she was had captured his heart. *As long as I breathe, baby, I'll be yours in mind, body, and soul.*

Chelsea handed Tommy back to Kendra and walked over to Paco. "What are you doing all alone over here? Don't you want to come join the party?" she asked, standing close to him.

Heat radiated from her, and the scent of pralines and honeysuckle wafting around him had him simmering for her touch. "I love you so much," he rasped into her hair.

She wrapped her arms around his neck and tugged his head down. "I love you, too." Her lips met his and she kissed him passionately as she pressed closer to him.

"Fuck, baby. I need you in the worst damn way."

"Maybe we can sneak off for a quickie," she whispered.

He laughed and hugged her tighter. "As tempting as that sounds, I want to take my time with you. I want to savor each inch of your luscious body."

"I don't mean to break in on your fun, but Raven and I are gonna take off," Muerto said.

Chelsea drew back and turned toward him, smiling. "Thanks for coming by. Raven said that next week you're having a potluck. Count us in."

"Are we?" he asked as he glanced over at Raven, who winked at him.

"That's what she said," Chelsea answered.

"I never know what the fuck's going on until someone tells me. Raven still thinks she's flying solo." He laughed and motioned for her to come over.

Raven slipped into his arms and gave him a quick kiss on his mouth. "Ready to go?"

"Yeah. I didn't know we were having a get together next week." He smacked her butt lightly.

Desire laced through her eyes. "Yeah… I forgot to tell you. Oops."

"Bad girl," he said thickly. Turning to Paco, he bumped his fist against his. "Later, bro."

"Thanks for a wonderful party," Raven said. "We're going to have to go out to lunch soon. I know you're swamped with your classes and volunteering at the teen shelter, but maybe we can do it on a Saturday. Fallon, Hailey, and Breanna want to go too."

"Next Saturday works for me," Chelsea replied.

"Really? Great. Let's do it. I'll tell the others. Are you game for Mexican? I love Alfonso's. They have the best shrimp and enchiladas in town."

"Paco and I love that place. What time?"

"One o'clock?"

"Perfect." Chelsea, grasping Paco's hand, walked Raven and Muerto to the door.

Soon all the guest started leaving, and Paco rounded up Matt and Diego as Kendra gathered the toys she'd brought. She slung the large tote over her shoulder and took Tommy from Chelsea. "Thanks so much for a lovely party."

Chelsea beamed and hugged her quickly. "You're welcome. I love having you and the kids over. Do you want to join me and the other old ladies for lunch next Saturday? Paco can babysit."

"What the fuck are you getting me into, woman?" Paco pretended to be pissed but the smile twitching on his lips gave him away. Chelsea laughed.

Kendra glanced at him. "Are you sure you'd be good with that? I'd love to go with the women and be kid-free for a bit."

"As long as you're good with the boys hanging at the club," Paco said as he walked Kendra to her car.

"I'm okay with that as long as there's no nasty stuff going on or super drunk guys around."

He shook his head. "Give me some fucking credit. I'll make sure that while Matt, Diego, and Tommy are there, it's like a church's community center on a Sunday." He bent down and kissed her cheek, ran his fingers over Tommy's soft hair, and hugged his other two nephews. "Drive safely and text me when you get home." He helped her settle in the boys then closed the car door. He watched the car until it turned the corner.

When he came back in, Chelsea and her mother were laughing and talking as they cleaned up.

"I'm going upstairs," he said to Chelsea.

After a half hour, she came into their bedroom, smiling at him. With the back of her hand, she brushed off stray wisps of hair stuck on her forehead. "I'm going to freshen up," she said as she went into the bathroom. A few minutes later, the sound of running water filtered into the bedroom.

Leaning against the headboard, his hands behind his head, an image of Chelsea's body wet, naked, and glistening filled his mind. He pictured her hands gliding over her soap slick breasts, sliding down further to wash the sweet parts that always made him crazy with desire. *Dammit!* His dick was hard enough to pound nails. "Fuck this," he growled under his breath as he threw off the sheets and stood up. He wanted nothing more than to step into that shower, wrap his arms around her and yank her sleek, naked body to his. Before he crossed the room, the bathroom door opened and Chelsea came out, steam curling out around her. Her gaze fell on his erection and a devilish smile tugged at her lips as she shrugged off the bathrobe. Sucking in his breath, his gaze took in her pink, freshly scrubbed skin, drops of water trickling down her body, and her hardened nipples. Arousal clawed at him and he gripped her upper arms and jerked her toward him. The subtle scent of her shower gel and the rich nutty scent of her arousal flooded his senses, and he fisted her hair and yanked it. Small moans came from her throat, landing on his pulsing dick.

Tilting her head back, he crushed his lips against hers, dipping his tongue in and out of her mouth. She curled her arms around his neck and rubbed her pebbled nipples on his chest.

"Fuck, baby," he rasped, cupping her ass and squeezing it.

He gently pushed her backward to the bed, easing her down on it then hovering over her. She reached down and circled her fingers around his cock and a guttural groan erupted from his throat. Reaching down, he grabbed her wrists and pinned them above her head then lowered his and sucked her nipples hard. "You want it hard tonight?" he breathed as he lightly bit the delicate skin of her tits.

"Nipple clamps, restraints, and whatever else you want to do to me," she said hoarsely as she writhed beneath him.

Desire and love shot through him, and he rolled off her and went over to a large hand painted trunk. Opening it, he took out a shimmering butt plug, restraints, clamps, and a purple feather teaser. When he walked back over to the bed, Chelsea still had her hands above her head, her inky eyes brimming with heated desire. *She looks beautiful.* Straddling her, he slowly slipped the cuffs on her hands then spread lube on his cock and nestled it between her tits, pressing them tight around him. As he teased her hard buds with his thumb, he slid between her tits, pushing so far that it hit her lips; each time he brushed her lips, she licked his cock's head, squirming and moaning beneath him.

"You look so fucking hot," he said, thrusting his hips as he moved between her breasts.

"It feels so good. Don't stop. Go harder," she said raggedly.

"We've got all night, baby." Winking, he bent down and sucked her bottom lip into his mouth.

A few hours later, they lay tangled together, sated and spent. He ran his fingers lightly over her shoulder, loving the way her skin pebbled under his touch.

"That was awesome," she murmured.

"Yeah. You ignite the fire deep in my darkness, baby." He kissed the top of her head.

She snuggled closer to him.

Her breathing deepened and he rested his hand on her shoulder. *I can't imagine my life without her.* She was the half that made him whole. His demons played well with hers and together they made magic.

On a cold rainy night, his world had been turned upside down by a quiet but strong woman. Love had slipped into his life when he'd least expected. There wasn't any fanfare, just genuine respect and understanding that had blossomed until he couldn't live without her.

He inhaled deeply then closed his eyes.

Make sure you sign up for my newsletter so you can keep up with my new releases, special sales, free short stories, and other treats only available to newsletter readers. When you sign up, you will receive a FREE hot and steamy novella. Sign up at: http://eepurl.com/bACCL1.

Notes from Chiah

As always, I have a team behind me making sure I shine and continue on my writing journey. It is their support, encouragement, and dedication that pushes me further in my writing journey. And then, it is my wonderful readers who have supported me, laughed, cried, and understood how these outlaw men live and love in their dark and gritty world. Without you—the readers—an author's words are just letters on a page. The emotions you take away from the words breathe life into the story.

Thank you to my amazing Personal Assistant Natalie Weston. I don't know what I'd do without you. I value your suggestions and opinions, and my world is so much saner with you in it. You make sure my world flows more smoothly, and you're always willing to jump in and help me. I appreciate the time you took in reading and offering suggestions with the book and the cover. And a big thank you for watching out for me when I'm in writer mode and live life with blinders on. I'm thrilled you are on my team!

Thank you to my editor, Kristin, for all your insightful edits, excitement with my new series, Night Rebels MC, and encouragement during the writing and editing process. I truly value your editorial eyes and suggestions as well as the time you spend. You're the best!

Thank you to my editor, Lisa Cullian, for helping me out when I was in a jam. I appreciate you fitting me in and making my work shine. I couldn't have done it without you.

Thank you to my wonderful beta readers, Barbara Hoover, Crystal Earl, Rebecca Allman, and Jeni Yeager. Your enthusiasm and suggestions for PACO: Night Rebels MC were spot on and helped me to put out a stronger, cleaner novel. Your insights and attention to detail were awesome.

Thank you to the bloggers for your support in reading my book, sharing it, reviewing it, and getting my name out there. I so appreciate all your efforts. You all are so invaluable. I hope you know that. Without you, the indie author would be lost. And thank you to the bloggers who have been with me from my very first book, "Hawk's Property: Insurgents Motorcycle Club." Your continued support for my books is beyond awesome!

Thank you ARC readers you have helped make all my books so much stronger. I appreciate the effort and time you put in to reading, reviewing, and getting the word out about the books. I don't know what I'd do without you. I feel so lucky to have you behind me.

Thank you to my Street Team. Thanks for your input, your support, and your hard work. I appreciate you more than you know. A HUGE hug to all of you!

Thank you to Carrie from Cheeky Covers. You are amazing! I can always count on you. You are the calm to my storm. You totally rock, and I love your artistic vision.

Thank you to my proofreader, Rose, whose last set of eyes before the last once over I do, is invaluable. I appreciate the time and attention to detail you gave to my book.

Thank you to Ena and Amanda with Enticing Journeys Promotions who have helped garner attention for and visibility to the Night Rebels MC series. Couldn't do it without you! Also a big thank you to Book Club Gone Wrong Blog.

Thank you to the readers who continue to support me and read my books. Without you, none of this would be possible. I appreciate your comments and reviews on my books, and I'm dedicated to giving you the best story that I can. I'm always thrilled when you enjoy a book as much as I have in writing it. You definitely make the hours of typing on the computer and the frustrations that come with the territory of writing books so worth it.

And a special thanks to every reader who has been with me since "Hawk's Property." Your support, loyalty, and dedication to my stories touch me in so many ways. You enable me to tell my stories, and I am forever grateful to you.

You all make it possible for writers to write because without you reading the books, we wouldn't exist. Thank you, thank you! ♥

PACO: Night Rebels Motorcycle Club (Book 5)

Dear Readers,

Thank you for reading my book. I hope you enjoyed the second book in my new Night Rebels MC series as much as I enjoyed writing Paco and Chelsea's (Misty's) story. This gritty and rough motorcycle club has a lot more to say, so I hope you will look for the upcoming books in the series. Romance makes life so much more colorful, and a rough, sexy bad boy makes life a whole lot more interesting.

If you enjoyed the book, please consider leaving a review on Amazon. I read all of them and appreciate the time taken out of busy schedules to do that.

I love hearing from my fans, so if you have any comments or questions, please email me at chiahwilder@gmail.com or visit my facebook page.

To receive a **free copy of my novella**, *Summer Heat*, and to hear of **new releases**, **special sales**, **free short stories**, and **ARC opportunities**, please sign up for my **Newsletter** at http://eepurl.com/bACCL1.

Happy Reading,

Chiah

SANGRE
Book 6 in the Night Rebels MC Series
Coming April, 2018

When Sangre, the tatted and built officer of the Night Rebels MC, agrees to be the bodyguard of Isla Rose, he has no idea what he's in for. It's just an ordinary gig: a bodyguard for a temperamental, difficult, diva who thinks a fan is out to get her.

Sangre doesn't have time for drama and decides there's no way he's going to indulge the spoiled rock star. He'll do his job and be out of there. Does he believe her? Not really. In his opinion the whole crazed fan scare is a ploy to garner more attention in the papers. But he isn't there to analyze her, just play bodyguard until she goes back to LA.

But when he sees her on stage, the blue and red lights bouncing off her sequined jeans, he's mesmerized. Then she starts to sing and her voice intoxicates and captivates him. The sound of her voice is thick and sweet like warm honey dripping over him.

In that moment he realizes this isn't going to be any ordinary gig. He's definitely screwed.

As he watches her, something familiar pulls him in. Something from his past....

Isla Rose's life is spiraling out of control. She needs to relax and get away from all the hype.

So she runs away and finds a slice of peace in Alina, but it is short-lived. Creepy fan letters invade her peaceful oasis. At first she blows them off, but as they become more sinister, fear consumes her.

When she first lays eyes on her bodyguard, she can't help but notice his tanned, muscled arms covered with wicked tattoos. The way women flock to him tells her he's bad news.

A heartbreaker in a leather jacket.

She needs his protection and nothing more.

But she can't stop him from invading her thoughts. The way he looks at her, she knows he wants to take her body then her soul.

And she hates to admit it, but she wants to give him her all. To make matters worse, he reminds her of someone from her past. Someone she yearned for in silence. Maybe she's safer taking her chances with the creepy fan and forgetting all about the tattooed hunk who's turning her life upside down. And that's the last thing she needs right now.

This is the sixth book in the Night Rebels MC Romance series. This is Sangre's story. It is a standalone. This book contains violence, sexual assault (not graphic), strong language, and steamy/graphic sexual scenes. It describes the life and actions of an outlaw motorcycle club. If any of these issues offend you, please do not read the book. HEA. No cliffhangers! The book is intended for readers over the age of 18.

Wheelie's Challenge
Coming June 2018

A member of the Insurgents MC, Wheelie is a chick magnate. Having a ripped body, mesmerizing tats, and a boyish grin, he can have any woman he wants. Except for one: Sofia. Ever since he laid eyes on her, he was taken in by her sparkling eyes, her sweet laugh, and her pretty face.

There's just one very big problem: she belongs to another Insurgent.
He knows that means she's off-limits, but he can't get her out of his mind.
The memory of their kiss consumes him.
He now knows how soft and perfect she is.

Pursuing her will get him kicked out of the brotherhood, and the club is his life. He can't betray another brother even if he's a cruel, cocky jerk. He has to be strong, but the more time he spends with Sofia the more tempting it is to cross the line.

Sofia can't get the handsome biker out of her mind. Married to Tigger, she is unhappy and tired of his cruelty and manipulation. She longs to be in the strong arms of Wheelie, but she knows what the consequences are for him if they give in to their desire.

Tigger made Sofia his old lady years ago and she knows he will never let her go. If she ever leaves him, she has no doubt that he will kill her. He's told her that more times than she can count. Is she willing to risk her life and Wheelie's in order to be happy?

Wheelie's fortitude is waning, and he wants nothing more than to claim Sofia and make her his even if that means going against another brother. Will he be able to turn his back on the Insurgents MC without any regrets? Is he prepared to love and protect Sofia from the demons of her past and present? Will Tigger make sure Sofia and Wheelie never get their happily ever after?

The Insurgents MC series are standalone romance novels. This is Wheelie's story. This book contains violence, abuse, strong language, and steamy/graphic sexual scenes. It describes the life and actions of an outlaw motorcycle club. If any of these issues offend you, please do not read the book. HEA. No cliffhangers. The book is intended for readers over the age of 18.

Other Books by Chiah Wilder

Insurgent MC Series:

Hawk's Property
Jax's Dilemma
Chas's Fervor
Axe's Fall
Banger's Ride
Jerry's Passion
Throttle's Seduction
Rock's Redemption
An Insurgent's Wedding
Outlaw Xmas
Insurgents MC Romance Series: Insurgents Motorcycle Club Box Set (Books 1 – 4)
Insurgents MC Romance Series: Insurgents Motorcycle Club Box Set (Books 5 – 8)

Night Rebels MC Series:

STEEL
MUERTO
DIABLO
GOLDIE

Steamy Contemporary Romance:

My Sexy Boss

Find all my books at: amazon.com/author/chiahwilder

I love hearing from my readers. You can email me at chiahwilder@gmail.com.

Sign up for my newsletter to receive a FREE Novella, updates on new books, special sales, free short stories, and ARC opportunities at http://eepurl.com/bACCL1.

Visit me on facebook at facebook.com/AuthorChiahWilder

Made in the USA
San Bernardino, CA
03 January 2019